A TIME
for the
HEART

OTHER BOOKS BY NANCY CAMPBELL ALLEN:

Love Beyond Time

No Time for Love

A TIME for the HEART

A Novel

NANCY CAMPBELL ALLEN

Covenant Communications, Inc.

Published by Covenant Communications, Inc.
American Fork, Utah

Printed in the United States of America
First Printing: September 2000

07 06 05 04 03 02 01 00   10 9 8 7 6 5 4 3 2 1

ISBN 1-57734-678-5

*To my brother, Craig, who
always thought that whole Titanic thing
was as amazing as I did, even before they made it
into a blockbuster movie.*

Chapter 1

The young woman carried the small basket of fruit into her queen and set it before her, curtseying as she did so.

"Thank you, Queliza," the queen murmured, smiling at the young servant. She was seated upon her ornate throne in her personal quarters in the spacious palace, which was positioned to the right of the ceremonial temple.

Queliza liked the new queen. The king's first wife had been thoughtless and demanding. After her death, the king had chosen for his bride a young woman from a neighboring city. The new queen was young and kind, and treated her servants well.

"That is all I will need for now," the queen said. "I will have you summoned should I require something further."

Queliza curtseyed again and quietly left the room, her heart giving a little leap of excitement. She had some time to herself! Perhaps, if she wandered around the plaza a bit, she might spy the object of her recent affections . . .

* * * * * *

Claire O'Brian viewed the empty spot on the shelf with something akin to dismay. She was either losing her mind, not altogether a far-fetched possibility, she wryly admitted, or someone had moved the artifact without her knowledge or authorization. Surveying the room, she looked carefully over each possible hiding place before turning again to the shelf where she'd last placed the ancient pottery bowl that had been unearthed and documented the day before.

A pesky, pulsating ache that began behind her eyes gave Claire the promise of more intense pain to follow. She pinched the bridge of her nose with her thumb and forefinger, closing her eyes and muttering, "I am a competent adult. I am an extremely competent adult."

She turned at the sound of the door behind her being opened and closed. Claire narrowed her eyes as a young woman entered with an unnecessarily dramatic flourish.

"So you're missing some stuff?" the girl asked without preamble.

Claire mentally sighed and attempted to fix a smile on her face, hoping the expression didn't look as much like a grimace as it felt. "Hello, Devon. Nice to see you, too." Devon Stark had a habit of bursting upon the scene, any scene, with an air of faux importance. Her presence at the Guatemalan archaeological dig called "Corazon de la Ceiba," or "Heart of the Jungle," was a nuisance, but a necessary one, as it was her uncle's money that funded the project. Devon herself had been the first stipulation. "I'll supply money for the project if you can find a position for my niece," had been the less-than-subtle demand. Needless to say, Claire had given Devon a job.

Too much personal garbage attached to this place, Claire mused as she rubbed her forehead. Devon's wealthy uncle was the other half of Claire's former relationship. It had ended on a good note, though a slightly unsettled one—at least on his part. Claire had wanted out, he'd wanted her to stay, and she had to suspect that he'd agreed to fund this dig more as a means of keeping track of her than out of respect for her abilities.

"Yes, Devon," she finally replied. "I'm missing some stuff. I don't suppose you've seen it? The most recent thing missing is a piece of pottery, a bowl, cracked in many places but largely intact. The main piece is gone, and so are the smaller pieces that need to be reattached."

Devon shook her brown hair off her shoulders. "I haven't seen anything," she stated, then turned and left, slamming the door.

Claire stared at the vacated spot, pursed her lips, and nodded slowly. Everything in life was attached to a price. In order to continue unearthing the ancient city of Corazon de la Ceiba, or "Corazon," as the staff had come to refer to the place, they had to put up with Devon. A seventeen-year-old girl wonder who had never bothered to crack a science textbook, who insisted on wearing full makeup and leaving her hair down in humid, ninety-degree weather, and who was "enjoying the experience of a lifetime her friends would just be so jealous of," in her own words.

Claire raised her eyebrows and blinked, turning her attention to her former dilemma. The artifacts were carefully catalogued and marked, placed in the temporary lab Claire supervised, then readied for transportation to a more formal lab in Guatemala City. The current incident of missing artifacts marked the third time the site had seen theft under Claire's direction. The five or six pieces that had previously gone missing had yet to be found, and Claire literally lost sleep over the fact. She closed her eyes in resignation. She was destined for a restless summer, it seemed.

She left the lab, locking the door behind her, and made her way to the office of her employer and the head of the dig, Justin Hodges. She didn't bother to lift her eyes to the splendor that surrounded her—the lush green colors of the jungle, the thick trees surrounding all sides of the ruins. The large Mayan temple positioned approximately a football field away from her current position, flanked on either side by two smaller but equally impressive buildings, was partially buried in mountains of dirt and rock that receded into the dense jungle overgrowth.

The floor of the site was a grassy expanse, punctuated periodically by large, carved pillars that rose from the earth, each with its own story to tell. Several buildings, nearly a dozen, were positioned around the ancient plaza of Corazon de la Ceiba. The archaeologists could only speculate as to the purpose of some; many were still partially buried in the earth and needed to be excavated.

Part of Claire's frustration with the limited number of her staff was that this process would take a long, long time. The buildings still holding their many secrets would have to wait until the crew and their helpful workers could get to them.

At the center of the dig was a ball court—a long strip of stone resembling a concrete athletic court that looked from the air to be the shape of an "I," flanked on either side by two small, rectangular buildings situated atop tiered staircases.

The lab where Claire did much of her work was one of several buildings Darren Stark had taken upon himself to have built on the site, with the intention of turning Corazon into a "research" site of sorts in the years to come. These buildings were temporary but sturdy. They were wooden, whitewashed, and red roofed, and were positioned at the end of the ruins opposite the ancient temple, where they would be out of the way and unobtrusive.

There were two larger buildings to be used for dorms; there was a small but functional kitchen in another building, where dinners were cooked by a woman named Rosa who lived in a nearby village; and there were several small, separate units to be used for offices. The electricity necessary for running machinery and equipment was supplied by generators, and the site boasted two very nice latrines, as latrines go, and a private, but not *entirely* primitive outdoor shower, which functioned by filling a large tank on the "roof" with rainwater.

For the time being, Darren wanted the staff kept small, and so the buildings were empty, for the most part. Justin Hodges used one for his office, Claire claimed another small building for a bedroom, and the remainder of the buildings were divvied up amongst the remaining staff, which consisted of three masters students, Darren's annoying niece, and a world-famous French epigrapher.

One benefit to having so few people on hand was that everyone was entitled to his or her own bedroom. One serious drawback, however, was that there was so much to be done, and not enough people to help.

She usually found amusement in the contrast between the splendor of the ruins and the crisp charm of the more modern buildings; however, at present, her brow furrowed in a deep frown as she reached the small building that housed the office, and gave a perfunctory knock at the door before cracking it open and peering inside. The object of her quest was seated behind his desk, staring into space. He blinked at Claire's greeting and motioned her to enter.

Justin smiled wearily as Claire took a seat opposite his desk. "Any luck?" he asked, his expression hopeful.

"No, but then I haven't exactly torn the place apart, yet." Claire wiped at her forehead, shoving her damp bangs out of her face. "I've decided I wouldn't be nearly so stressed about this if it were cool outside."

Justin chuckled and glanced at her in sympathy. "Only a few more hours 'til the temperatures start dropping." He paused at Claire's grim expression. "It's not hopeless, you know. It's probably just the local amateurs at their best. And if that's the case, we'll put a stop to it, and the artifacts will stay where you put them."

Claire shook her head. "I don't know," she admitted. "I can't see pothunters getting into the lab so easily. I always lock it if I'm leaving and the students aren't there either." She paused, frustrated. "It's making me angry. More than just a little."

Hodges nodded. "We'll figure it out, Claire. Just keep doing your job, and we'll get things figured out."

Claire nodded, trying to hide her stress. Her job. Lately, her job description seemed to be growing by leaps and bounds.

* * * * * *

Bump St. James smiled at the man who was perusing Bump's wet bar, which was full of nothing but diet drinks.

"Where's all the good stuff?"

"I got rid of the good stuff. You'll have to make do with what's there, I'm afraid." He laughed at the expression on the face of his young companion, who had formerly gone by the street name of "Doc." Bump currently used the man's given name on a regular basis in an effort to help the younger man make a new life for himself.

"It's not so bad, Jon."

"Not so bad! Man, I've only been gone for six weeks! What have you done?" Jon's face was the very picture of panic.

Bump's mouth quirked into a gentle smirk. "You've been in rehab. You're not supposed to go looking for alcohol the minute you walk in the door."

Jon scowled. "I was just going to smell it."

"Smell it?" The hoot of laughter was loud and contagious. Jon's answering smile was quick in coming, and it warmed Bump's heart. "Buddy, you go around smelling the stuff and you're done for. Stay away from it, trust me."

Bump's mirth died away and he motioned for Jon to sit in the overstuffed chair, opposite his own position on the couch. "It wasn't just for your sake, actually."

"What wasn't?" Jon made himself comfortable in the chair, propping his feet on the matching ottoman with a sigh and settling back.

"Getting rid of the alcohol. I've made some, um, lifestyle changes since you've been gone."

Jon's eyebrows shot upward of their own accord. He cleared his throat. "What kind of changes, exactly?"

Bump absently rubbed the arm of the couch. "I've joined the Mormons."

The pause was lengthy and defining, in and of itself. When Jon finally found his voice, the incredulity within it was blatant.

"Why?"

Bump laughed. Why indeed? "I'll explain it sometime soon. Let's just say that neither of us is going to be doing any drinking anymore."

Later that evening, Bump asked himself the same question Jon had given voice to earlier. Why? He knew the answer, had felt the rush of emotion when he'd been given the missionary discussions under the tutelage of his friend, Liz O'Brian, and her new husband, Connor. But *why* was probably a question he'd be asking himself for some time to come.

As he wandered around his Seattle high-rise apartment, switching the lights off and readying for bed, he reflected back on his baptism of a month ago. The feeling had been extraordinary. He believed the principles he'd been taught, was still studying his new scriptures with the single-minded goal of learning as much as he possibly could, and he felt the truthfulness of it all when he prayed.

It was the Mormon culture he was having a hard time with. The Church members had been extremely nice in welcoming him into their fold. They'd been kind and friendly and more than a little curious. He was just so different, and felt it himself. They all seemed very content to . . . *conform.* His life had been anything but ordinary; his acquaintances worldwide were varied and often odd.

He wondered how he'd ever fit in enough to feel like he belonged.

Queliza stepped out of the palace and into the bright sunlight, looking over the whitewashed plaza in hopes of spying the young man who had sought her attention time after time in the recent past. Of course, he was the son of the king, and therefore hopelessly out of reach, but her heart thumped when he spoke to her. He was so very handsome . . .

* * * * * *

C laire entered the office with a single-minded purpose the following morning. She sat at Justin's request and regarded his tired face. His eyes were lined and careworn, making him appear older than his mere forty years. She was determined that the recent mishaps in her laboratory not affect him.

"I'd like to bring someone in on this, Justin."

His thoughts were obviously elsewhere; the effort it took to bring the present into focus was evident. He blinked. "What? Bring someone in on what?"

She leaned forward, catching his glance and holding it. "I know you're stressed. I understand your responsibilities to this dig, and I know the funding is precarious, at best. We don't need pothunters making things worse." She paused for breath, searching his face for signs of agreement. "My brother and his wife are good friends with a high-tech security expert. They've suggested he may agree to a trip down south for awhile."

Justin braced his arms on his desk with a sigh. "I don't know, Claire. If Stark gets wind of any problems, he may back out altogether. What's he going to think if we can't handle things on our own? If we have to count on an outsider to help us take care of a few pesky problems?"

"They're not pesky, Justin. The police have basically told us we're on our own with this. We're missing valuable artifacts that are of no use to us gone. I know my work." She ran a hand through her hair and sat back. "I don't make mistakes with important things. I rarely make mistakes with unimportant things." She punctuated her remarks subtly by tapping her palm on the arm of her chair. "I don't like what's happening; I feel like something's just not right."

She shook her head at his silence. In the short time they'd worked together, he'd shown himself to be an archaeologist of immense talent. She valued his friendship. He was one of the few people she could relax around. With other people, she felt the necessity to maintain a cheery exterior at all costs, and the demands she placed on her own performance were high. Justin was one of the few people who knew she was a perfectionist to a fault. Everyone else found her carefree and highly entertaining; it was a burden that was beginning to wear.

Claire knew she wasn't the only one who was having problems. In addition to the issues they faced with their volatile benefactor, she knew Justin was going through a messy divorce that was tearing at his heart. He rarely saw his child, a daughter, and when he did, it was under the close scrutiny of his estranged wife, who seemed determined to drain his very lifeblood before their relationship formally reached an end.

"Please, Justin." Claire's brow creased in concern. "This is one more thing you just don't need. Let me take care of it. I'll have Connor contact the guy and see if he's even interested."

"And what would a high-tech security expert be able to do for us here?"

"Well, it's not just that; he's also an excellent PI. I've heard nothing but rave reviews about him from Connor and Liz ever since their debacle with drug dealers in Peru." Claire shrugged. "I don't know. I keep thinking he might be able to see things around here clearly because he'd be fresh and new to the place, you know?"

"And how do we pay the man? You'll never get this past Stark."

Claire smiled grimly. "How 'bout you let me handle Stark. If I can get him to agree, will you support me on this?"

Hodges shook his head in resignation. "You are persistent, Claire. Yes, I'll support you. Just don't get your hopes up; Stark will never go for this in a million years."

* * * * * *

"So what you're telling me is that there are problems beyond your control, Claire? Is that what I'm hearing from you?"

Darren Stark. It was so very like him to be sanctimonious. Claire gritted her teeth, clutching the phone until her knuckles whitened. All thoughts of showing a happy face to the world came to an abrupt halt each time she spoke with her ex-boyfriend. She hoped the air escaping her flared nostrils wasn't evident to the man on the other end of the line. She didn't want him to know that her reaction to him mirrored that of a stampeding bull. She was certain he'd find a way to turn it around on her, to suggest that she was just unable to handle life without his controlling presence.

"You know, Darren, there was a time I thought you understood just what it is I do for a living. I help run an archaeological site. I'm an on-site Conservator. I'm busy with the preservation of extremely old and valuable artifacts. I don't have time to scout around, playing detective." Claire sat in the chair behind Justin's desk, grateful he'd given her some space to make the call. Had he been witness to her end of the conversation, she feared he'd have mouthed the words, "I told you so." Justin had been right; Stark would never agree to spending money on an outside PI.

"I'll tell you what, Claire. You come to Paris and we'll discuss it."

Claire rolled her eyes, then closed them in frustration. It was his favorite request, and one he repeated every time they spoke, which was as little as she could manage without jeopardizing her job security. "I don't need to go to Paris to discuss this with you. I can do it from here." She paused. "You know I can't leave, Darren. I need you to stop asking the impossible of me. I have work to do here, and I'm doing a job you're paying for."

"I miss you, Claire." The voice was soft and vulnerable. She knew it too well; he'd perfected it and used it on her before. Fortunately, she was wiser for it.

"You don't miss me, Darren. You miss having someone to lord over." *I never did fit well into that role. It's a wonder we lasted as long as we did.* "Now give me the go-ahead to call this guy and we'll see if we can't save you some money. You do realize that each artifact that goes missing costs you, if only in name recognition? Everyone who's anyone in archaeology knows the great Darren Stark is funding this dig and will be generously donating the finds to museums. Every little piece of pottery that's stolen is one less artifact with your name on it."

The responding chuckle was subtle. The ensuing pause was lengthy and wasn't subtle in the least. It was designed to make her hold her breath, hoping, and she hated the fact that she was. "You call your PI, Claire, and see what he can do," he finally responded. "But I'll only give him a month or so. I'm not going to pay the man to sit around forever if he doesn't start turning up something."

"Thank you, Darren." To be forced into thanking him for anything was galling, but necessary. "I'll let you know what I find out."

"You do that. Incidentally, how is my niece?"

"Oh, she's great. Devon's great. Quite the little helper."

"Well, good. I'm glad to hear that. You take good care of her for me, will you? She's an awfully long way from home."

Yes, at whose insistence? "That she is." *You probably sent her here as a way to wreak your revenge on me . . .*

"You take care of yourself, Claire. I'll see you soon."

What did that mean? She didn't think she'd be able to control her temper if he visited the site. It was her first venture into the professional world of archaeology outside her years at school, and the fact that the experience was tainted with Stark's presence at all was something she continually forced herself to overlook. If he actually showed up in the flesh, she might be forced to stab him through the heart with one of the small pick-axes in plentiful supply in the lab. She smiled grimly at the image as she disconnected the call. Life in prison just might be worth the expression on his face—complete and utter disbelief that she was not still under his spell.

Her mood lifted substantially as she left the office and headed in the direction of the ancient temple that currently had workers swarming over its surface like a hive of bees. She smiled. This, really, was what it was all about for her. The love for things ancient, past, and gone—evidence of lives lived and a burgeoning curiosity about those individuals who had conducted their daily activities in the midst of the very structures that currently surrounded her. The thought that human minds devised the architecture, and human hands put it all together, over a thousand years ago, was testament to the consistency of life; it existed, sometimes triumphant, sometimes tragic, but it always moved forward and the world never stopped spinning.

Claire took great comfort in that fact; she viewed science and religion in perfect harmony. *God is God, and is in His place, and the world continues along its path, at a twenty-three-and-a-half-degree tilt.*

"Where are those thoughts, Dr. Claire?"

Claire turned at the familiar voice. "Dr. Luis," she said with genuine affection. She clasped his proffered hand and smiled broadly. "It's been awhile since we've seen you here!"

The man grinned, his white teeth a contrast to his handsome, dark, Guatemalan complexion. "I've been busy with the missionaries," he said. "They keep me hopping."

Claire laughed. "I'll bet it's the other way around," she stated. "You have enough energy to keep ten missionaries hopping. I hope all is well with your family?"

Luis nodded. "Maria is healing nicely after the surgery and Marco is being her 'big helper,' or so he says." He smiled fondly. "Hard to believe a little boy of six believes he can take care of his mother, but he truly does."

Claire's expression changed to one of concern. "And Maria is feeling okay about . . . things? I know a hysterectomy is often hard on women psychologically . . ."

Luis nodded a bit and they walked slowly toward the large temple. "She was upset when she first came home," he said, "but is doing much better now. We're both grateful for Marco, and grateful that Maria is well."

Claire nodded. "Well, I'm happy to hear that. I'll pay her a visit soon, if you think she wouldn't mind."

"I know she wouldn't mind. She would be happy to see you again."

Claire regarded the young man as they strolled, marveling at his current role in her life. He had grown up in a small village approximately thirty miles to the south and had left to attend medical school in California, only to return home to his native village to offer his services to those he knew and loved. The village itself was growing at a rapid pace, and Luis found himself plenty busy with work between those who lived in the older parts of the area and with other newcomers, many foreign, who were a bit more affluent and who found the charm of the countryside and its nearby coastline irresistible.

He had stumbled across the ancient ruins of Corazon de la Ceiba quite by accident one year ago, although many of the older locals had known of its existence for years. He recognized its worth as an incredible asset to the archaeological world and had notified the missionary who had baptized him while in college. That same missionary was an Anthropology student at Brigham Young University and also happened to be a close friend of Justin Hodges. Justin had recently formed his own private archaeological business and had been looking for a contract, and the site was ripe for exploration. Once funding became available through Darren Stark, the rest was history.

Luis's occasional presence at the site was welcome and, Claire felt, poignant. When he was around, she had only to look at him to feel a connection with the people whose lives they were currently attempting to unearth. He was bright, a devoted family man, and loved working with the young missionaries assigned to the area. He often accompanied them as they taught discussions, lending his spirit to the meetings and offering medical advice when it was needed as well. He was gentle and good, and Claire valued their association.

That she also liked his wife was icing on the cake. Maria was a fantastic artist, working her craft with a variety of mediums including clay sculpture and watercolor paints. She was a bright woman, and Claire had enjoyed the few visits they'd had.

"So have you anything new to show me?"

Claire grinned. "Do I ever. Come here." Her step quickened and she briskly made her way to the left of the ancient temple where the ground began to slope upward in a gentle climb. Much of the thick vegetation had been cut back, and as they finally approached, Claire bent down to the ground and placed her hand upon a row of stone, approximately five feet wide, that was taking on the appearance of a step as the earth was removed from atop and around it. The color was almost a deep red, and upon careful inspection, it became obvious that the front was adorned with a series of epigraphs.

"Can you believe this?" Claire's eyes betrayed an excitement she didn't bother to try to hide. "I'll bet we have a staircase here that goes right up the hill." She gently scraped at the dirt atop the step to reveal a similar configuration just above it that tiered back. "See?" She stopped her exploration when her hand reached a white string, attached to a stake, that divided the hill into a curious grid.

Luis nodded and smiled with her, crouching down low to examine the pictures. He shook his head. "It's amazing," he murmured. "Can you read the glyphs?"

She shook her head in regret. "Very little," she admitted. "I wish I could read more of them myself. Etienne, however, is moving along quite nicely. He knows his stuff." She wrinkled her nose in faint distaste. "The problem is that he wants *everybody* to know he knows his stuff."

Luis laughed. "Where is he going, by the way? I thought I saw him leaving as I came in."

"Something's come up at home; he didn't want to say, I guess. He said he'll be back as quickly as he can."

"Well," Luis told her as he straightened, "this is impressive. I'm happy for you."

Claire dusted her hands as she rose. "Thanks," she said, all traces of her earlier disappointment and frustration fading. "I'm thrilled with it. You should have seen me yesterday when I found it. I was doing a happy dance all over the place."

He laughed. "I'm surprised you weren't out here at the crack of dawn, digging the whole thing up yourself."

Her face clouded, almost imperceptibly before she shrugged and offered a half smile. "I had to take care of some things," she said. "As much as I'd rather play in the dirt, there are issues on the business end we can't ignore." She hesitated, not wanting to dampen the mood.

"Something else was missing from the lab yesterday morning," she finally admitted.

"Oh, no. What was it this time?"

"A vessel we found in a burial pit with several skeletons." She shook her head. "I was pretty bummed. It was a good thing there was a silver lining to the day," she said, motioning to the "staircase." "I needed something positive."

"Can nobody help with this?"

Claire looked off into the distance and nodded. "We're trying to bring someone in from the States," she said. "Someone my brother knows and trusts." She shrugged and looked back at her companion. "Let's hope he knows what he's doing."

* * * * * *

"Well, if it isn't Boy Wonder!" Bump laughed at the resounding snort on the other end of the phone line.

"Aren't you funny." Connor O'Brian's voice held a smile. "One of these days, buddy, you're going to mess with the wrong guy."

"Now that, I seriously doubt." Bump knew his friends considered his ego to be beyond large and definitely out of control. He indulged their opinions regularly, much to the amusement of everyone involved, himself included. "So to what do I owe this great honor?"

"Well, do you remember me telling you about some problems at Claire's dig?"

"Yeah."

"They're not going away." The smile in Connor's voice had disappeared. "I'm not so much worried about that as I am about her."

"What's wrong with her?"

"She gets . . . she gets uptight when things go wrong." Bump waited patiently as Connor paused, apparently weighing his words. "She's a perfectionist, beyond belief, and she internalizes everything." Connor sighed. "She's extremely smart, and can usually handle anything thrown at her. She's also a very funny person who, for the most part, enjoys life. She makes people happy and they flock to her because of it." He paused again. "But when things under her control get *out* of control, she stresses to the point of self-destruction."

Bump frowned. "What, she gets suicidal?"

"No, it's not like that. But she's volatile in a different way. She's had some issues that are hers to divulge, if she chooses to, and I'll leave that up to her. Anyway, I thought I'd check with you first. I mentioned you to her once before, and she said she'd approach her superiors and see if they were interested in outside help. She called last night and said she has the go-ahead. Stark agreed to set aside some money for a PI."

"Stark is the guy funding the dig?"

"Yeah. He's also her ex-boyfriend."

"Mmm. The water gets murky."

Connor's laugh was absent of any genuine humor. "You wouldn't believe how murky. Anyway, you think about it and let me know. And if you do decide to take the job, will you do me a favor?"

"Sure."

"I'm worried about her—if she thinks I'm asking you to check up on her, she'll freak. But will you, and be discreet about it?"

"Of course. I'll go over some things and call you back tonight. This may actually be a good time to leave for awhile. I could use a break."

* ** * ** *

Claire paused at the door to the laboratory, viewing the scene inside with a smile. The good-natured bantering amongst the lab workers was just what she needed to take her mind off of her earlier conversation with Stark. After Luis had left, she had worked on the staircase, but had been unable to keep thoughts of the thefts at bay. She didn't figure that was a good sign. She never let anything interfere with her work. Of course, she had to admit, she'd never had artifacts up and disappear on her before.

There were several lab assistants, the number varying on any given day. There were three masters students stationed at the site; one was from England and two were native Guatemalans. The remainder of those working were locals who loved the history of the land and the extra money the work supplied. She loved the variety in people and culture.

She wandered through the room, looking over shoulders as she went, observing the processes being applied. It had always fascinated her—the natural transition from learning principles in a classroom and then applying those principles in the field. She adored her role as teacher. It satisfied her to no end to see the enjoyment in the eyes of her colleagues as they reverently studied the pieces of the past they were so tenderly attempting to preserve.

She watched carefully as Sue, the masters student from England, carefully cleaned a small pottery vessel that had recently been discovered along with the skeletal remains of one of the ancient site's prior inhabitants.

Claire eventually left the laboratory and wandered back out onto the site where the most active excavation was currently taking place. She viewed with satisfaction the differing strata alongside one of the partially unearthed buildings. The bits and pieces of the ancient people's lives were coming together, small amounts at a time.

She looked toward the setting sun, a fireball of bright orange that shed its majestic light for a few final moments before finally giving in to the inevitable and sinking beneath the horizon. It was so beautiful, the sun. So full of hope, so bright in its glory. She resented the fact that it left her presence, if only for a few hours. Nights were never easy for her.

She narrowed her eyes in anger at the feelings she thought she'd conquered. Her stomach clenched involuntarily in protest to her stresses that began with her emotions and made themselves manifest in a very physical way. *I've already dealt with this,* her mind screamed in frustration. *I've been through therapy, I've fixed it! It isn't supposed to crop up again . . .* But she knew that to be untrue. Relapses were not uncommon; her therapist had told her to be vigilant and remember the things she'd learned so that she could help herself as the years progressed, should she fall back into her old patterns.

And falling, she was. Rapidly. She noticed, with a small amount of fear, the first outward signs as Sue approached her with a friendly smile.

"Aren't you going to eat? Dinner's ready."

Claire's answer came of its own volition without conscious thought or intent, and was at odds with the growling of her stomach. "Not tonight, thanks. I'm not hungry."

*When she finally saw the prince, Queliza smiled and shyly walked
near the ball court where he was sitting with his friends. He saw her and
smiled in return, leaving his friends for a moment and approaching her.*

*"I see my father's wife isn't working you too much today," he said in
greeting.*

"No, not much," Queliza agreed.

"I was hoping I would see you today."

Queliza smiled again, but said nothing.

*"I wonder, would you cheer for me if I were to participate in the next
Game?"*

*Queliza gasped. "But . . . but . . . you're the son of the king! The
penalty for losing is death! He would never allow you to play!"*

*The prince laughed. "Have you so little faith in me? You believe that
I would lose? Besides, I would play in disguise. My father would never
guess it to be me on the court. And then when I win, I will show him I
am a force to be reckoned with . . ."*

* * * * * *

Claire sat quietly in the lab, having assigned several of the workers
to carefully dig out what she was coming to regard with affection as The Staircase. As much as she wanted to do it herself, she was
torn between duties, and was aware of the artifacts recently unearthed
that needed timely attention before being shipped off to a bigger lab.
The artifacts themselves were not used to the harsh environment they
now found themselves in; treatment was required quickly to help

them adapt from the soil they'd existed in for years upon years to the new reality of outside air.

She was bent over a broken clay pot, so intent on her work in piecing it back together that she missed the sound of the lab door opening and closing. She looked up with a start at the voice that greeted her.

"I'd like to talk to you, Claire," Devon Stark stated and made her way into the room, taking a seat opposite Claire's lone position at the long table.

Devon, from now on, you're to address me only as "Dr. O'Brian." And that's only if I speak to you, first. Claire squinted at the girl and barely refrained from spurting her thoughts aloud. The impertinence in the girl's voice made her mad; Claire wasn't one to stand on ceremony, but something about Devon's attitude made her want to shove her varied diplomas in the girls face and shout, "You're a seventeen-year-old wart! You're squirly and obnoxious. If it weren't for Darren, you'd not be let within ten miles of this place, due to your stupidity alone! Don't you dare act as though you have something over me!"

As it was, she merely sighed and laid down the glue she held in her hand. She wiped her fingers on a nearby cloth and looked Devon squarely in the face. "Devon," she began with a forced smile, "I realize that you have a position of some importance at this site because of your uncle's money; however, I'm tired of your attitude toward me. You are not my boss. Do we understand each other?"

Devon's eyes blazed briefly before she spoke. "It's my uncle I'm concerned about, actually. You broke his heart, and now you're making off with his artifacts."

Claire was so shocked by the statement that she stared at the girl for a full ten seconds before finding her voice. When she did, it came out in a dangerous whisper.

"What did you say?"

Devon flipped her dark, voluminous hair over her shoulder, a gesture Claire had come to recognize as defiance. "I think you're the reason the artifacts are disappearing, and as soon as I can prove it, I'm telling Darren everything. I just thought I'd give you fair warning."

Claire was hard-pressed to remember a time when she'd been angrier. She wouldn't have believed it was possible for her to feel such virulent disdain toward another human being. She carefully counted to ten and collected her thoughts.

"Devon," she began, "let me tell you something about myself. I love archaeology, and I have a deep and abiding respect for the artifacts we find. I would never do anything to jeopardize my moral beliefs about the care of these things." She paused, taking a deep, cleansing breath. "I don't owe you any explanations at all, but I will say this; I'm not behind the thefts. I don't know who is, but I have someone coming from the States to help us figure it out."

She leveled a glare at the young woman and continued before she could be interrupted. "Let me tell you something else. I rarely, if ever, repeat myself. If you *ever* again accuse me of such a thing, I'll personally put you on a plane home. I can't have you undermining my authority here with idle threats. I don't care if your uncle shuts the whole operation down; you'll be out of here. I'll find other funding. Am I clear?"

Devon turned several interesting shades of red and purple before finally responding. "You're going to be very sorry for this." She launched herself from the chair and left the room, banging the door with a significant, if slightly childish, final parting shot.

Claire replaced the object she'd been working on, left the lab after locking the door behind her, and made her way to the site where she knew she'd find Justin.

"I need to speak with you," she muttered upon finding him behind the lens of a 35mm camera. He'd been taking pictures of one of the sections currently under excavation, immortalizing it on film before the artifacts were removed from their resting places in the earth.

He glanced at her quickly, surprised. "Can't it wait?"

"It's fairly urgent."

Hodges finished snapping two more pictures, then moved off to one side, pulling Claire gently by the arm as he walked.

His eyes were a picture of concern as he studied her face. Claire wasn't sure how she appeared, but if her visage displayed the hostility she felt, she was certain she looked more than a little frightening. "What is it?" Justin asked in an undertone.

Claire carefully recounted her conversation with Devon, making sure to mention every detail that had transpired. "I just wanted you to know what she's thinking," Claire finished. "She's seemed relatively harmless this far, but I think she's bored and looking for some dramatic excitement."

Justin rubbed a hand across the back of his neck. "She shouldn't be here at all," he responded, his voice quiet and tinged with disgust. "Don't worry about it, Claire. And you were right; if it should come down to either you or her, she'll definitely be the one to go. I stand behind you completely."

Claire's fingers were restless, fidgeting and intertwining in movements completely at odds with the self-assured outward appearance she usually maintained. "You know I'm not taking the artifacts, don't you?"

"Oh, Claire." Justin pulled her close for an affectionate squeeze before releasing her and looking into her eyes. "I know you're not. You would never."

Claire nodded and fought at the unfamiliar sting behind her eyes. "I just wanted you to know."

"I do know. I never questioned it for a minute."

* * * * * *

Bump answered the knock on the door and took the bags full of delectable-smelling Chinese food from the deliveryman who stood in the hallway. He handed the man a wad of money and smiled at the resulting outpouring of thanks the man gushed at being told to keep the change.

He nudged the door closed with his shoulder and carried the fare to his living-room coffee table where he promptly began dispersing the contents. His eyes closed of their own volition at the smells emanating from the cartons.

"Am I interrupting a private moment?"

Bump smiled and motioned for Jon to sit. "I didn't know how hungry you'd be, so I ordered a lot."

"A lot? You ordered enough to feed the entire building." Jon sat and picked up a carton of shrimp fried rice. "Good thing, though," he said, grabbing a fork and digging in. "I'm starved."

"There are plates, here," Bump motioned with his hand, the corner of his mouth quirked into a smile. "Some of us use them on occasion. You're more than welcome to try one yourself."

"Nah. Waste of time."

"And since when are you concerned with time?"

"Things have a way of changing when you're not stoned."

Bump nodded sagely and began dishing heaping servings of sweet and sour pork, Szechuan chicken, and fried rice onto his plate. "One good thing about the plate theory, though," he lifted his food in salute, "is that you can eat more than one thing at once."

Jon thoughtfully chewed his rice. "I'll have to consider that," he finally responded with a smile when he swallowed.

Bumped looked carefully at his friend. Jon had changed, outwardly and inwardly, since Bump had rescued him from a life on the streets of Chicago. He had met Jon nearly ten years ago when Jon had been a young boy of fourteen, living with a mother who was always high, and a series of her boyfriends who paid him attention only as an outlet of drunk or drugged aggression.

Jon had left home shortly after to take his chances on the streets. Bump had contacts the world over that he utilized for information when doing his private investigative work. It was through some of these people that he had met Jon. The young man had been too proud and sneaky then and in the years that followed to accept help from Bump or a series of well-meaning social workers. It was only recently when Bump had hauled him out of a gutter late one night where he'd fallen prostrate with a needle sticking out of his arm that Jon finally conceded the point that life couldn't get much worse.

His appearance then had been beyond frightening; his cheeks had been hollow and gaunt, his skin sallow, his eyes flat and lifeless. Bump had taken him to his apartment in Seattle and, after cleaning him up, enrolled him in a six-week rehab program.

Those six weeks had served him well. Bump had pushed him into the program, but Jon had stayed of his own free will. He was regaining a healthy color, he had gained some much-needed weight, and fortunately, his brain didn't seem any worse for the wear.

Bump had noticed one problem, however. Where his eyes before had seemed dull and lifeless, they now were haunted. Whenever the look was most pronounced, Jon changed into running shoes, shorts, and a T-shirt. He would take to the streets of Seattle, running down past Pike Place Market, which he loved, along the piers and around to the spot where the recently demolished Kingdome had stood. More often than not, he ran for a good long time, pounding his unspoken thoughts into the pavement and returning to Bump's apartment, famished.

"How was your run?" Bump chased a mouthful of spicy chicken with a long swig from his diet drink.

"Good. Who knew?"

"Who knew what?"

"That I'd like running so much." He returned the half-empty carton of rice to its former position on the table and reached for some chicken chow mein, this time doling a large portion of it onto a plate. "Not a bad way to pass the time."

Time again. Suddenly it was an issue. "What are you thinking you'd like to do from here on out?"

Jon frowned. "I don't know. I've never done anything."

"Well, okay. What did you do when you were young before you started shooting up?"

Jon opened his mouth to say something, then closed it abruptly and stirred his food.

"Yes?"

"Nothing."

"You were going to say something."

Jon shoved a mouthful of chow mein noodles into his mouth and chewed. When he swallowed, he shrugged. "It's not exactly masculine."

Bump fought back an instinctive smirk. "Okay. Let's have it."

"I used to . . ." The last was lost on a mumble.

Bump squinted. "You what?"

"Draw, okay? I used to draw. Until one of my mom's boyfriends found my sketchbook and said I'd never be a real man."

"Yeah, that Michaelangelo. What a wuss."

Jon shook his head. "You don't get it. When a man twice your size tells you you'll never be a man because you draw, and then he beats the tar out of you, you don't draw anymore."

Bump sobered. "Jon, you were more of a man as a kid than any of those boyfriends your mom brought home."

Jon nodded, and Bump knew he hadn't heard a word. "You don't believe me."

Jon looked up from his plate. "Sure I do." He rose and took his plate into the kitchen. "I'm taking a shower and going to bed." He stopped and looked at Bump apologetically from the hallway. "I'm sorry," he said. "I'm not very good company tonight."

Bump waved his hand. "Forget it. We'll talk tomorrow."

He sat in the silence for a long time, his food laying untouched on his plate. He had intended to broach the subject of Jon entering therapy and staying at the apartment while Bump went to take the job at Claire O'Brian's dig. Suddenly it seemed extremely foolish to leave the man to his own devices.

Bump shook his head, set his plate on the coffee table with a sigh, and leaned back into his chair. Jon Kiersey was twenty-four years old and hadn't a clue what he wanted to do with his life. He'd been one of the most unpleasant teenagers Bump had ever known. The reasons for his behavior were no mystery, however. Bump had seen Jon's mother and knew of the life the young man had lived. Jon had cleverly eluded Bump and the system for four long years until he was eighteen years old and legally on his own.

Bump thought back on the haunted look in eyes that shouldn't have appeared so old. *Why was it all allowed to happen? To an innocent child?* He directed his thoughts heavenward, not expecting a dramatic answer. Although an angel or two might be nice every now and then, he mused wryly, he didn't imagine that was realistic. He'd figured out his own relationship with his Maker. The answers came softly and without fanfare. It was probably that way for the majority.

"Tell me what to do, and I'll do it," he said aloud. The feeling in his heart mirrored what his mind had already decided.

Take him with you.

Chapter 4

Queliza watched as the prince and his friends made their way across the plaza and into the palace. She couldn't believe he would risk his life for the Game, merely to prove himself to his father. The king was a harsh man, true, but it was well known amongst the citizens of the city that he loved the prince very much. He had great plans to make the prince one of his many military advisors when the young man came of age; apparently that wasn't soon enough for the prince himself.

Queliza turned as she heard someone behind her calling her name. She smiled at her old childhood friend, Palome, who was the son of the court astronomer. He seemed to be the only person she felt close to since the death of her father, several months earlier. Her father had been crushed during the renovation of the sacred temple, and her mother had died of a broken heart not long after. Queliza imagined they were happier now than they were when they were alive; her family had been but poor workers. That Queliza had caught the eye of the former queen and been asked to act as a servant for her had been an amazing thing.

Palome smiled and brushed his hand across her cheek. "Are you well today, Queliza?"

"I am."

Palome's gaze darkened a bit as he followed the line of her eyes. "Surely you're not thinking about the prince again," he said.

She sighed. "I'm not. Not really, anyway. After all, he's the prince . . ."

* * * * * *

C laire gripped her pen, determined to write her frustration out of her system and thereby force herself into some semblance of relaxation.

I feel completely out of control. I see my professional life slipping away by degrees every time another artifact disappears, and it's slowly killing me. I worked too hard for this; I sacrificed so many things to come this far. I've wanted this career, this life for as long as I can remember. I'm afraid if I lose it, I'll lose myself.

Claire took a deep breath and stretched her aching and tensed muscles, glancing back at her journal entry. It had been a long time since she'd regularly written; in fact, she hadn't done so since she'd used it as therapy. When she'd been in the throes of her treatment, she'd been required to write down all her thoughts, to look for patterns in her behavior and to try to recognize the signs that signaled she needed to do something to make things right for herself.

She reluctantly continued, hating the honesty she knew would pour forth from her pen.

I skipped dinner again tonight. I just couldn't make myself eat it. I looked in the mirror earlier today and felt sick. I saw an inept woman who can't keep track of anything. I know it's not true. I know logically that I never lose anything, that I always stay completely organized. It's just that I always know, in the back of my mind, that something's wrong. I can't get rid of the oppressive feelings. I check the lab fifty million times a day to make sure nobody's in there, pilfering stuff.

I don't feel as badly this time around as I did last time I quit eating. I know who I am, I really do. And even though I don't want to eat, I know intellectually that I should love who I am. I'm proud of myself. I love what I've done with my life. Maybe it just seems worse, now, because I have so much more to lose.

Claire got up from her bed where she'd been sitting cross-legged with her journal. She reluctantly walked to her trunk of personal belongings and picked up the ornate, hand-held mirror that had been her grandmother's. It was a lavish affair—silver backed with a carved ivory handle. Her mother had given it to her when Claire had been deep into therapy. *I want you to see yourself as I see you, Claire,* her mother had said through her tears. *You're so beautiful. You're killing yourself and it makes me hurt so much inside . . .* Claire knew what the words had cost her mother. She was not a woman given to emotional fits, or admission of deep feelings.

She gazed into the mirror and objectively studied her reflection. Her hair was thick and jet black, and hung straight down her back to rest below her shoulder blades, with a fringe of bangs on her forehead. Even in this intense heat, she couldn't bring herself to cut her hair, so more often than not it was secured in a ponytail at her crown. Her eyes were large and a deep cobalt blue in color. They were fringed with lashes so dark that she had no need for mascara, which was actually a good thing given the fact that she wasn't exactly in an environment that was conducive to a lot of makeup. *Unless you're Devon*, she mused.

Claire's lips were full and her teeth white and straight, much like every American kid of her generation; she remembered well the phase in junior high school where everyone who was *anyone* had braces. She smiled grimly at the memory, knowing that reflections on junior high and high school were places she didn't want to go.

All in all, she decided while studying herself in the mirror, it wasn't a bad face. She closed her eyes and rubbed them, carefully placing the mirror back in its proper spot amongst her other belongings. *A place for everything and everything in its place . . .* It was a phrase she lived her life by, which was probably why the recent thefts from the lab were so frustrating. In addition to the fact that valuable, irreplaceable artifacts were missing, she hated that something under her jurisdiction was out of order.

She turned at the sound of a knock on her door.

"Hi, Sue," she said pleasantly to the woman on the other side, carefully and effortlessly pasting her "people face" into place. "What has you up this late?"

"Well," began the other woman, "I thought I'd come by to see if you wanted any leftovers from dinner. I told them to leave something for you . . ."

Claire smiled again. "Sue, you're too thoughtful. And thanks, but I'm okay. I snack so much during the day that I'm not always hungry for dinner."

Sue nodded, seemingly unconvinced. "Well, if you're sure," she answered. "I'll see you in the morning, then."

"Thanks again, Sue. You're sweet." Claire thoughtfully closed the door. She felt the old, familiar relief at not being discovered. She'd felt that way before when her family finally clued in to the fact that she was starving herself. *This isn't the same,* she tried to convince herself. *I'm stressed. Lots of people lose their appetites when they're stressed.*

Yeah, a voice in her head answered back, *but lots of people don't nearly kill themselves in the process . . .*

She shook her head as though to banish the traitorous thoughts and turned again to her journal. With a sigh of resignation and perhaps a bit of disgust, she closed the book and gathered her bag full of things she needed to shower and brush her teeth in preparation for bedtime.

Tomorrow, she thought. *I'll deal with it all tomorrow . . .*

* * * * * *

Two days had passed since Claire's bout with honesty in her journal and she still hadn't dealt with her problems. She found herself eating less and less, and because she was hungry and worried she became internally irritable. Her "people face" that usually came so easily for her was requiring more and more energy to summon. That nobody around her seemed to notice her subtle distress was a miracle in itself and one for which Claire was extremely grateful.

Devon was a continual and increasingly obnoxious source of Claire's discontent. Claire was examining some pottery on one of the shelf labs when she heard the door slam behind her. The sound of Devon's voice had her flaring her nostrils in disdain.

"You'll never guess who I just saw," the girl announced breathlessly to the room at large. "The most gorgeous man in the world!"

Claire raised her eyebrows at the enthusiastic pronouncement and slowly turned. One corner of her mouth quirked into what she hoped was a smile. "Really? Someone you'd like to run away with?" *Please?!*

"Oh, don't I wish!" Devon's face was flushed and her eyes positively glowed. *Humph,* Claire muttered mentally. *Now who really has eyes that glow? Leave it to this kid . . .*

"Anyway," Devon was saying, "This guy is some kind of insurance adjuster. I'm going to offer to show him around." She turned and made a quick exit, nearly knocking down Miguel, one of Claire's students, who was in the process of carrying several artifacts into the lab.

Claire nodded slightly. She and Justin had figured it would be good idea to hide Connor's friend's reason for his visit to the site and keep his true purpose a secret. If Devon knew, it would be all over the site by sundown. Claire slowly walked toward the door, shaking her head as she went. Devon had a mouth that rivaled the Grand Canyon in size.

She paused at the entrance, quickly viewing the artifacts that Devon had nearly creamed when she left. Miguel was one of the Guatemalan students who was working on his master's degree. She joined him in his admiration.

"These are incredible," she murmured to him in Spanish, enjoying the opportunity to speak the beautiful language although Miguel was fluent in English.

Miguel nodded in agreement. "We just uncovered them," he said with obvious pride. "The colors must have been fantastic in their day."

She smiled at the young man. She appreciated people who loved the work the way she did. "Have fun with it," she said as she turned and left the building.

Claire wandered slowly over the site until she spotted Justin. He was standing again behind a camera that was poised on a tripod, viewing the items still embedded in the hard earth. She came quietly up behind him and said, "So Devon found a new friend, huh?"

Justin turned to her and rolled his eyes. "Poor man doesn't know what he's in for," he said.

"I take it he's our security guy?"

Justin nodded. "Seems nice enough—I talked to him briefly, and I'll sit down with him in a little bit to kind of give him the rundown. For now, though, Devon's giving him the grand tour."

"Mmm." Claire winked at Justin. "Which way did they go?"

"Over that way, toward the far side of the temple." Justin pointed with one hand as he leaned down to focus the camera lens with the other. "You might want to go rescue the poor guy," he said into the camera. "He brought a friend with him, too. They both might need some help."

Claire laughed and moved toward the temple. She walked around the current area of excavation to the right side, which had been the easiest to uncover, having been the least buried by trees and undergrowth. It didn't take long to spot Devon and her hapless companions. Claire approached quietly from behind, shaking her head again as Devon's dialogue with the men became clear.

"This is the area we just finished cleaning up," Devon was explaining as she pointed. "Sometimes we find all this really old stuff in the dirt using some itty-bitty shovels."

Claire cleared her throat as she neared the trio. They turned and as Claire opened her mouth to introduce herself, her breath caught in her lungs. Darn her, Devon had been right. The man standing directly to Devon's right was undoubtedly the most beautiful man she had ever seen. He looked to be an inch or two over six feet tall with shoulders that could stop a train, a nicely built torso that tapered to a trim waist, and legs that were long and perfectly proportioned to the rest of his impressive frame.

Claire realized to her horror that she'd just looked the man up and down. When had she ever done that? She'd *never* done that! She hoped the flush she felt internally wouldn't manifest itself on her face. She ordered herself to stop ogling his body, and her eyes flew to his face. Which was another mistake. His hair was a rich, chocolate-brown in color and was cut short and casually styled off his forehead as though a hand had recently combed its way through. His skin was nicely tanned over high cheekbones, his nose and mouth utter perfection. The eyes, though, were what kept her riveted to the spot. They were a golden color that glowed. Rather like a tiger.

Well, Claire thought when she managed to pull herself together, *I guess Devon hasn't cornered the market on the glowing-eye thing.* She wondered what she should say when she noticed the man's expression. His mouth was quirked into a half-smile, one eyebrow raised in obvious amusement.

She didn't have to formulate an introduction; as it was, this model of male perfection stepped forward and offered his hand. "You would be Claire O'Brian," he said.

She nodded.

"You look just like your brother," he said, grasping her fingers in a warm clasp. "Although he's not nearly so pretty," he admitted with a smile.

Claire cleared her throat. "Yes," she finally said. "I'm Claire. You would be Mr. St. James?"

The man laughed. "Call me Bump."

"Oh, that's right," she said. "Connor said you had an odd name." She paused. "Uh, I mean . . ."

He laughed again. "It's okay. It is odd. I like it that way."

Devon elbowed her way closer to the pair. "Claire," she said, "I was just showing them the site."

Claire turned her attention to Devon. "Thank you, Devon. I'll take it from here."

"Oh, no. I don't mind."

Claire smiled. "Devon, what I want you to do is find Justin and see what he needs to have done before lunch."

Devon's expression was mutinous, but she turned and left anyway. With a mixture of irritation and foreboding, Claire watched her retreat. Bump's deep voice seemed to rumble behind her.

He chuckled. "She's been telling us all about the old stuff you've been finding with itty-bitty shovels . . ."

Claire shook her head. "You'll have to excuse her," she said. "That girl dines on a steady diet of idiot sandwiches."

Bump snorted in appreciation, his guffaws ceasing only as Devon cast a flushed glare over her shoulder.

"Oops," he said.

Claire closed her eyes. "I've gotta learn to keep my mouth shut."

She turned back to Bump and noticed, for the first time, the young man standing next to him. He stretched his hand out and introduced himself.

"I'm Jon Kiersey. I'm Bump's friend—I'm just kind of along for the ride," he offered by way of explanation.

Claire took in the man's appearance as she shook his hand. Not at all bad either, she had to admit, although his looks leaned more to the blonde, hot-dog snowboarders she'd known at home. *Paige would like this one*, she mused with an inner smile. He looked like a life-size Ken doll, she decided. Unfortunately, in her mind, he paled in comparison to his companion. She reluctantly turned her gaze back to Bump, hoping she wouldn't find herself speechless every time she set eyes on the man.

He smiled, as if reading her thoughts, and she found herself instinctively falling back on what she knew worked. Her charm with people. It was a family trait that never failed.

She grinned. "Well, you come highly recommended by my brother and Liz," she said. "I can't thank you enough for taking time out of your schedule to help us out here."

"It's my pleasure. Your brother's a good man. We were in need of a change of pace anyway, weren't we?" Bump addressed the last to Jon, who was standing casually at his side, hands in the pockets of his khaki pants, taking in the surrounding jungle.

Jon nodded slowly and turned his face back to Bump and Claire. "Yeah, we were," he answered. Claire looked at Jon's hazel eyes and read something in them she saw every time she looked in a mirror. The man was in some kind of pain.

Well, she mused as she guided her companions toward the main area of the encampment, there was something about the land that was soothing and peaceful. It had seen thousands of lives pass away over thousands of years; maybe, somehow, they'd all find what they were looking for.

Chapter 5

Queliza walked around the plaza with Palome. The place was teeming with people; it was afternoon, and the people liked to gather at the plaza to talk, debate, place wagers on the next Game, and who knew what else. Palome placed his hand under Queliza's elbow and guided her through the throngs of people.

Palome himself commanded a certain amount of respect because he was the son of the court astronomer, but he was a humble man. He'd befriended Queliza when they were children, and he had been kind and considerate to her ever since. She had never kept secrets from him before, but she couldn't bring herself to openly share the strange feelings she was experiencing for the prince. Somehow, she knew Palome didn't approve, but it wasn't because she was merely a servant; somehow, it was the prince he didn't care for . . .

* * * * *

Bump deposited his belongings on his cot in the small building he and Jon were given to share as a bedroom. Jon had already dumped his bag and said he wanted to walk around outside for awhile. Bump ran a hand through his hair and mentally reviewed the events of the past hour.

First of all, Connor O'Brian was a big, fat liar. "You'll know my sister," he had said on the phone. "She looks a lot like me." Well, Claire O'Brian *did* resemble her brother, but resemble was about as far as Bump would take it. The woman was stunning. Bump couldn't ever remember a time when he'd looked at Connor and found him stunning.

She was small, much smaller than he'd have expected given the size of her brother. He'd be surprised if she stood an inch taller than five foot two, and she was very slight. Her skin was tan from hours spent in the hot sun, and she'd looked the very epitome of a Healthy American Woman as she'd approached them on the site. Her eyes were the same intense Mediterranean blue color as her brother's, but somehow on her, the effect was much more startling.

Just when Bump had been sure his eyes would roll back in his head if he had had to listen one more minute to that young pseudo-tour guide, Devon, Claire had approached them like a vision in her white T-shirt and khaki pants, a red-plaid flannel shirt tied around her waist.

And looked Bump up and down like she'd consider eating him for lunch.

To say he'd been startled by her obvious appraisal would be an understatement. Had he not known Connor so well, he might have taken Claire's perusal for an open invitation. And who knew? Maybe it was. Just because her brother was the saintly type didn't mean she necessarily was.

Bump laughed out loud. Unfortunately, *he* was now one of those saintly types and had agreed when joining the LDS church to avoid any sexually intimate relationship until marriage. Now why couldn't he have met this woman *before* he was baptized? He turned his eyes heavenward and chuckled. "I'm just kidding," he apologized, and left to find the building he had been told served as the "mess hall."

The site itself was impressive. He'd been many places in his life, and had experienced a great many things; this, however, was new. He'd never actually seen an ancient Mayan ruin before, and he decided that all the PBS specials he'd ever seen on the magnificent buildings didn't do them justice. They were large, solid, and breathtaking.

From what he could gather as he observed, the whole process seemed to combine traditional digging with computers and other various pieces of handy technology. He cast an appreciative eye over the wide array of equipment; he was a seriously addicted gadget man himself.

He found his way to the mess hall and looked around at the people who were eating their lunch. They sat together around a large table, enjoying a meal of sandwiches and soda. He moved forward as the man he remembered as Justin Hodges motioned to him.

"This is Bump St. James," Justin said to the people seated at the table. "He's an insurance adjuster, here to look over some of the particulars of the site."

Bump nodded to the group, who seemed to accept his presence; if they doubted his purpose, they were wise enough not to say anything in front of him. He smiled as Justin introduced each member of the team, committing their names and faces to memory. When the introductions were concluded, Bump, at Justin's suggestion, made his way to the counter that flanked one wall and made himself a sandwich. He joined the people at the table, wondering if he'd need to send a search party out later to look for Jon.

* * * * * *

Claire was examining a piece of what was presumably an ancient tool of sorts that was protruding from the earth next to one of the smaller buildings on the site when she caught movement out of the corner of her eye. She turned and saw Jon walking slowly around the site, apparently taking in detail as he went. She smiled when he finally saw her, and raised from her crouched position on the ground, stripping off her latex gloves as she stood.

He approached her as she'd hoped he would; she was more than a little curious about this one. "Hi there," she said as he moved closer.

"Hey."

"So what do you think?"

He finally stood before her, his hands in his pockets, eyebrows raised. "About the site?"

She nodded.

"It's incredible. I'm really amazed at the whole process, actually."

"It's not always very exciting," she admitted with a grin. "Most of the time it's a long, tedious process and sometimes we go for ages without finding anything substantial, but it means so much." She gestured with her arm. "All of this was once inhabited by other people and we're lucky to have the chance to figure out how they lived."

She laughed. "I get carried away, I know. I just really love finding stuff people used thousands of years ago. It's like putting together a puzzle."

He shook his head, smiling. "You have every right to get carried away. It must be nice to be so passionate about something." He looked out over the landscape, his smile fading.

He didn't say anything else. The silence was unnerving.

"So where are you from?" she finally asked.

He turned his attention back to her. "Seattle, right now. I'm living with Bump. But I was born and raised in Chicago."

Claire nodded. "I've been to Chicago," she said. "It's a wonderful city. What did you do there?"

His brow creased. "Nothing worthy of mention."

"Oh." Okay. Time to shift. "So how did you meet Bump?"

Jon's mouth quirked into a semblance of a smile. "I met him when I was fourteen. I was between homes at the time."

"I see." Well, not really, but he didn't seem to want to offer anything further. "Are you hungry? They're having lunch in the mess hall right now . . ."

He nodded and fell into step beside her.

"So, Bump," she said as they walked, "that's his name?"

Jon laughed. "Yeah, and don't ask me what his real one is. Nobody knows. It's a secret I think he'll take to his grave. For all I know he's had it legally changed to 'Bump.'"

"What does his driver's license say?"

Jon looked at her in surprise. "I have no idea, actually," he said. "I never thought of looking there."

"So all you have to do is grab his wallet when he's not looking, and . . ."

Jon's laugh demonstrated the first real expression of true mirth she'd seen in the man. "That's a good one," he finally said. "Nobody gets *anything* from Bump, whether he's looking or not."

Claire smiled. "What is he, some kind of superman?"

Jon nodded, a grin still on his face. "Yeah, actually, he is."

* * * * * *

Bump finished his lunch and stood to leave. As the other members of the team filed out, Justin Hodges stayed behind. He was a healthy-looking man in what Bump judged to be his mid-forties, with dark-blonde hair and a medium build. His eyes were a soft blue color, and Bump didn't know him well enough yet to ascertain whether or not the lines around them were due to the natural processes of age, or from stress.

"I appreciate your being here," Justin began and ran a hand across the back of his neck. The man looked extremely tired. Bump waited patiently for him to continue. "Things have been crazy, lately. I don't know how much you were told on the phone . . ."

"Not much," Bump admitted.

"Well, all I can really add to that is to tell you that artifacts are disappearing from the lab."

Bump quirked an eyebrow. "I was told that much on the phone."

Justin nodded. "I know. Unfortunately, that's *all* we know." He paused for a moment. "Claire O'Brian is actually the person with the closest contact to the lab—she's our on-site conservator and this is really her domain. She might be able to tell you more than I can."

"Okay." Bump nodded. "Would you mind just giving me a brief rundown on who you have here at the site and what their jobs are?"

"Not at all." He motioned for Bump to sit beside him. "The operation at this site in terms of people is relatively small, primarily at the request of Mr. Stark, although he's made arrangements for much bigger operations in the future—you can see that in all the new buildings we have here that aren't being used yet. He agreed to give us the money with the stipulation that we keep the publicity limited, at least for now."

"Any idea why?"

Justin shook his head. "None. But money talks, so we cooperated. We have two archaeologists here at this site—which would be Claire and me. We also have three masters students: Sue Chastain, Miguel Robaina, and Ricardo Valez. Etienne DuBois is our on-site epigrapher, but he's currently back home in Paris dealing with a family crisis. He's been with us from the beginning. Guatemalan law requires that for every foreign archaeologist on the site, there also has to be a native Guatemalan archaeologist. As graduate students, Miguel and

Ricardo fill the bill for two of those requirements, and for the third, we use Etienne. He's not actually a Guatemalan citizen, but he's worked and lived in the country for so long that we can get away with it, for now, at least."

"I see a lot of other people around as well; are they workers?"

Justin nodded. "We have a team of approximately fifteen people who live here in the area and are paid for part-time work as their schedules allow. We also have a cook who is paid to come in and cook dinner for us and clean up the kitchen each evening. Oh," he paused, quirking his lips into what was probably supposed to pass for a smile, but resulted in more of a grimace. "We also have one general . . . assistant . . . of sorts."

Bump smiled. "Would this be the young lady I met this morning?"

"Yes. Devon." Justin checked his watch.

"Don't let me keep you," Bump said, waving aside Justin's embarrassed response. "If you'll just show me where the lab is so I can talk to Claire, I'll get out of your way."

Justin led Bump to the entrance of the mess hall and pointed to a building close by. "That's it," he said. "Claire's usually in there or somewhere on the site."

Where else would she be, Bump wondered as he thanked Hodges and made his way toward the lab. *It's not like there's a mall on every corner, here.* He noted the countryside, remote and far away from current, modern civilization. There was something amazingly tranquil about the place.

He entered the lab and allowed his eyes to adjust to the reduction in light. He viewed shelves upon shelves of what he assumed Devon probably referred to as "that really old stuff," and tables where several people sat, busily cleaning the artifacts.

His gaze finally came to rest upon Claire, who was seated at one of the tables, close to a young male student. She talked as she demonstrated something she was doing to a piece of pottery with a rag and what Bump assumed to be some sort of cleanser. He watched her, quietly, and quickly noticed several things about the woman.

First of all, her face was animated and alive; she gestured gently with her hands, pointing to the object she held, the perpetual touch of a smile on her face as she spoke. She obviously loved what she was doing.

Secondly, she commanded a presence with her colleagues; in the short amount of time Bump had stood watching, several others had gathered behind her to listen as she talked. She noted their presence, and turned to speak over her shoulder in an effort to encompass the entire group. Many of the others also wore latex gloves, as did she, and held rags and artifacts in their hands, apparently performing duties similar to those she was demonstrating. It appeared that even those who already knew what they were doing were drawn to her.

She must have said something funny—the people around her laughed, and he caught the good-natured bantering that can only occur when people are familiar and comfortable with each other. She then handed the rag to the young man seated beside her and stripped the gloves off her hands, tossing them into a nearby garbage can. She rose, offering another comment that must have amused the masses; they laughed as though she were the most brilliant person alive. She ended with a final admonition the group had probably heard before, given their smiles and nods. "Don't clean *anything* I haven't authorized," she stated.

Bump smiled slightly from his vantage point near the door, off to one side. It was how he liked to observe—close enough to almost touch, but far enough removed to see it all clearly. It was from this position that he made his final observation about Dr. O'Brian. He saw her face as she left the table, and the others resumed their duties. She was tired. She moved toward him but still hadn't seen him standing there. He noticed the weary movements that were at odds with her prior performance; she rubbed a hand across her forehead and down behind her neck, rotating her head as she did so. As she got closer, he saw the slight circles under her eyes that probably would have been much more prominent had she not been so tan.

Yes indeed, the doctor was tired. Or stressed. Who could blame her—she obviously loved her job and it was being stolen from under her nose. She walked steadily toward the door and didn't see Bump until she was nearly upon him. She stepped back, startled.

"Oh!"

"Hey," he said, stretching his hand out to catch her arm. "Sorry about that. I just got here, and you're actually the person I was looking for."

She smiled, straightening her spine. "Really? Well, that makes me feel special."

He took a good look at her face, trying to read sarcasm. He didn't find any, and being cynical himself, could usually spot it a mile away. What he saw was a pleasant smile and a wink. She reminded him of her brother. Those O'Brians possessed charm in spades. Funny, but her version of said charm affected him differently than Connor's ever had. Connor was just a nice guy. His sister was darling.

Darling. Now there was a word he hadn't known he possessed in his vocabulary. As nauseating as it was to admit, he couldn't really find another word to describe her. Well, maybe if he thought about it for a minute. Beautiful. Yes, that one would work. Athletic. *Yeah, that one would work too*, he mused as he watched her precede him from the building. She was wearing shorts this time, and he noticed the firm outline of her calf muscles as she walked. He forced his eyes upward as she came to a halt just outside the building.

"I forgot something," she was saying. "Can you wait here for a minute?"

"Sure."

She ran back inside and came out a moment later with a notebook and pen. She quickly jotted some notes and turned to him again. "I assume you'd like some information?"

He nodded. "Yeah, that would be nice."

She looked around the site, tapping her pen against her lip. "Hmm," she said. "Why don't we walk for a bit."

He followed her as she walked toward the center of the ruins, and then off to the side and into some of the thicker vegetation that sloped gently upward, surrounding the entire site like a bowl. He mentally shrugged and followed her without question. "I'd like a little privacy," she explained. "Some of the people around here have big ears."

He nodded, content to follow her lead, and finally sat beside her on a large boulder situated in the midst of several thick trees.

She sighed and leaned back against the trunk of a tree and smiled. "Well," she said, "what can I tell you that you'll find useful?"

He wasn't sure whether she was asking him or herself. He leaned forward and rested his elbows on his knees, loosely tapping his fingertips together. "Why don't you just start from the beginning and tell me everything you can think of," he offered.

Claire nodded and rested her head against the tree, closing her eyes for a moment. "I've been involved with this particular site since before we got permission to do it a few months ago," she began, opening her eyes. "Before I graduated from school, I was dating a man who's made quite a name for himself in the field; he likes to donate large sums of money and claim all the glory." Her voice was notably void of emotion.

"When our relationship ended," she continued, "I didn't think I'd ever see him again. After hearing nothing from him for quite a long time, he came out of the woodwork and offered to fund this dig. Of course, Justin jumped at it." She paused, pursing her lips and apparently weighing her words.

"His name is Darren Stark and he's . . . he's . . . well, he likes things to go his way, let's just say that. I've been more than a little worried about his reaction to these thefts. I really don't want to have this dig shut down because he pulls his money."

Bump nodded. "Why don't you tell me what you know about the thefts themselves."

"Well, they started about seven or eight weeks ago. At first I just assumed they were local pothunters, but now I'm not so sure."

"Pothunters?"

"Amateur 'archaeologists' who go around digging up stuff for their own private collections."

"I see."

Claire scowled. "They exist all over the world and they ruin sites everywhere. When we dig up artifacts," she explained, again using her hands, "we take photographs and draw pictures of them, carefully documenting their location and positioning before we ever even lift them out of the ground. We have to know exactly where they come from in order to formulate theories about the ancient societies these things were a part of. When pothunters come along, they destroy that whole process and steal what isn't theirs."

"So what makes you think these pothunters aren't behind your missing artifacts?"

She sighed. "I don't know. I lock the lab, so you'd think that would take care of it, but I suppose anyone can pick a lock." She shrugged. "I guess it's the things that are missing that make me think it's not just some schmuck."

"You think it's someone on the inside?"

Claire looked off into the distance at a point over his shoulder and shuddered, probably involuntarily. "I sure hope not," she finally said, bring her gaze back to meet his. "I don't know what else to think, though."

"How well do you know these people?"

"Really well, I thought. All of them." Her gaze clouded and the muscles along her jawline tightened. "Except for one."

"Let me guess. My tour guide from this morning?"

Claire nodded. "Devon Stark."

"Stark? I suppose that's not a coincidence?"

"Not a coincidence in the least. She's Darren's niece."

"Mmm. Nice. How did that happen?"

Claire laughed. "What, the fact that she's his niece?"

"Well, no," Bump's mouth quirked into a smile. "I think I can figure that part out. How did she end up here?"

"Oh, she just had to have this experience, and her sweet Uncle Darren was all too happy to see that she got it." Claire shook her head. "Truthfully, and it probably wouldn't take a rocket scientist to figure this one out, she's driving me out of my mind."

Bump nodded. "Do you think she's the one lifting the stuff?"

Claire tilted her head to one side and shrugged a shoulder. "She's the only one I have reason to suspect, but that's just because I think she's a complete dork, not because I necessarily think she's dishonest. But," Claire paused, softly tapping her pen against her forehead, "somehow I don't think she's bright enough to pull it off, you know?"

"She may not be. Or she could just be trying to make you look bad. It was pretty obvious this morning she doesn't think much of you."

Claire laughed. "No, she doesn't. She hasn't from the start." She sobered and grimly recounted the story she'd already shared with Justin concerning Devon's suspicions and threats to go to her uncle.

"Have you gone to the local police with any of this?"

She nodded. "We have, but they've been unable to help much at all. Besides," she motioned with her hand, "they've got other, more pressing things to worry about. A few missing pieces of pottery are low on the list."

Bump nodded. "Have the people who are currently here been here since the artifacts started disappearing?"

She nodded, pursing her lips thoughtfully. "I think so. Yes," she decided, "they've all been here the whole time. The only one who has been here but isn't here right now is Etienne DuBois, our epigrapher. Well, no," she commented, thinking, "he hasn't been here for all of the thefts. He wasn't here for the last one. I guess that puts him in the clear."

"Maybe, or maybe not. You never know."

She nodded, looking glum.

"Well," he said, "that at least gives me some place to start. You don't mind if I watch you work and ask pesky questions, do you?"

Claire smiled. "No, I don't mind at all. And I promise to try not to bore you with unnecessary details about my work. Sometimes I get a little carried away."

When Bump made no move to immediately leave the comfort of his perch with her beneath the tree, she assessed him carefully, apparently trying to decide whether or not she should speak.

"Connor speaks highly of you," she finally said. "And I'd really like to take the opportunity now that we've met to thank you for taking care of things in Peru for him and Liz." She nodded slowly, emotion clearly written on her face. "I really love him, and I'd have missed him . . ."

Bump smiled softly. "Well, I can't really take too much credit. He's a bright guy and he just about had things figured out when I got there."

"Well, at any rate, thanks."

"You're welcome."

Claire cleared her throat and moved off the rock, dusting the seat of her pants as she rose. "So," she said as he joined her to walk back, "Connor tells me you're a new convert."

Bump nodded. "I was baptized just a few weeks ago."

"Wow! You're *really* new!"

He laughed. "Yes, I am. Frighteningly new."

"Welcome to the fold, brother," she laughed.

"Thanks."

She gave him some background on the site, motioning with her arm to the main area of the site they were approaching as they walked. "This is a smaller version of some of the bigger, more impressive Mayan ruins. This one has been hidden in the jungle for thousands of years; it was only *formally* discovered a year ago by a man who lives here in the area. His name is Luis Muños, and he's the reason we're here at all." She shared Luis's history with Bump as they walked.

"And how do you know Justin? Did you go to the "Y" also?"

She laughed. "No, I wanted to get a little farther away than that. I went to Arizona State University. When I was nearing the end of my doctoral work, I went home for a quick vacation and did some homework on who was working in the area. I found Justin, and met with him; he offered me a job upon graduation, and here I am."

"Do you trust him?"

Claire glanced at him in surprise. "Justin? Implicitly," she said without hesitation.

Bump nodded. "That's good to know." He took in the ruins as they walked back to the lab. They stood on the floor of the green valley, the trees and undergrowth crowding to the edges of the site. The ancient temple soared above them and touched the sky. "It's amazing," he murmured.

"Isn't it? I'm in awe every day at how incredible this place is. I wonder constantly about the people who lived here." She shrugged, grinning, and he had to smile in return. Her enthusiasm was engaging. "That'll be one of my questions on the other side," she said. "I'm going to want to know whose stuff I was digging up."

Chapter 6

"It's not that I don't like the prince," Palome whispered to Queliza as they left the plaza and wandered toward some of the smaller structures that comprised the homes of the area citizens. "But he's young, and he feels he has to impress his father. I think it makes him reckless."

"He's very friendly to me."

Palome glanced at Queliza, his expression grim. "I'm sure he is; you're very beautiful, Queliza. But be careful how you give away your heart; he may not treat it with care. He has much on his mind, and it all involves himself. There is not much room for others . . ."

* * * * * *

Claire sat in the lab alone, her head bent over a piece of pottery she had just cleaned and was currently documenting. She detailed in her notebook the appearance of the piece and exactly what had transpired in attempts to preserve it since it had left its former home in the dirt.

Her shoulders ached from being hunched over for a long period of time, and the rest of her body was beyond fatigue. She knew she should try to get some sleep, but it had been elusive lately; she was afraid she'd go lie down on her bed, only to stare at the ceiling for hours on end, her stomach clenched in knots and her mind refusing to rest. That had been the pattern over the past few weeks, and it wasn't getting any better.

So she stayed up, later than anyone else, and concentrated on parts of her job she *could* do. It was beginning to wear on her emotionally as well as physically and she knew she couldn't keep her current pace, but she shoved aside any concerns for her own well-being and instead tried to pretend there was nothing wrong. Nobody pestered her about eating; she'd never had a huge appetite to begin with, so the fact that she wasn't eating much at all didn't seem to arouse suspicion amongst her colleagues. They also assumed she was a night owl and left her alone to do her work while the rest of the world slept.

She was so intent on her work that she didn't hear someone enter the building. When he finally did make his presence known, she was so startled she dropped her pen.

"Sorry," Bump apologized. "I didn't mean to scare you—I should have knocked, or something."

Claire gave him a tired smile. "No problem," she said, picking up her pen.

He gestured to a chair opposite hers at the table. "Do you mind if I sit here for a minute?"

"Not at all." She tried to smother a yawn. "I'm not sure I'll be very entertaining company tonight, though." As he sat down at the table, she viewed him through half-open eyes and cursed her heart for giving a leap at the sight of him. He shoved the chair back a bit as he sat and rested one ankle across the other knee. He was casual and self-assured; he looked as though he owned the world.

She felt as though she barely owned her composure from day to day. For a small moment, she resented him his self-confidence. His was undoubtedly real. Hers was a façade. She felt her smile slip from her face and couldn't find the energy to bring it back.

"I don't mean to interrupt you," he said.

She shook her head. "It's really not a problem. I'm just a little tired. I should probably go to bed but there's a lot to be done, here."

"I thought I'd talk to Devon Stark tomorrow, as well as the rest of your staff. I figured it'd be a place to start, if nothing else."

Claire nodded and set her pen down on the table, rubbing her eyes. "That sounds good," she said. She leaned back in her chair and stretched her sore muscles. "I've been wondering how you'll go about all this without making people wonder why an insurance adjuster is asking such personal questions . . ."

Bump wiggled his eyebrows. "I have ways . . ."

I'll bet you do . . . Claire closed her eyes and rotated her head around in a full circle, cursing her fatigue and hoping she hadn't murmured the thought aloud. She opened her eyes and looked at his face, again struck by his incredible appearance. Those tiger-like eyes seemed to see everything; at that very moment he was probably reading her thoughts. She shook her head.

"It's none of my business," he said, watching her actions, "but I think you could use some sleep."

She shrugged a shoulder. "I don't have time."

"Sure you do." He quirked a brow. "Can this not wait until tomorrow?"

She tamped down a surge of irritation at the fact that he was presuming to tell her what to do. She chose to ignore the fact that he was right. "I like to get things done as quickly and as well as possible."

He nodded. "I'm sure you know your job better than I do. I just know that I, personally, function much better after a good night's sleep. I have a nasty habit of assuming everyone else does things the way I do."

She smiled and blinked slowly, feeling herself grow more and more weary. If she wasn't careful, she'd fall right out of her chair. "I do too, actually. I'm always surprised to find people have systems different than mine." She blinked again.

"Claire, you're falling asleep."

"Mmm?"

"Come on." His chair scraped against the floor as he stood. "I'll walk you to your room."

She opened her eyes when she felt his hand on her shoulder. She looked up at his face and blinked again. "What?" Had he asked her something?

"I said, do you need to do anything with this stuff, here?" He motioned to the artifact and notes she'd been working on.

She nodded and looked at the table. *Claire, for crying out loud, pull yourself together!* She rubbed her eyes again and stood, carefully moving the artifact to its proper place on the shelf against the wall. She gathered her notes and gave the entire lab one final, cursory glance.

"I'm ready," she told Bump and led the way to the door. After carefully locking it behind her, she made her way to her room, barely managing to lift a hand to Bump in farewell. She went inside, dropped her notes on the floor by her trunk and fell on the cot, surrendering to sleep almost instantaneously.

* * * * * *

Bump entered his room, shaking his head.

"What?" Jon was reclined on his own cot, reading an archaeology magazine.

"Connor's sister. She's running herself into the ground."

"Can you blame her? Someone's stealing her stuff."

Bump shrugged. "Yeah, but she's not going to be of any use to anyone, including herself, if she doesn't slow down a little." Connor had warned him, he mused. He'd said she was self-destructive.

"What's she doing?"

"She's up before the crack of dawn, for starters, and she stays up later than anyone else on the site, working herself until she can't keep her eyes open."

Jon smiled and flipped a page. "Bump St. James, to the rescue."

Bump scowled and gathered the sweatpants and T-shirt he planned to sleep in. "What's that supposed to mean?"

"Nothing."

Bump pawed through his large, heavy-duty duffel bag. "Where's my towel?" he muttered to no one in particular. He finally found the towel and a small, zippered pouch containing his toothbrush, shampoo, soap, shaving cream, and a razor.

"I'll be back," he threw over his shoulder to Jon as he left the room, still scowling. To the rescue. Whatever. He was doing a favor for a friend. Connor had asked him specifically to check on Claire and make sure she was okay.

There was nothing wrong with looking after the welfare of a friend's sister. So what that she was so physically attractive he found himself distracted. And so what that she was smart and funny, and cared enough about the people around her to put on a brave face rather than let the world view her stress.

And just because the rest of the people he'd watched all day were completely mesmerized by her magnetic personality didn't mean he was.

He was just doing a favor for a friend.

* * * * * *

When Claire awoke the following morning to the sharp chirping of the alarm on her watch, she felt as though her head had been split in two by something very large and very sharp. She groaned, bringing herself to a sitting position and fought a wave of nausea that accompanied her empty stomach. She'd cut back on her food intake gradually in the past several days so that she barely noticed the hungry feelings anymore. But nausea that occasionally accompanied an empty stomach was something that had plagued her since childhood.

She took several deep breaths and pulled herself from her cot, glancing at her watch. It was obscenely early, but she wanted to check on the lab. She stretched and yawned, pulling a sweatshirt over her head before leaving the building. She pulled her hair from the ponytail elastic that had remained in place from the night before and quickly retied her hair, hoping nobody would be up and view her disheveled state.

The morning air was crisp and clear. She took a deep breath and turned an appreciative ear to the chirping birds. At least something was glad to be up early. She held her breath as she approached the lab, and unlocked the door. It was with no small amount of relief that she viewed the artifacts placed on the shelves precisely as they should be.

She quietly left the lab, locked the door behind her, and made her way back to her tent to collect clean clothes and things she'd need for a shower. Maybe she'd feel a little more awake after washing her hair. Upon entering her room, however, she looked longingly at her cot and sighed. Maybe just a few more minutes of sleep wouldn't hurt.

She lay down and settled comfortably into her pillow and blankets. And waited.

Her traitorous mind wandered. Someone was stealing artifacts. Precious pieces of the past that could never be replaced. Those artifacts were in her care. Devon suspected her of something Claire considered morally heinous. Devon was Darren Stark's niece. Devon had threatened to go to Darren and ruin Claire's career. Darren was a jerk. He wanted to see Claire fall on her face because she'd had the audacity to leave him.

Claire sighed and got up, scooped up the things she'd gathered for her shower, and headed out the door, stomping as she went. Anger was good, she decided. Anger gave her energy. Thinking about Darren always made her angry, so if she dwelled on him all day, she just might be able to get something done.

Her theory saw her through her activities until about 8:00 that morning when she ran, quite literally, into Bump St. James. All memory of Darren Stark promptly fled. Bump was leaving the mess hall, presumably having just had breakfast, and she was making her way from the lab to find some food herself, her head buried in her notebook. She ran into what she assumed was a tree, only to be corrected as a pair of hands caught her arms.

"I'm sorry," she said, laughing. "I do usually try to watch where I'm going."

"I don't mind, actually," he returned with a grin.

Her breath caught in her throat. *Claire, this is getting ridiculous. He's just a man, for crying out loud.* When she finally remembered to breathe, she managed a little laugh and a quick explanation that she was on her way for some breakfast.

"Okay," he nodded. "I'm going to talk to some people and then be around to harass you a bit later on, is that all right?"

She nodded and cursed herself for a fool, feeling much like a student in junior high school again, her heart thumping every time the best-looking boy in school walked down the hall. She gritted her teeth and shoved her way into the mess hall, hoping to find a piece of wheat bread somewhere.

Bump moved away from the entrance to the mess hall, casting a final glance over his shoulder at Claire as she stormed her way inside. He fought the smile that twitched at the corners of his mouth and lost the battle. He'd flustered her. It was nice to know he still had it.

He whistled a cheery tune as he ventured onto the site where the team of archaeologists was busily at work. His eyes roamed the group until they stopped upon the object of his quest. Devon Stark. He was looking forward to his interview with her the least, so he figured he'd start with her and get it over with.

She was all smiles when he asked if he could talk with her for a few moments, and moved off to one side of the activity. "Should we go somewhere and sit?" she asked.

"No, this'll be just fine. It won't take long."

The look of disappointment on her face was almost comical, and if he'd had a minute, he might have wondered why he found the idea of Claire enamored with him much more appealing than the thought of Devon similarly struck. Well, no, it wouldn't really take more than a minute to figure that one out, he decided.

"I'm just wondering what you know about the artifacts that have turned up missing lately. The insurance company I represent is anxious to get to the bottom of it."

"I'm sure they are," Devon replied, her eyes wide. She tossed her hair over her shoulder. "I don't actually know who's been taking them, but I think I have a pretty good idea." She leaned in close, forcing Bump to tilt his head down an inch to hear her whispered admission. "I think it's Claire."

"Dr. O'Brian?"

She pulled back, the expression on her face a mixture of dislike and triumph at blowing the whistle. She nodded. "She used to date my uncle, and I know that she comes from a . . ." she leaned forward again, whispering, "middle-class family."

Bump raised his eyebrows and said nothing.

"Don't you see? She could use the money! She steals the artifacts, sells them and gets rich!"

"Wow."

"I know." Devon glowed. "The more I thought about it, the more sense it made. Oh, and it's not like I'm going behind her back, telling you this," she hastily explained. "I told her to her face that once I had proof I was going to my uncle."

"And what did she say to that?"

Devon scowled. "Nothing. Well, she denied everything, of course, but what *could* she have said? It's not like she's going to admit to it."

"Mmm." Not only was the girl dumber than a box of rocks, Bump decided, she was mean and spiteful. And probably horrifically jealous of the good Doctor. "So you're close to your uncle, then?"

"Oh, yes. He's always taken really good care of me." Her smile was wistful. "I think he's always wished he had a daughter of his own."

"I'm sure."

"Are you sure you don't want to go sit somewhere and talk? I'd *love* to hear all about your work."

"Well, unfortunately I have to keep doing that work, so I don't have time to sit down right now. But Devon, while we're talking, I really do need to tell you that to go around accusing Dr. O'Brian of theft probably isn't a very smart thing to do."

Her eyes narrowed.

He continued speaking in an even tone. "I'd suggest you keep your suspicions to yourself until we know more about what's going on here."

"But my uncle . . ."

"I know about your uncle; in fact, he's grateful I'm here, doing this job. I promise you, I'm looking after his best interests."

The girl nodded, looking decidedly furious. "If that's all you have, then I'll be getting back to work."

"You do that," he said with a smile and watched her walk back to the site. He wondered if Devon would stoop to pilfering the artifacts herself and then casting the blame on Claire. It probably wasn't outside the realm of possibility.

Chapter 7

If Queliza had been paying closer attention as she walked with Palome, she might have noticed the way his eyes were reluctant to leave her face, that he often placed his arm under hers, that he had always been considerate of her feelings and curious about her thoughts. If she had noticed these things, she might not have turned her attention so much to the prince in the days that followed . . .

* * * * * *

"S o how long have you been with the dig?" Bump was talking to Miguel Robaina, a serious young archaeology student who was working on site for a short time as part of his masters program.

"Let's see," Miguel mused in heavily accented English as he pushed his wire-frame glasses up on his nose. "I've been here since the digging on this site began."

"And how well do you know everyone here?"

"Quite well, actually. There's not all that many of us, and we're pretty close."

Bump nodded and gave the young man his spiel about the "insurance company he represented" being concerned about the thefts. "Do you have any information that you think I might find useful?" he finished.

Miguel's brows drew together in a picture of concentration. "I really don't know what to tell you—we're all really confused by it." He paused. "I know it's bothering Claire, especially. She takes her work very seriously, and justly so."

"How well do you know Claire?"

Miguel straightened a bit. "In the short time I've been here I've grown to know her very well, I believe. I respect her as an archaeologist and I support her without question." He flushed. "I know there are those who are jealous of her, but I don't trust them."

"'Them' or *her*? I assume we're really talking about one person, here."

Miguel lifted a shoulder in resignation. "Okay, her. I don't trust Devon Stark as far as I can throw her."

Bump grinned in appreciation at Miguel's dry sense of humor; Miguel was a thin man who *maybe* stood five inches taller than Devon's own five foot five. Miguel's answering smile was reserved, yet sincere.

He patted Miguel's knee, then stood up from the large, overturned crate where they had been sitting. "I thank you for your time, sir. Let me know if you think of anything else, will you?"

Miguel nodded, his expression once again serious, and returned to his former duties.

* * * * * *

Claire was in the lab, frantic, and trying to hide it. "Sue," she said, "are you sure you didn't see it this morning?"

Sue stood alongside her mentor, apparently noting her agitation. "I'm sure, Claire." Her face bore an expression of extreme concern. "When did you see it last?"

The two women stood before the shelves, staring at a spot that should have contained the very clay pot Claire had been documenting the night before, and had been sure she had seen in its place that morning when she checked the lab before her shower.

Claire fought tears. "It was here when I left for breakfast just before, oh, roughly eight o'clock, I think."

"Oh, Claire." Sue threw an arm around Claire's shoulders and gave a squeeze. "We'll get this whole thing figured out, really we will."

Claire closed her eyes and hastily wiped at a tear that escaped and left a trail down her cheek. She blew out a puff of air and tried to laugh. "I know," she said. She glanced at Sue and gave her a small smile. "Thanks for the support. I appreciate it."

Sue gave her shoulder another small squeeze. "I'll go tell Justin," she said.

"So," a voice behind the women stated as Sue turned to go, "something else is missing, huh?"

Sue's fists clenched and she marched over to Devon, who had slipped in unnoticed. "You watch your step," she said to the younger woman.

Devon looked Sue up and down. "Is that a threat, Ms. Chastain?"

Sue looked back at Claire in frustration, knowing full well she had no power over Darren Stark's niece. She moved to leave, but turned back when she reached the door. "Leave her alone, Devon." She motioned toward Claire who had turned her back and was busying herself with some papers on one of the tables.

"Or what," Devon laughed, "you'll tell on me?"

Sue couldn't contain her smirk. "That's not a bad idea, really."

Bump was approaching the lab with Jon at his side just as Sue Chastain was leaving, in an apparent hurry. He'd yet to talk to her and made a mental note to do so when she was looking a little less harried.

The scene he encountered when he reached the entrance to the lab went a long way toward explaining Sue's flustered exit. He saw Claire standing behind a table, a fistful of papers clutched in one hand, her eyes bright with unshed tears and her jaw clenched.

Devon Stark stood on the other side of the table, her back to him, and was unleashing a torrent unlike anything he'd ever heard.

"Missing, Claire? Is that what you're saying? Something else is *missing*? Isn't that just convenient for you! You have access to this stuff all the time, you have a key, and everyone just thinks you're a goddess!"

She paused for air, and Claire made no attempt to answer her, merely glared.

"Well, I'm on to you. You thought you could just march in here and make money off my uncle. You're doing this, and I will prove it! Now who's eating idiot sandwiches?!"

Bump had heard enough. "Sharing your cuisine are you, Devon?"

He took savage satisfaction at the shocked expression on her face as her head whipped around to face him. Her shock was swiftly replaced with apparent outrage.

"Are you *defending* her?"

His answer was calm and quiet, but if she'd have known him better, she'd have realized she was treading on thin ice. "Why don't you go cool down somewhere and we'll discuss this later."

She moved toward the entrance where he still stood with Jon a step behind him. "I'll cool down," she flung at his face when she reached him. "I'll cool down while I call my uncle!"

Bump and Jon moved to one side and watched as she stormed past, then turned around once she was outside. She leveled a finger at Bump and pointed emphatically as she spoke. "You'd better watch yourself," she said through clenched teeth. "If you get too close to Claire, you'll go down with her when it all hits the fan!"

Bump shook his head. Poor, poor girl. If she had any idea of the power Bump wielded amongst his network of associates worldwide, she'd be shaking in her Doc Martens. Very few people ever threatened him, and it was only those who didn't know better. Jon's snort beside him was a testimony to that fact.

They watched her retreating form with interest. "She stomps around a lot," Bump finally stated.

Jon rolled his eyes. "Why don't you let me take care of this. I assume we don't want her calling the uncle?"

"That's right."

"Done."

Bump left the problem of Devon in Jon's capable hands and turned to Claire. She was still standing where she'd been before.

"Hey," he said softly.

"Turn around," she replied.

"What?"

"Turn around. Please. Don't leave, just turn around."

"Okay." He complied and wondered at the sounds he was hearing behind his back. Scrapes and clunks.

"All right," she said. "Turn back around." When he did so, he saw that she had moved several of the artifacts off their positions on the shelves and onto the tables, creating large gaps where they had once stood.

"Do you remember watching me put away that artifact I was working on last night when you came in here and I was all but asleep? You had to remind me to put it away."

"I remember."

"Show me where I put it."

Bump moved forward and located the spot he remembered Claire placing the pottery just before they'd left the lab the night before. "You put it right here," he said.

She nodded and began replacing the other artifacts she'd taken off the shelves, presumably in an attempt to throw him off—to be sure he wasn't just picking the only vacant spot on the shelf where the most recently missing piece was supposed to have stood. She sank into a chair when she finished her task and rested her head on one hand, her elbow braced on the table.

He sat in a chair next to her. "Did you put it in the right spot?"

She nodded. "I did. I was afraid that maybe I'd put it in the wrong place. Justin and Miguel packed up some of the artifacts this morning to be shipped to a bigger lab in Guatemala City." She pinched the bridge of her nose with her thumb and forefinger. "The things that are ready to go are put on those shelves over there . . ." she pointed with her finger. "I was thinking maybe I put the missing one in with those . . ."

She shook her head, still thinking, apparently. He stayed quiet, letting her talk.

"In some ways, it would have been good if I had," she admitted. "Then we'd know where it is. But if I *had*, then it would mean I'm slipping, and that," she tried to laugh, "is just not okay."

"It's okay to slip every now and then," Bump offered with a wry smile.

"Not for me." She sniffled. "It's not okay with me."

Connor apparently hadn't exaggerated the fact that his sister put pressure on herself. Bump wondered if the family knew to what extent. They probably did, he mused. Connor had always struck him as a family-friendly kind of guy. He was probably fairly close to his sister. Close enough anyway, Bump remembered, to know that she might need someone to check up on her. Bump was a man of his word.

"You're not alone here, Claire." He kept his voice pitched deliberately low, in case someone should come in or overhear. The fact that she didn't seem to want others noting her distress or unhappiness spoke volumes about her pride. He meant to try to help her preserve it. "I'll help you with all of this."

He turned his chair so that it faced her directly and rested his elbows on his knees, taking the hand that lay listlessly on her lap and holding it between both of his own. He leaned in close so that she turned and looked at him. Her expression was unguarded, and bleak.

"I'm very, very good. There's nothing that I can't figure out, given enough time."

She bit her lip and lightly cleared her throat. "I appreciate your candor and your arrogance," she said, trying for a smile, "but time is one thing we just may not have very much of. Devon's on her way to call Darren right now."

"Jon's on it."

She raised her eyebrows. " 'Jon's on it'?" She laughed in spite of herself. "What are we, cops?"

He snorted and patted her hand. "I'm not kidding," he said through a chuckle, "Jon will stop her."

"How?"

Bump shrugged, grinning. "I leave that up to him. If you haven't noticed, he looks like he just stepped off a surfboard. With a girl as impressionable as Devon, I have no doubt that when he says he'll take care of it, he'll take care of it."

Claire nodded with a small shrug. "I hope you're right."

"I am. Jon will keep her occupied. In the meantime," he continued, "I'm going to talk to the rest of your people, here. If we can't narrow it down to someone on the team, we'll have to assume it's being done from the outside. That may actually be easier to figure out. Do you get many other people wandering through here?"

Claire sighed, thinking. "Yes," she mused aloud, her brow wrinkled in a frown. "We get locals from neighboring towns, curious about what we're doing. I guess it could be any of a number of people . . ."

He nodded. "Well, at least we have some places to look." He patted her hand again. "You give me a week, two at the most. I'll have it taken care of for you by then."

She shook her head, a reluctant smile tugging at the corners of her mouth. "You're incorrigible," she said.

"So I've been told."

Chapter 8

The prince was especially attentive to Queliza over the next several days, seeking her out when she wasn't with his stepmother and fawning over her as though she were a princess. He brought her small gifts and showered her with his smiles and his charm. And all the while, he spoke to her of how he would surprise his father and be on the winning team when the next Game was played.

Such talk made Queliza extremely nervous; she wondered if she should tell the queen what the prince was planning to do . . .

* * * * *

"I'm sleeping in here."

"You're what?"

Claire stood stubbornly in the lab before Justin, her features set in a mask of determination. "If I sleep in here, then whoever is taking the artifacts will have to step over me to get to them."

Justin shook his head. "Claire," he said yawning. "It's late. Everyone else is in bed, and I came over here on my way to my tent to see why the light was on. Now you're telling me you're going to *sleep* here?"

"I am."

Justin looked her in the face, his eyelids half closed from his own fatigue. "I don't suppose there's any way I can talk you out of this?"

"Nope."

Justin shrugged. "We'll talk about this tomorrow. I need some sleep." He left, still shaking his head.

Claire closed and locked the lab door behind him. "We may talk," she muttered as she tried to make herself comfortable on her cot after extinguishing the lights, "but that's all we'll do. And I'll still be sleeping in here from now on."

Had she been conscious two minutes later, she'd have been amazed she fell asleep so quickly. Her peaceful slumber was interrupted the next morning by a loudly insistent knock on the door. She tossed her messy braid over her shoulder and rubbed her fingers across her eyes, rising on unsteady feet to answer it.

Bump St. James. Darn him, did he ever not look perfect? He stood in the open doorway, the bright sunlight spilling in behind him, looking freshly showered and combed; he even smelled nice. The expression on his face, however, had her retreating a step or two.

"What are you doing in here?"

She scowled. Obviously Justin had seen things differently in the light of day and had shared his thoughts with the "insurance inspector." She turned and left the doorway, yawning as she went. "I see you've been talking to Justin," she said as she sank down on her cot and drew her blanket around her shoulders.

Bump entered the lab and closed the door behind him, none too gently. He pulled a chair over next to Claire's cot and plunked himself onto it unceremoniously. "Why are you in here?" he repeated.

"Isn't it obvious?" She rubbed her burning eyes and tried to focus. "If I'm in here, nothing will get stolen."

Bump was quiet. Too quiet. She looked up at him after finishing her weary eye massage to find him staring at her with an unreadable expression on his face. "Claire," he finally said in measured tones, "we hardly know each other. But I'll tell you this; there is no way I'm going to let you sleep in here knowing there's someone out there willing to steal this stuff." He shook his head. "If it's as old and valuable as you claim, then it's worth some money, am I right?"

She reluctantly nodded.

"Then whoever's making money off this deal isn't going to give up just because you're sleeping in here."

She sighed. "I can't sit by while this continues to happen. I've been doing some thinking," she continued, "and other than that piece that was taken yesterday morning, the rest of the thefts have happened at night." She spread her hands wide. "Maybe they'll think twice before breaking in at night if they know someone's here."

"Yeah, maybe they'll just shoot you or club you over the head instead."

Claire screwed up her face. "Let's not be melodramatic."

He eyed her evenly. "I am never melodramatic."

She tried to smother another yawn and waved a hand at him. "I don't see what the big deal is," she said. "I really can't sleep in my room anymore." Her expression sobered. "I literally can't sleep in there. I need to be in here. I worry too much, otherwise."

"I'll tell you what. If it'll make you feel better, *I'll* sleep in here. There is no way, in good conscience, I can let you do it. I promised your brother I'd make sure things were okay, and I don't see that happening if you're putting yourself right in the line of fire."

She narrowed her eyes. "You promised my brother what?"

Uh oh. "Nothing."

Claire looked at the shelves beyond Bump's shoulder and shook her head slightly. "What else did he tell you? That I'm a freak who doesn't eat?"

"No, he didn't tell me anything." He paused. "You don't eat?"

"Yes, I do," she answered a little too quickly. Her chin rose a notch.

Bump sat back in his chair. *So that's it,* he mused. Connor had alluded to something about Claire that was "hers to divulge, if she chose." He slowly allowed his eyes the freedom they desired to wander over her small frame. She was thin. He'd noticed that before, and presumed she was genetically small; that much was easily discernible merely from taking a good look at her bone structure. However, things took on a whole new light now that she'd all but admitted she didn't eat well. The dark circles under her eyes and her look of constant fatigue he'd noted in the short time he'd observed her may well have been signs that she'd been skipping meals, along with sleep.

"What are you looking at?" she snapped, and drew her knees up to her chest under the blanket. "I swear," she fumed. "Connor, I'm going to kill you . . ." She buried her face in her knees and pulled the blanket up around her ears. He heard angry muttering and caught a few choice words he assumed were directed at her brother.

Bump briefly closed his eyes and considered quietly leaving the lab, giving her pride the privacy it probably needed. Just as he was about to rise, she lifted her head, her eyes flashing. "It's nobody's business," she said quietly, harshly. "He had no right to tell you that."

Bump stayed firmly in his seat. He carefully leaned forward. "Claire, he didn't tell me anything. Okay? All he said was that he was worried about you because you're a perfectionist and you put a lot of pressure on yourself." *And he may have mentioned that you're a bit self-destructive. Nah, better leave that part out.*

She bit her lip, and her face suffused with color. "He didn't tell you I recently recovered from an eating disorder?"

Bump carefully shook his head, making sure he held her eye contact. "No, he didn't. He didn't say a word about that."

She nodded stiffly. "I'm sorry I snapped at you," she said. "It's not something I like to have broadcast to the world."

"Understandable."

"I'm better now," she said, sounding defensive. "I went through therapy and everything."

He nodded, thoughtfully pursing his lips. "You're right," he said. "It's none of my business, and you're a big girl. You can do what you want." He paused, leaning forward with his elbows resting on his knees. He lightly tapped his fingertips together. "I did promise Connor, though, that I'd make sure you were doing okay."

"I'm doing fine."

"You didn't have dinner last night." He paused again. "Come to think of it, I didn't see you having lunch yesterday, either."

"Are you watching me?"

One corner of his mouth quirked into a subtle smile. "How can I not?"

Her face again flooded with color. She cleared her throat, apparently at a loss for words. She opened her mouth and closed it again, not making the slightest sound. She rubbed her forehead with a hand that snaked its way out from underneath the blanket she still clutched around her bent knees.

"Look," she finally said. "I'm twenty-five years old. I don't need a baby-sitter. I know what I need to do."

"Well, tell ya what," he answered. "I'm going now to let you get your clothes changed. When I come back, we'll go have breakfast together. Then I'll feel better because I've watched you eat, and I can get off your back about it."

Her nostrils flared slightly, but she shrugged. "Sure. Whatever." Her face then clouded. "I don't know how I'm going to get anything done, worrying about this stuff all day," she murmured, looking about at the artifacts.

"Do you have responsibilities outside that take you away from the lab during the day?"

She nodded. "I do a lot of the actual digging and recording," she answered, running a hand over her hair.

"Well, let's do this; I'll spend the bulk of my time in here for today, at least, and talk to some of your colleagues that I haven't interviewed yet. When you're gone and I'm not in here, let's make sure you have someone in here you trust so you can get your other work done. Will that help?"

Claire nodded. She chewed on her lip, fidgeting with the blanket she held between her restless fingers. She must have finally come to some kind of resolve. She straightened and looked at him. "Again," she said, "I'm sorry for snapping at you. I do appreciate your help."

He nodded with another of his characteristic half-smiles. "No problem," he said and rose from his chair, walking to the door. "I'll be back in ten minutes. Will that give you time to change?" He motioned to the duffel bag she had placed next to her cot the night before.

She nodded.

"Okay. I'll see you in a few."

* * * * * *

Claire tried to choke down her toast while looking as though it wasn't killing her. He had *buttered* it. Ack. He was sitting there next to her, chatting animatedly with Jon Kiersey about who knew what while she was trying not to think about how many calories and fat grams were worming their way into her system, via her unwilling mouth.

She recognized the signs; it was identical to the way it had happened the time before. She had been stressed while in school, wanting perfection from herself in every aspect of class and field work, and had started obsessing about her food, figuring her weight and appearance were, if nothing else, things she had absolute control over. And then, seeing the results of her obsessive dieting, she became intoxicated with the heady power of that control.

She supposed some of the problem stemmed from the fact that she was short, and always had been. She and Paige had pored through fashion magazines as young teenagers, wanting to look like the models on the glossy pages. They were lucky, both of them, in the sense that they possessed extremely good genes, and they both had a natural love for all things outdoors, which lent itself to plenty of exercise.

But they were short.

Short was hard to swallow when the world appeared to judge glamour and beauty in terms of height and visible skeletal structure. Paige moaned along with Claire about the fact that they'd quit growing at five foot two, but she'd let it go. Claire couldn't. She remembered thinking, *if I can't be tall, I can at least be really thin.*

And so she dieted on and off through high school and college, carefully watching the things she ate and never indulging to excess. It wasn't until graduate school, however, that the weight and control issues spiraled out of control. When her parents had realized the extent of the problem, they intervened, and in a big way. Even though they lived hundreds of miles apart, Claire's mother had threatened to come to Arizona where Claire was going to school and move in with her.

Claire had acquiesced, and quite honestly, had been to the point where she was afraid for herself. She had sought counseling. She was referred to a therapist who had experienced some of the same problems herself, and Claire had benefited from this woman's experiences, taking her advice to heart and working through the issues that were buried far beneath the surface. Her therapist had warned her to be careful and use the things she'd learned to prevent future problems.

The thefts at the dig had caught her off guard. Her life had been going so well that when the artifacts began turning up missing, she had not dealt with it effectively. The fact that she actually *knew* that was helpful, she supposed as she continued tearing off pieces of her toast and stuffing them into her mouth, but it wasn't going to be easy. She had fallen back into some of the same old patterns and she knew it was altogether too easy to want to stay there.

Except that she knew she wouldn't be happy. She sighed. *Come on, Claire,* her mind urged. *Pull yourself out now before it gets any worse.* She nodded slightly to herself and resolved to fix things. *I can do this,* she mused and stole a sideways glance at Bump, *and I can do it by MYSELF. I don't need any help.*

He must have sensed her quick perusal; he finally looked at her with a smile.

"Almost done?" He nodded toward the last bite of toast she held between her fingers as though it were covered in mold.

"Mmm hmm," she murmured, chewing. She swallowed and put the last bit in her mouth. She chased it down with a gulp of water from her water bottle and stood, palming the apple she was also supposed to have eaten. Unfortunately, she'd been eating so little lately that her stomach had shrunk and left no room for anything larger than one piece of toast, it seemed. She placed her water bottle in the small backpack she wore when she worked on the site; it contained a pencil, notebook, a few plastic bags for artifacts, some tissues, a camera, and a measuring tape.

"I'll eat this outside, later," she said, waving the apple as she rose. She motioned her head to Jon as she worked her way to the door. "You coming with me today?"

He nodded and rose, following her out the door carrying his own water bottle. "We'll catch you later," he said to Bump as they left. Claire managed to grunt in agreement as she stepped outside.

. . . sitting there, watching me eat like I'm some child . . . It was all she could do to keep from muttering her thoughts aloud. *Well, Claire,* her practical inner voice finally sighed, *if you didn't act like a child, you wouldn't have to be treated like one.*

Okay, you can shut up, now. Really, who needed practicality when it was so much nicer to be irrational? She shook her head at her thoughts as she walked toward the site with Jon at her side. He was content to say nothing at all, and she was grateful to have a few more moments to herself before she felt compelled to put on her "people face."

They walked onto the main area of the site, approaching one of the smaller buildings flanking the ancient temple. Claire felt herself relax as they approached; in the heart of all the activity was where she felt most at home.

She turned to Jon with a smile. "Ready to play in the dirt?"

Chapter 9

Queliza studied the queen carefully before finally gathering the courage she needed to speak freely. The queen seemed to sense her reluctance; she beckoned the young girl forward and bade her speak.

After several attempts, Queliza finally found her voice and managed to try to explain her fears concerning the prince's safety.

The queen's reaction was one of gentle mirth. "Oh dear child," the woman said, "I'm sure the prince would never be so foolish. Even if he were to win, the wrath of the king would fall upon him; he would never risk such a thing . . ."

* * * * * *

Claire shoveled dirt gently into a bucket, using a small trowel; it was flat, the same kind a bricklayer would use. She talked to Jon, who was kneeling by her side, as she worked. "We use these smaller tools for the detail work," she said. "We can sift through, layer by layer, and hopefully not miss or dismantle anything."

She handed Jon a small broom and dustpan with a grin. "You sweep while I pick."

He laughed. "Am I supposed to believe I have the fun part?"

"Of course! Kind of like white-washing Aunt Polly's fence."

"You'd make Tom Sawyer proud." He commenced sweeping the dirt she was sifting away and motioned when the dustpan was full. "Into these buckets, I suppose?"

She nodded, wiping at her cheek with the back of her hand and leaving a smudge of dirt in the process. "Yes, and then we'll dump the bucket into one of those wheelbarrows," she said, motioning with her hand toward several wheelbarrows that sat situated in groups around the site. "We take all that excess dirt to a dump site."

She and Jon worked side by side in companionable silence until Jon cleared his throat and apparently sought to make an attempt at conversation."I was reading one of your archaeology magazines and I saw pictures of sites with all kinds of square holes."

Claire looked up when he offered nothing further, appreciating the fact that sometimes silence was unnerving. He didn't seem the chatty sort; she quickly realized she'd better come up with some kind of comment to keep him from feeling stupid. Fortunately, talking about her field was one of her favorite topics of conversation.

"Yes," she said. "Square holes keep things neat and organized. We grid everything off with the string and stakes to make it easier for recording purposes. When we make note of where we find something, we do it according to its position on the grid. We take pictures, we draw what we find; we have to completely document everything. We dig square trenches according to the grid, and we dig straight down, not tapered at all. I'm sure you've noticed all the string and stakes we've got set up all over the site."

He nodded. "It's an interesting process," he commented, sweeping dirt into the bucket.

"It is. I never get tired of it. This site is a little different," she explained, "in that the bulk of the ruins are already above the surface. They're only partially buried, so we have a pretty good idea of what we're dealing with." She turned and pointed with her trowel at the ancient temple, situated to their right. "Now *that's* an interesting thing to see," she said. "I need to work in the lab this afternoon, but I'm reserving tomorrow for another trip inside. Do you think you'd like to see it?"

He shrugged. "Sure. What's it like?"

"Oh, it's amazing. I love it. I'll let you be surprised."

The building they were currently sifting through actually housed its main level at a height approximately six feet off the ground. There were columns flanking the outer walls, much like one might see in Greek or Roman architecture, and the foundation of the building was currently encased in mounds of dirt. It was from this vantage-point that Claire and Jon turned their heads upward at the sound of harsh coughing. Claire moaned in sympathy. "Are you gonna be okay, Ricardo?" she called out.

"I don't know," came the faint reply, followed by more coughing.

Claire's brows drew together in a frown. She rose and walked to her left until she found a good place to climb up to where Ricardo was crouched near the ground over a notebook.

She reached him and placed her hand on his shoulder. "It's getting worse," she said quietly. "Why don't you go lay down. This can wait."

Ricardo murmured a faint protest but didn't complain when Claire insisted. She held out her hand for the notebook. "I'll see what I can do with it," she said as she viewed the sketches the young man had made thus far. He stumbled from the site, coughing and expressing his thanks as he went.

Claire returned to her former position beside Jon and placed the sketches on top of the backpack she had shed upon arrival.

"What's wrong with him?" Jon asked.

"Well, he's had this nagging cough for a long time, but today he seems almost feverish. He's an avid swimmer, and yesterday he went swimming in a nearby river where there are always lots of mosquitoes . . ." She pursed her lips, thinking. "I wonder if he doesn't have malaria." She shook her head. "He needs to be examined, but he's too stubborn to do it on his own. I'll have to talk to Justin about it . . ." she added the last as though making a mental note. "In fact," she said as she rose, "I think I'll do it now before I forget. Do you want to just wait here for me?"

Jon nodded. "Sure, no problem. I'll just keep sweeping." His mouth quirked into a wry smile.

She laughed and walked away from the site.

Jon watched her retreating form and then looked down at the notebook she had placed on her backpack. Apparently, Ricardo had been making a sketch of the area he'd been viewing when he'd had his coughing fit. Jon's fingers moved of their own accord and picked up the sketches, examining them closely. Without thinking, he picked up the pencil that had dropped to the ground beside the backpack and cautiously climbed to where Ricardo had been working.

He crouched in the same position Ricardo had occupied and carefully looked at the figures and pictures carved into the wall mere inches from his face. He backed up a bit and examined the picture before him from a wider perspective. He glanced down at the drawing, which did the job, as he supposed was its purpose, but it was missing . . . something.

He flipped to a fresh sheet of paper and began to draw, his mind thinking in images, not words. His hand flew over the page, and all of the surrounding sounds of the site and its people faded away into a distant place. Finishing the sketch and growing impatient with the small segment of wall that was his subject, he flipped to another clean sheet of paper and turned his body so that he had a commanding view of the site.

He sketched the layout of the entire dig as he saw it, with its differing layers and levels: the carved pillars situated around the grassy floor of the small valley; rock walls; and the gargantuan temple standing out against the brilliant blue sky, the stairs leading to its pinnacle and seeming to go on forever. His eye caught every detail, every nuance of the scene and transferred it unerringly to the notebook he held comfortably in his right hand. He filled in the gaps, giving the picture depth as he added the equipment present in every nook and cranny: wheelbarrows, countless buckets and shovels, machines and devices whose names he did not know, and the rough outlines of people as they went about their activities.

He had lost all sense of time. When Claire finally returned and stood before him, he blinked.

"What?" he said.

She crouched down next to him on the ground. "What's that?" she repeated, motioning with her hand toward the notebook.

He cleared his throat. "Nothing." He attempted to tear the sheet from the notebook.

"No, you don't," she said. "Please, may I see it?"

He hesitated, then handed it to her, looking off to his left into the distance. She was silent for several long minutes, confirming his worst fears. She thought it was ridiculous.

"Jon," she finally said, lifting her head. "This is fantastic. Why didn't you mention that you're an artist?"

He looked at her in surprise, taking a moment to formulate his words. "An artist?" He laughed. "I'm not an artist."

She snorted. "Yeah, and I'm not an archaeologist." She shook her head at him. "I can't believe how wonderful this is; it looks like a photograph!" She paused, her lips pursed. "Ricardo is sick. He's going into town today to see a doctor. How would you like a job?"

"A job?" He blinked.

"Would you be willing to sketch whatever I ask you to?"

He shrugged. "I guess so. I've never done much drawing, though . . ."

"Are you kidding me?" She laughed, her eyebrows raised in disbelief. "Well, Jon," she said, sobering, "that's a shame."

He shrugged again.

"We really do need someone to sketch this stuff," she said. "We take pictures with cameras, and draw and document everything we come across. I can do it, but only passably well. This," she said, motioning to the notebook with her hand, "is art. And you did it in the, what, fifteen to twenty minutes I was gone?" She shook her head again. "My friend," she said as she stood, "you've got yourself a job whether you want one or not. This is just incredible."

She paused for a moment and then rose, waiting as he stood next to her, dusting off his pants. "Would you mind if I kept this?" she asked.

"Not at all." The dubious half laugh that accompanied his statement suggested he was surprised she'd even want it.

"Will you sign it for me, then?"

He raised one eyebrow. "Sign it?"

"Well, yeah. Someday you'll be famous and I want to be able to say I own a Jon Kiersey original."

He snorted, but took the notebook and signed his name in small script on the bottom right-hand corner of the picture.

She smiled and took it from him, gently tearing it from the notebook. "Okay," she said, "would you be willing to start right here where Ricardo left off with his sketch?"

"I already have." Jon took the notebook from her and turned to the page where he'd sketched the scene they stood beside.

She stared at the picture, eyes wide. "Well then," she murmured. "Let me see where else we need to put you."

As Claire examined various trenches while speaking to her fellow colleagues, Jon's eyebrows drew together in thought. Someone actually *wanted* him to draw. They *needed* him to do it. He couldn't remember the last time he was needed for anything.

* * * * * *

Bump was seated in the lab with Sue Chastain, completely unaware that his traveling companion was on the brink of an epiphany. "So tell me about your responsibilities here," he was saying. His casual scrutiny of her appearance revealed dust-stained shirt and pants, hazel eyes, and a smattering of freckles across her nose and cheeks that, Bump assumed, had made their home on her face at the bidding of the bright Guatemalan sunlight. She had a small nose, and a wide mouth that was quick to smile or assume pleasant conversation, despite the serious expression on her face.

Her hair had the look of a woman blessed, or alternately cursed, with curls. In a dry climate, it might have been manageable, but in the humidity of their current conditions, he supposed that the best she could manage without bothering with equipment meant to tame it into submission was to brush it back off her forehead and tie the resulting mass together in a very large, very fuzzy-curly ponytail. She didn't strike Bump as the type who would mess with her hair even in convenient conditions; she was very no-nonsense, very practical, and seemed to be very much unimpressed with herself.

"Well, I'm working toward my master's degree," Sue replied, "and I've been here for about two months. I assist wherever I'm asked; I work a lot with Claire."

"And can you think of any specific details about the thefts of the artifacts I might find interesting?" He watched her carefully, without appearing to, monitoring body language, tone of voice—all the subtleties that tended to betray a person.

She pursed her lips in thought. "I wish I had some definitive thoughts, but there's nothing I can put my finger on," she finally stated on a sigh. "As I recall, all the thefts but the most recent have occurred at night, and the pieces that have been taken are those that seem to be the most intact, with only small pieces missing. Let's see," she mused, "they've mostly been pieces of pottery. Claire has a detailed listing of exactly what's been stolen and when."

I'll bet she does. Bump nodded. "I'll talk to her about that," he said. "I appreciate your help. I wonder if you'd let me know if you think of anything else?"

Sue nodded. "Of course." She rose with a smile and resumed the duties she'd been performing when he'd found her in the lab. He knew Claire trusted Sue; she'd told him as much and designated her as the person she wanted to be in the lab should Claire or Bump not be available.

He'd spoken to half of the staff already, and had been content to observe their activities as well as speaking to them briefly, if only to ascertain their reactions to him. He'd expected them to be nervous; even the most innocent of people often felt edgy around him when they knew he was investigating something.

There was a difference though, he usually found, between innocent nerves and the look in someone's eyes when there was something to hide. If this were a quality that was easily discernible, he'd have marketed the methods of detection to PIs worldwide and made a killing. As it was, he was content to be able to recognize the signs himself and make a comfortable living at it.

To his discouragement, he had to admit that he hadn't seen that "look" in the faces of anyone he'd interviewed. He was a patient man, however, and wasn't one for wallowing in despair. He also didn't discount those he'd spoken to. Just because he'd marked them for innocent at first glance didn't always mean such was the case. He'd keep his guard up, as always, and trust his instincts, which had yet to fail him.

Bump fought the smile twitching at the corners of his mouth at his recollection of young Devon Stark and her reaction to him earlier in the day. She'd scowled at him, but had said nothing. Jon had indeed worked his magic, and the dreaded phone call to Uncle Darren had never materialized.

When Bump had questioned Jon about it the night before, he'd been met with a smug expression.

"I told you I'd take care of it," Jon had said.

"How?"

Jon shrugged. "I told her she was much prettier when she smiled."

"That's it?"

Jon grinned. "Well, that, and I told her I imagined she must have been the most popular girl at her high school . . ."

Bump laughed. "And she took off from there?"

Jon nodded. "Talked for a good twenty minutes before I could get another word in. I now know that not only was she a cheerleader, but she was also active in student government and voted 'best dressed.' Apparently, her biggest dilemma now is whether or not she wants to pursue a career of any sort—she thinks it might be fun to just 'take a break.'"

"Take a break from what?"

Jon shrugged. "A break. That's all she said. She's been thinking it would be good to take a break."

"Yeah, I bet she's had it pretty tough. Did you tell her about where you came from?"

Jon snorted. "Yeah, and I showed her the track marks on my arms to prove it."

"You did?"

"Nah. But that would have been funny."

Bump laughed. "Well, try to restrain yourself for the time being."

Jon nodded, his lips twitching. "I don't suppose we want her calling her uncle and telling him there's a junkie at the dig."

"A former junkie."

"Yeah. A former junkie with no more direction in his life than the girl who was born with a silver spoon in her mouth and thinks she'd like to 'take a break' for awhile."

Bump sobered and lightly punched his friend in the arm. "You'll figure it out, man."

Jon had nodded absently and then stood, stating that he needed to change his clothes and go for a run. Bump had left the room and given him the privacy he needed. When Jon had returned an hour later, he was sweaty and exhausted, but then he showered and slept in his cot like the dead. Running appeared to be therapeutic for the man, and Bump figured the more he did it, the better off he'd be. Everyone had demons to work through at one time or other; Jon had found a way to sort things through.

And what of his own demons? Bump mused over the thought as

he sat in the lab, watching the students at their work. He'd been lucky, he supposed; he'd never really had many problems. He'd had a wonderful mother who, as a single parent, had supported him by working two jobs so he could have the education she felt he deserved. His father had died when Bump was six.

Well, there's a bit of a demon, he conceded, though he rarely thought of it on a conscious level. He had been old enough when his father had died to miss him horribly. There had been times in his childhood and subsequent adolescence that he'd felt a loneliness so crushing sometimes he couldn't breathe. And just when it always seemed at its worst, he'd feel his father in his heart, and relax.

Perhaps that was why, when the LDS missionaries had been teaching him their "Plan of Salvation," it had sounded familiar. Because when he had sat through that lesson, and the others that followed, he'd felt his father in his heart. It felt right and true, and he had welcomed it impulsively—albeit calmly—as was his style, into his life.

He'd probably always find the Mormon culture part of the whole thing gently amusing. That whole canning, quilting, Young Men, Young Women, raucous church basketball business was new to him, and wasn't at all what he was used to. The Book of Mormon figures, however—the men who fought to the death to protect their families and their freedoms, the fathers who loved their sons and prayed for them and blessed them—this he could feel in his heart. Had his own dad lived to see his son into adulthood, he'd have blessed him and prayed for him, of that he was certain.

He'd have been proud, too, Bump reflected with a surety. *My dad would be proud of the man I've become.* He viewed his surroundings and pulled himself to the present, gruffly clearing his throat and rising from his seat. Rather than sit there and miss his dad until he felt sick, he decided to go outside and find Claire.

She made him smile.

And aside from that, he told himself, he had to be sure she'd eaten that apple she'd passed over at breakfast. It was as good an excuse as any, and he'd take it. He smiled inwardly, wondering when he'd last needed an excuse to see a woman. Well, he figured as he walked from the lab and to the site, she wasn't just any woman.

This one was unique.

Chapter 10

Palome looked at Queliza in concern as they walked the length of the plaza. "How . . . comfortable are you becoming with the prince?"

Queliza blushed. "Not so comfortable that you should have cause for concern as one of my oldest and dearest friends," she said. "I'm not ignorant in the ways of men and women; I know what happens, and we have not engaged in such activity."

Palome shook his head. "I would not wish to cause you discomfort over this matter, Queliza. It is that I care for you so much . . . promise me that you will be careful."

"I will be careful," Queliza murmured, and laid her hand against Palome's cheek. Her attention turned from her old friend at the beckoning of the prince; he was across the plaza, walking toward them with a smile on his face.

"Ah, Palome," the prince said when he reached the couple. "And how are you today?" The prince never imagined Palome to be a rival for the attention of a woman; after all, Palome was nothing but the astronomer's son.

"I am fine, your highness." Palome turned away as the prince offered Queliza his arm and led her toward the palace.

* * * * * *

Claire was hard-pressed to remember a time she'd ever felt so dowdy. She was kneeling in the dirt, her clothing filthy and her cheeks smudged, squinting up into the grinning face of Bump St. James.

"Are we having fun, kids?" he asked and looked from her to Jon, who knelt at her side, sweeping dirt into the dustpan.

Claire glanced at her companion, noting the smudges of dirt on his face and the filthy state of his clothes and didn't feel quite so badly. She laughed.

Jon smirked up at his friend. "Why don't you come down here and join us, pretty boy? Afraid to get your hands dirty?"

"Oh!" Claire exclaimed, swiftly cutting off any reply Bump might have managed. "Your neck, Jon!"

"What's wrong with it?"

"Ooh, we're going to have to find you a hat. You're as red as a lobster."

Jon snorted. "Well, I'm not wearing one of those goofy-looking straw things," he said, motioning to one of Claire's colleagues, who stood off in the distance, wearing a wide-brimmed hat, as did many others on the staff.

"Yeah, we'll see how you're feeling tomorrow, tough guy," Claire answered with a grin. "We don't wear those as fashion statements, you know. The brim keeps the sun off the face and the back of the neck. They serve a good purpose."

"I don't see you wearing one."

"I happen to have long hair," she said, flipping her ponytail for emphasis, "that covers my neck. And when the sun gets really bright or I know I'll be in it all day, I wear a baseball cap."

Jon wrinkled his nose. "I've been sunburned before."

Claire laughed. "This sun is hot, my friend. Hot and merciless." She shook her head. "Suit yourself, but you'd do well to take my advice."

She glanced up at Bump, who was taking in the scene surrounding him. He shook his head. "I'm amazed that Stark won't let you employ more people to handle all of this. It's huge."

Claire nodded, then shrugged a shoulder. "Well, we've been able to handle the bulk of it. There were parts we had to bring in some big equipment for, and for that we enlisted the help of some qualified outsiders, but that was near the beginning. We've done the rest ourselves with the help of many of the interested locals who like to see what's buried under all this." She smiled. "That's always fun. I like to see them get all excited when we uncover something, even if it's just a little thing. We get more and more volunteers every day, in fact, in addition to the ones we pay." She made a face. "I haven't told Darren that, but Devon probably has."

Bump nodded and continued to peruse the countryside. "Well, it's impressive."

"Thanks. But actually, this site is a relatively small one. I've seen many of the larger Mayan sites; they're just gargantuan."

"So what drew you to this one?"

She smiled. "I don't know. I just . . . I don't know." She tipped her head to one side and studied the land. "There's something special about this place. When we found out about it I was so excited, but we had to go through all the motions of getting permission from the government and trying to drum up the money."

"And the funding magically appeared, so you were good to go."

Her brow wrinkled. "Yeah. Magic funding."

"With strings attached."

Claire's laugh was hollow. "Well, supposedly not, but sometimes I wonder." She turned to Jon as an afterthought. "I meant to thank you," she said, "for taking care of Devon yesterday. If she'd have called her uncle, he'd have given me grief."

"It was no problem," Jon replied as he continued his methodical sweeping. "She's easy. It didn't take much to figure out how she ticks."

"Well, you saved my hide, that's for sure." She turned her attention back to Bump, who had moved to squat next to them on the ground. "How are things in the lab?"

"Good. I still need to talk to Ricardo Valez and Etienne DuBois, if he ever returns. Sue and Miguel were both very cooperative."

Claire nodded. "Have you discovered anything . . . interesting?"

He shook his head. "Nothing yet."

"I'm almost relieved." She wiped at the sweat on her forehead with the back of one hand. Unzipping her backpack, she hauled out her water bottle and took a long swig. "I like Sue and Miguel. I trust them both, too." She shook her head with a frown. "I'm more inclined to believe an outsider is doing this, the more I think about it," she said.

"I thought you said it was probably someone on the inside."

"I did," she admitted. "But I've been truly giving it some thought, and I just can't imagine it's someone I've been working closely with, day in, day out . . ."

"Well, give it some time. I still have some ground to cover, but we'll get it figured out. In the meantime, how about some lunch?"

Jon abruptly stood, dropping the dustpan and broom. "Great," he stated. "I'm tired of chewing on dirt."

Claire laughed and placed her water bottle and the sketch pad into her backpack. "We'll put you to work sketching after lunch. You're more suited to that, anyway." She shook her head as she rose, hefting the pack onto her shoulder. She turned toward Bump and said, "Has he ever shown you any of his artwork?"

"His artwork?" Bump raised a brow and considered Jon, who rolled his eyes. "No, I don't believe he has."

"You wouldn't believe it," Claire gushed as the trio began walking from the site toward the mess hall. "He's a master."

Jon muttered something unintelligible under his breath.

"Anyway," Claire said, casting an irritated glance at Jon, "Ricardo is sick, and Jon's going to take his place until he gets back."

Jon shrugged, looking embarrassed. "She asked me to . . ." he offered lamely to Bump.

"Hey, man, I think it's great! Do I get to see any of this 'artwork'?"

"Yes," Claire promptly responded.

"No," Jon snapped simultaneously.

Claire heaved an exaggerated sigh as they reached the mess hall. She transferred her backpack from her shoulder to her hand and turned to Jon. "It's not like I'm asking you to do a naked self-portrait and show the world. All you're doing is sketching the site, and if your friend wants to see it, I don't see why he shouldn't."

With that, she offered a small shrug and a grin as though the discussion were closed, and turned and entered the mess hall.

Bump and Jon stared for a moment at the spot she'd just vacated. Jon slightly shook his head. "It's embarrassing," he finally said.

"Nothing to be embarrassed about. But I would like to see the pictures when you're done, if you don't mind. And I won't think you're anything less than masculine for having done them."

Jon rubbed the back of his newly sunburned neck and lightly

winced. "Do we have to discuss this in great detail?"

"No."

"Good." He turned and headed for their tent. "I'm going for a quick run before lunch."

Bump speculatively watched Jon's retreating form before finally turning and entering the mess hall. Claire barely knew either him or Jon, yet had all but ordered Jon to share the results of his sketch work. He couldn't stop himself from seeking her out at the counter where she stood, dishing a meager amount of food onto a plate.

"You insisted he show me that stuff," he said to her without preamble.

"Yes." She placed a lone piece of fat-free turkey breast lunch meat on a barren slice of wheat bread.

"Why?"

"Because he needs it." She looked up from her plate, questioning, and yet not.

Bump finally nodded. "I think he does."

Claire nodded as well, and turned her attention back to her plate. She placed an orange beside her sandwich and reached for a napkin. Taking her plate, she turned and walked to a table, talking over her shoulder as she went. Bump followed to be sure he heard her.

"He needs to share that talent," she said, shaking her head as she sat down. "I can't even describe it to you—you'll have to see it for yourself. It's obvious," she added, peeling her orange, "that he's never been encouraged in it."

Bump's derisive snort confirmed her statement.

"So if he's ever going to feel comfortable doing it, he's gotta know he's good. I think he respects you enormously, so I figured he if he could get some good feedback from you, he might keep at it."

Bump nodded a bit to himself. "He does need to find something."

"Well," Claire said as she bit into an orange slice. "This is definitely something. The guy is incredible."

Bump looked closely at Claire. "Really?"

"Really." She nodded, her eyes wide as she chewed.

Incredible, huh? Bump told himself it wasn't a spurt of irrational jealousy that had him suddenly wishing he could sketch. Anything. He couldn't even manage stick figures.

He watched her lick a drop of orange juice from the tip of one finger and vowed to take an art class.

Chapter 11

Queliza walked along the paths that led to the outskirts of the city center, moving farther away from the bustle that surrounded the plaza. She looked with some sorrow at the meaner, cruder homes that so resembled the one she'd been raised in. She came to a stop in front of one particular dwelling—her former home.

She thought sadly of her parents—her father who worked so hard to please the king, and for so little. To have his life so hopelessly and literally crushed had been beyond bearing for her mother. She had been a worker who created clothing for the queen, along with several other women in the neighboring homes. She had gone to work each day in the palace, slaving away to make beautiful garments she would never wear, her young daughter by her side.

Queliza missed her parents. They had loved her and cared for her and tried to spare her some of the horrors so prevalent in court life. The king was not a nice man, the society was harsh, and the royal aims were to conquer and amass as much surrounding territory as possible. Slaughter and sacrifice were ways of life, and oddly enough, her father and mother had never thought it right.

She didn't think it was, either. But the prince was different; somehow he wasn't as bloodthirsty as was his father, the king. He was immature, undoubtedly. But he was also somehow a bit more gentle. She worried at her lower lip with her teeth as she thought of him competing in the Game, unbeknownst to his father . . .

* * * * * *

T he stars were out in droves. From her position atop the steep staircase of the ancient temple, Claire felt she could see forever into the universe itself. The sky was an inky black, and she couldn't resist the impulse to lay flat on her back and stare into the vast expanse. "What's it all about?" she murmured with a smile.

Her grandfather had always asked her and Paige that very question as they'd sat perched on his knee. "What's it all about, girls?" he'd ask in his Irish brogue, and appear to take great interest in their responses, even as small children. As they grew older they refrained from sitting on his knee, but still managed to think about the question and give him answers despite the fact that they grew embarrassed and awkward in their middle teen years.

The last time he'd asked Claire his favorite question was when she was nineteen and studying hard in school. "What's it all about, Claire," he'd said with a smile after dinner one Sunday afternoon.

"I don't know," she'd moaned, sprawled on the couch, her eyes red-rimmed from a late-night study session. "It's about life kicking my butt."

He'd laughed long and hard over that one and patted her knee, his eyes crinkled at the corners and turned upward in mirth. "Only if you let it, Claire, my girl. Only if you let it."

Claire smiled at the memory and felt moisture burning behind her eyes as she lay looking at the stars. "I miss you," she whispered. Her grandfather had died in his sleep one month following that last conversation. "I wish you were here right now."

It was almost dizzying, the effect the sky overhead had, given the fact that she could see nothing else. It was as though she was totally and completely alone, feeling extremely small in comparison, yet grateful to be alive and a part of the whole. A gentle breeze wafted through the air, gently blowing over her sun-kissed skin and dirt-laden clothing. She closed her eyes and reached behind her head, lifting it up as she released her hair from the ponytail, wincing as she ran her fingers over her scalp.

Breathing a contented sigh, she lay her head back down on the ground and reached her arms out from her sides, prostrate on the dirt and completely relaxed. *Yes, funny enough,* she mused, *relaxed.* She hadn't felt so much at ease for weeks, it seemed. The knot that had held her stomach in its vicious grip had relaxed quite a bit, and it didn't take long to figure the reason why.

Bump St. James.

He had told her he'd find the person or persons responsible for the thefts, and she was slowly coming to believe him. He had a presence about him that commanded respect. She couldn't help but have confidence in him; he acted as though he could solve any problem, given enough time, and she found comfort in his professed abilities.

* * * * * *

It was with some alarm that Bump finally found Claire. He'd been searching every building in the encampment, his concern growing with each negative response. He hadn't seen her for dinner, but had decided to give her a little space. However, as the hour had grown late, he'd become increasingly antsy until he found himself combing the entire site.

The impulse that had him climbing the bazillion stairs leading to the top of the old temple was one that paid off. There she was at the very top, lying flat on her back, spread eagle and looking at the stars. He approached her softly, not wanting to startle her and yet ready to throttle her for not at least telling someone where she was going. *She's not a child. She doesn't have to tell anyone anything if she doesn't want to,* spoke the voice of reason.

Yeah, well, it's common courtesy, he mentally argued. It wouldn't have killed her to mention the fact that she was going to become one with the cosmos for awhile.

He walked quietly until he finally reached her side. He looked down at her face, peaceful and beautiful in the moonlight, her hair spread about her like a great black cloud. She must have been sleeping. She apparently hadn't heard him walking. He stood still for a moment, wondering which approach to take; he couldn't very well let her sleep outside all night.

"Hey," he finally whispered.

She shot bolt upright, her eyes huge.

"Oh, I'm sorry," he said immediately on a half laugh, and crouched down to sit next to her. "I thought you were asleep."

Her breath came out in a huge, heaving *whoosh*. "I . . . I . . ." she stammered. She took a deep breath. "Thank you for the heart attack!"

"I'm sorry," he repeated again with a grin.

"Yeah," she grumbled, running a shaky hand through her tangled hair. "You don't look very sorry."

His grin faded. He'd never seen her hair down. It was long, thick, and straight. The fringe of bangs on her forehead framed her eyes, making them look huge, and the long strands she combed with her fingers shimmered in the moonlight. He shook his head. *Shimmered in the moonlight?*

"What's wrong?" she asked, finally tossing the mass over her shoulder and batting at the resistant strands that blew across her face in the soft breeze.

"I'm thinking I suddenly have the soul of some idiot poet," he muttered.

She arched a brow in question.

He shook his head again. "Must have been something I ate." He inclined his head toward her. "Speaking of which, you never showed up for dinner."

She sighed. "It's a good thing, apparently. Otherwise I might be feeling like 'some idiot poet.'"

"Not funny."

She rubbed her forehead and wrinkled her nose. "I just couldn't," she finally said. "Nothing sounded good."

"Claire," he began, and searched for the right words. He found himself at a bit of a loss. The right words usually came to him quite easily. "Is there someone or something you need? Can I get you anything? There's not much of anything I can't get—I know a lot of people . . ."

She laughed, sounding delightfully . . . well, delightful. He wanted to smack his palm against his forehead in frustration. He hadn't *ever* used the word "delightful."

"That's very sweet of you to offer," she said, "but I'm doing okay." She sobered a bit, a smile still hovering around the corners of her mouth. "I finally decided to let you do your job, and I'll get back to mine. Now that you're here, I can just transfer all my worry and stress onto your shoulders," she said, gesturing with her hands, "and quit fretting about what I can't seem to fix."

He wasn't convinced. "So you're all better."

Her half laugh turned into a moan. She rubbed her eyes with her fingers and yawned. "I don't think I'll ever be all better. But at least I'm functioning."

He paused, watching her closely. "Can I ask you something really blunt?"

"Sure."

"Do you think you're fat?"

She laughed again, this time long and hard. When she finally sobered enough to form words, he had to wonder what was so dang funny. "I really hope," she said on a chuckle, "that you've never asked any other women that before. And if you have," she said, holding up a hand to forestall his defensive response, "I can tell you right now why they never went out with you again."

He smirked, mostly at himself. "I'm not usually so blunt," he said by way of apology.

She still smiled. "Sure you are. I'll bet you're every bit that blunt and then some. But," she said with a sigh, "to answer your question, no, I don't really feel all that fat." She shook her head. "With me it wasn't always about weight. Well," she amended, "it started out that way. I realized I'd never be tall, so I decided to be thin instead. The minor dieting kind of, well, intensified when I was in grad school, and then it just became a control issue." She had the grace to look slightly chagrined. Had the light been brighter, he guessed he'd have seen her blushing. "I think that's what's been happening with me here these last few weeks. I'm kind of a control freak," she finished.

"No, really? I'd never have believed it."

She waved a hand at him in irritation. "You don't understand what it's like," she said.

"Sure I do. I like things to go my way."

"Yeah, but do you obsess about it until you can't sleep at night? Do you let it affect your appetite so much that even if you didn't care about your weight, you wouldn't be able to eat anyway?"

"Well, I'd have to say no to that one. But again, speaking of food . . ." He reached behind his back and pulled forward a paper lunch sack. "I made you a sandwich and brought you an apple."

Claire took the proffered sack with a smile. "You're sweet," she said.

He grunted. "That's a new one."

She pulled the sandwich out of the sack and tried to examine it without being too obvious in her intentions.

"It's turkey breast on wheat bread," he supplied for her. "Two slices of bread though, not just one. And I didn't add anything else to it—no mustard, mayo, butter, or anything. And there's only one slice of turkey breast on it. Now, if you ask me," he continued, "you're probably getting the same effect flavor-wise with that one slice as you would if you just asked the turkey to walk across the bread for good measure, but hey—what do I know?"

She laughed again, choking on the bite she'd taken from the sandwich. He pulled a water bottle from the sack and removed the lid, handing her the bottle and watching as she took a gulp. "Thanks," she sputtered. "And thanks for the dinner. I actually was starting to get a bit hungry up here."

"What were you doing, anyway—communing with nature?"

She smiled. "Something like that," she said, taking another bite of the sandwich. "I was talking to my grandfather. He's dead." The night was alive with the sound of crickets and other creatures of the night, combined with the sound of rustling leaves as the warm wind occasionally blew across the site. Claire continued munching her sandwich in the companionable silence that followed her pronouncement. She swallowed and took another drink before speaking again.

"He was my father's father. He emigrated to the States from Ireland when he was in his teens, and my sister and I thought he was just about the most wonderful thing ever. He passed away a few years ago, and sometimes I like to think he's listening to me, somewhere."

Bump nodded thoughtfully. "I can relate to that. My dad died when I was six."

Her brow wrinkled into a frown. "Oh, no. How awful for a young kid."

He shrugged, and nearly said *Nah, it was nothing . . .* but it wasn't "nothing." It had been a very big something that had haunted him his whole life. He finally nodded, clearing his throat. He looked around at the dark earth, the even darker sky, and the myriad stars that twinkled in their brilliance. His eyes finally came back to rest on her face. That beautiful face, those eyes that were so blue they almost weren't, and the black hair that occasionally blew like silk in the breeze.

"It was bad," he said quietly. "It was hard for my mom and hard on me." He took a breath. "But we did it," he murmured with a shrug, "and life goes on."

"Had he been sick?"

Bump shook his head. "No. He was hit by a car one morning while walking to work. Killed him instantly."

She had stopped eating. "I'm so sorry," she whispered, sitting there with him, looking for all the world like her heart was in her eyes.

"He didn't suffer," Bump finally stated, straightening a bit and trying to lighten the mood. "For that I'm grateful." ·

She nodded, apparently sensing his need to move on to other topics. She straightened a bit herself and took a bite of her apple after swiping it across her filthy shirt.

He laughed. "I don't think that little maneuver there did you much good."

She grinned and took a loud, crunching bite. "I have to at least go through the motions," she laughed, still chewing.

They again lapsed into silence, the noises of the night mixing with the sound of crunching apple. When Claire finally finished, she tossed the apple core back into her sack and chased the small meal down with one last drink from her bottle. "So," she said after wiping her mouth on the small napkin Bump had included in the sack, "what's your real name?"

She'd caught him so completely off guard he almost told her. Instead, he stopped himself and laughed. "My name is Bump," he said.

"Bump is your legal name?"

"It might as well be."

"That's what's on your driver's license?"

His mouth quirked. "No. My given name is on my driver's license."

"So how did you come up with 'Bump'?"

"My dad called me 'Bump.' I never remember him calling me anything else. I was clumsy as a toddler, the story goes, and I forever ran into the walls with my head. He called me Bump because of the perpetual goose egg on my forehead."

Claire smiled. "What a fun memory. Not the bumping into walls part, but having something like that from your dad must be nice." She paused. "Weren't you teased a lot as a kid?"

He snorted. "I'd have been teased either way. My given name is . . . well . . . I don't like it much."

"Must be pretty bad . . ."

"I hated my name so much as a kid that after my dad died, my mom let me go by Bump because it was what I wanted. After awhile, it just became a game; people always wanted to know and I've never wanted the game to be at an end, I guess. I've been at it for so long now, I wouldn't know how to stop."

"And you don't worry about what people think?"

"Nah. I don't worry too much about that."

She smiled. "I admire your fortitude. I worry entirely too much."

"You shouldn't."

"Easier said than done." She yawned.

He stood and brushed off his clothing, offering her his hand to help her rise. She took it and stood, carrying the paper sack and water bottle with her as they walked back to the camp. "Now," he said. "I'm sleeping in the lab, as is Jon. You'll have two of us in there, guarding your stuff. So you get some sleep and don't worry. Everything will be fine."

She glanced in his direction, clearly wanting to believe him.

"Trust me."

"Okay."

Chapter 12

He kissed her! The prince finally kissed her, under the stars on the ball court, right where he said he was planning to play the Game before the week was out.

"I am but a servant," she said to him with some trepidation when he pulled back, wondering what his intentions were. He had no obligation to preserve any sort of honor on her part; indeed, the society cared very little for honor. But it meant something to her, because her heart was involved.

The prince's face was sincere. "I know this, Queliza. But remember that I am the prince. I may not rule the city, but someday I will. And I will be free to choose my own queen. I am not so concerned with alliances. We have allies enough. I would like to have you at my side . . ."

* * * * * *

Bump observed Claire the next morning in the mess hall, regaling the staff with embarrassing tales from graduate school, and not eating. He shook his head and wondered if he'd spend his entire time at the site stuffing food in her mouth. As the crowd began to disperse and reluctantly leave her side, he made his way over to her and muttered in an undertone, "Where's your breakfast?"

Her smile froze on her face. She laughed at something Sue was saying over her shoulder as she left the building, then finally turned to Bump when Sue was gone. Replacing the smile was a decidedly irritated frown. "Okay, buddy," she said. "I have never, I repeat, never, been a morning person. I have to be awake at least two hours before I can stand to eat something. I ate yesterday morning because you looked big and forbidding," she said, motioning to his large frame absently with her hand, "but now I've decided you've basically got the heart of a small, furry animal."

With that, she stood and gathered her backpack, making her way to the counter and withdrawing an empty water-bottle from the pack. "You remind me of this guy I know," she said as she walked. He followed her out of morbid curiosity.

"Who?"

"A friend of my brother's. Actually," she amended as she reached inside the cooler for a fresh water bottle, "he's really a friend of the whole family. But Connor took to him and his wife like old friends and ended up living with them for awhile in Virginia right after he finished school." She finished as though the conversation were concluded and what she'd said made perfect sense.

"And?" he prodded with a growl.

"And what?"

"You can't just make a statement like that and expect me to know what it means," he said. "What is this guy, some kind of psycho? And what's all this about a furry animal?"

She laughed and closed the cooler, storing the bottle securely in her backpack. "He's not a psycho. He's just got this exterior that totally says, 'Don't mess with me man, or I'll take your head off,' and once you get to know him, you realize he's like this cuddly, furry thing on the inside that's really very mild."

She threw the pack over one shoulder and made her way to the door, grabbing an apple from the table as she went. She held it in the air and rolled her eyes. "I'll eat this in about an hour. Will that make you happy?"

He grunted in confusion. He was still stuck on the furry animal talk. "Wait a minute," he said, but she was already out the door. He caught up with her outside.

"Claire, stop," he said and pulled her to a halt. She was going a million miles a minute.

"What is it?" She looked up at him, shading her eyes with one hand to avoid the harsh glare of the morning sun.

His breath caught in his throat and he forgot what it was he wanted to say. So he said the first thing that came to mind. "I remind you of a psycho?"

She snorted. "I told you, he's not a psycho. In fact," she said, a look of surprise covering her face, "you probably know him. Or at least know of him; he's Liz's brother-in-law."

"Montgomery?"

She nodded, grinning. "Yeah, that's him. Have you ever met?"

He shook his head. "No, we haven't." He couldn't think of anything else to say.

"Well," Claire shrugged, still smiling. "Okay."

She started walking again toward the ancient temple and Bump closed his eyes in frustration. He felt like he was losing his mind. He ran the few steps it took to cover the surprising distance she'd gained in a few short moments and caught her arm again.

"Claire." He put both hands on her shoulders.

"What?" She didn't try to mask her irritation. "What is it?"

His breath came out on a frustrated sigh. What *was* it? There was something about her today, something restless he hadn't ever seen in her. "Have you had a lot of caffeine today?"

She looked him carefully in the eyes, her own eyes narrowing a fraction. "No," she said, tilting her head to one side, "but I might ask the same of you. What's going on with you today?"

"Me?" The word nearly exploded from his lips. "*You're* the one who's all . . . all . . ."

She shook her head a fraction in question. "All what?"

"All energetic-like." He felt like a fool; there was something different that he couldn't pinpoint. It was drawing him to her side and made him feel like he never wanted to leave.

She quirked one corner of her mouth into a grin. "Well," she said, "I felt a little different when I woke up this morning. I think I know what it is."

He raised his eyebrows, waiting impatiently.

"It's you."

He blinked. "Me?"

She nodded. "Now that you're here, I can concentrate on my job and let you take care of all the muck. I think I finally realized it last night when we were talking, but I really do mean it. I can actually transfer the worry of the thefts to you and get back to the things I need to be doing." She shrugged one shoulder. "I've been a little antsy all morning; I can't wait to get into the temple and do some exploring. In fact," she said, "Jon's coming with me to check things out; you can come along if you'd like."

He stared at her face for a moment, then motioned toward the old structure. "In there? That thing?"

She nodded. "It's kind of like an Egyptian tomb," she explained. "It's really fascinating."

He'd heard all he needed to. "Well, actually I needed to talk to some more of your staff this morning," he said, shoving his hands into his pockets. "I'll have to catch it another time."

"Okay, whatever." She started to walk again, and then stopped, turning back with a smile. "Can I leave, now?"

He nodded absently. He walked back toward the lab, turning twice to observe her as she made her way to the ancient building, examining the sky and the tops of the trees as she went, her body moving in effortless grace. It was then that he was finally able to define the difference in her behavior; she seemed genuinely happy and at peace. Excited, even. The happy performance he'd been observing since his arrival had been just that; only now did her outward show of joy seem genuine.

And he was responsible. Well, now, there was a bit of pressure. *It's nothing I haven't handled before*, he assured himself as he walked. But he wondered as he pushed open the door to the lab why suddenly the thought of failure seemed absolutely unacceptable. It wasn't as though he'd *ever* contemplated the notion of failing as an excusable thing, but he reflected on Claire O'Brian's stressed features of the days past and compared them with the woman he'd just seen.

No, failure was definitely not an option.

* * * * * *

Claire walked along the narrow passageway, speaking over her shoulder to Jon. "Apparently," she said, "the Mayans used to completely crush their old temples when they decided it was time for a new one, and simply fill the old, smashed structure with dirt and build right on top of the existing site."

She motioned with her hand as they turned a corner. "You'll see in a minute where we've been removing all kinds of dirt and rock to reveal an older structure underneath this one." She ran her fingers along the wall, envisioning the hands of those, aeons of time before, who had run *their* hands along that very spot.

"This flat wall to our right was once the outer wall of a former temple," she said, still trailing her hand along the smooth surface. "The jagged wall here on the other side," she said, motioning to their left, "is obviously the inner wall to the most current structure."

"Amazing." She heard Jon's hushed whisper behind her as they walked.

"I know, isn't it?" She had yet to meet anyone who wasn't impressed with the feeling of the old building. There was a presence, a lingering essence of the people who had lived before. She hadn't lied to Bump. She'd been feeling a restless energy since she had wakened that morning, and couldn't quite put her finger on the source, except to assume that she was no longer worried.

And in truth, she wasn't. She was so relieved to have shifted the burden of her stresses onto his capable shoulders that she wanted to sing. If she had been able to carry a tune, she might have attempted it. Perhaps the fact that she was willing to let him worry about her problems meant that she was avoiding them, but so be it. She'd take the peace where she could get it and the rest could take a flying leap. She had a job to do, and she was more than happy to let him do his.

She turned a series of corners, leading Jon deeper into the heart of the temple, standing to one side on occasion as workers pushing wheelbarrows full of dirt and rock passed by on their way outside. "We've found an inner sanctum of sorts in here," she said, "that seems to be harboring a lot of secrets. We've found some interesting artifacts, but nothing we haven't also found on the outside. I'm hoping we'll come across something really interesting one of these days."

They progressed toward a source of light; when they finally reached the center to which Claire had referred, they encountered Justin and several workers who were currently dumping buckets full of dirt into a wheelbarrow.

"Hi there," Justin said with a smile as they approached. He nodded to Jon. "Going to join in the fun?"

Jon nodded, taking in the awe-inspiring site of the temple walls, which were carved with odd-looking figures and faces, and were partially buried in dirt. "Yeah," he said, looking toward the ceiling, which seemed to stretch forever upward.

Claire laughed. "It's a little strange, isn't it? I'll never forget the first time I laid eyes on this place. This carved wall here is again part of the former structure that was buried beneath the new one. The odd thing we're finding about this one, however, is that it wasn't crushed, like the structure before it. The ancients simply built their new temple right on top of this one, leaving it completely intact." She moved past Justin and motioned for Jon to follow her to a more secluded spot that looked relatively untouched. The dirt was piled high against the wall, obstructing the figures carved beneath.

"Why don't we work over here," she said, grabbing an empty bucket and several shovels as she walked. "Now," she paused, setting her backpack on the ground, "you're sure you want to be in here? You can sketch outside if you'd rather."

He shook his head. "This is too weird," he said. "I'd never forgive myself if I went home without coming in here for awhile."

"Well, okay then. I don't want to be bullying you into anything you don't want to do."

He shook his head with a self-deprecating smile. "Trust me, I've been talked into worse."

Claire tipped her head to one side and eyed him speculatively, but said nothing as she moved a lantern situated on a rock to a more convenient spot. She sat down next to it, pulling the empty bucket and shovels close.

"So what are we doing, here?" Jon asked as he sat down next to Claire and grabbed a shovel.

"Well, we're chipping the dirt from this wall and watching for stuff."

"What kind of stuff?"

"Anything that doesn't look like an ordinary rock. We've found pottery and tools in here; we need to be careful we don't get careless and just start chucking dirt in the bucket. We may miss something. Let me know if you find something; don't just yank it up—I need to document where we find everything." She began clearing dirt and rock from the carved wall, still explaining as she went. "Chances are we won't find anything buried here up against the wall, but you never know."

"Where have you found the pottery and tools?"

She wrinkled her nose, thinking. "Mostly in some of the smaller 'rooms'; we passed some coming in. I'll show them to you again as we leave."

He nodded and dug his shovel into the dirt, depositing the resulting heap carefully into the bucket. They worked alongside each other in comfortable silence for several minutes while Claire debated indulging her curiosity. The man beside her apparently had no career, no profession of any sort, and never talked much about his past. She was dying to know what it was he *did*.

She cast a sidelong glance at his hands as he worked, noticing for the first time, in the light of the lantern, the needle marks along his veins. She felt his gaze on her and raised her eyes to meet his.

"They're track marks," he said blandly, without any traces of either humor or derision. "I'm a heroine addict." At that, he shrugged sheepishly. "Well, I *was* a heroine addict."

She offered a small, sympathetic smile. "Recovered, huh?"

"Yeah."

"Well," she said, nodding, "that's commendable. It's not easy; I can relate to addiction."

He nodded, and resumed his work. She figured he was through discussing the topic when he quietly broke the silence. "I grew up in Chicago with a junkie for a mother. I left home when I was fourteen and never went back."

"Where did you live?" Claire pried a chunk of dark earth from the ancient wall and carefully deposited it in the bucket.

"I lived anywhere I could find," he said. "I lived with people off the streets—prostitutes, mostly. They took care of me. More or less. Taught me how to avoid AIDS, if nothing else."

"How did you eat? What did you do for money?"

He shrugged and dumped another shovelful. "I had jobs here and there; what I couldn't earn, I stole."

Claire finally turned and looked him in the face. "So what made the difference? Why the change? Why did you get out?"

"Bump," he replied. "Bump made all the difference. He saved my life one night, and literally took me away from it." He shook his head, now making marks in the dirt with his shovel, but not really moving any of it into the bucket. "I was hardly ever sober and was almost always high. I couldn't really think clearly enough to get myself out of it."

Claire thought of her own recent relapse and current struggles to continue eating. "Do you think you'll ever go back?"

"What, to Chicago or the drugs?"

"Either one."

He shook his head. "No. I don't want to go back to Chicago because the only people I know there don't care enough about me to help me stay clean. As far as the drugs," he paused, examining the small rocks he'd picked up with his shovel. "Well," he admitted on a sigh, "it's not easy. Not a day goes by that I don't want a drink. And every time I think about memories I'd rather leave alone, I remember how it felt when the heroine went into my vein."

"So what keeps you from doing it?"

"Well," he said, his brows furrowed in a frown, "I guess I really don't want to die. And I know I'll kill myself eventually if I do it again." He shook his head. "There have been plenty of times I figured I wanted to die and get it all over with, but now that I'm dealing with a clear head, I'm thinking there's a few places I'd like to see, some things I'd like to try . . ." He trailed off, his reddening face visible even in the fairly dim light.

Claire nodded. "Well, I'm happy for you," she said, wanting to ease his obvious embarrassment. "You're lucky. Not everyone's that lucky."

He nodded. "I know."

She sensed his reluctance to speak further. "You'll figure it out," she said with a small pat on his arm. She laughed, mostly at herself. "We all do, eventually."

Chapter 13

"He says he wants to make me his queen! How can you say he cares nothing for me?"

Palome winced. How could he compete with a prince? He wanted to say, "Queliza, I love you. I've loved you all my life and will guard your heart as carefully as I would my own life . . ." but instead he said nothing. He looked off into the distance, and finally replied.

"I want you to be happy, Queliza. That is all I want . . ."

* * * * * *

"So how is it that this whole ruin went undiscovered for so long?" Bump asked as he walked alongside Justin to the mess hall.

"Well, it's been hidden completely for over a thousand years by vegetation; it took us forever just to clear enough trees and under-growth to get into the buildings themselves."

"Didn't the people living in the surrounding villages know this was here?"

Justin smiled. "They did. But I suspect they wanted to keep it a secret for as long as they could. It's the locals that named the place Corazon de la Ceiba. It's hard," he said, "wanting to respect their privacy and their ancestry, but dying of curiosity about the ruins themselves. It's an odd balancing act."

Bump nodded. "And how long will this whole process take?"

"Oh," Justin laughed, "it could take years, and probably will. It's a relatively small 'city,' in comparison to some of the others, like

Palenque, Copán, and Chichén Itzá, but it's been interesting to compare some of the similarities."

He motioned with his hand toward the center of the ruin. "That alleyway of sorts between the two small structures that look like buildings is what we consider to be a ball court. This is a common thing among many of the ruins. The ancient Mayans played a game with a ball—a game that we think may have been played to the death. The two teams faced each other and had to hit the ball to each other without using their hands or feet. They used arms, knees, hips, you name it. The losers were executed."

"Mmm. Nice."

Justin laughed again. "Interesting, isn't it? The ball court was the center of the plaza; the surrounding buildings were all part of a city square, of sorts, and the main focal point of the whole thing was, of course, the temple." He pointed to the ancient structure that towered over the other ruins. "I understand Claire took your friend in there today."

Bump nodded. "She did. He said it was cool. I believe that was his exact word."

Justin smiled. "Well, he's right. It is cool."

Bump paused as they reached the entrance to the mess hall. "I know how important this is to you. I want you to know I'll do my best to see if we can't recover your stolen artifacts."

Justin's smile faltered, and he suddenly looked tired. He nodded. "I appreciate that. I get so caught up in this work every day that lately I've forgotten there's been a downside to all of this." He accepted Bump's offered hand and shook it, recovering his smile as Bump clasped his shoulder, and the two men walked into the mess hall for dinner.

During the course of the meal, which nearly all the staff attended with the notable exception of Devon Stark, Bump was introduced to Luis Muños, the man Claire introduced him to as "the one responsible for the fact that we're all here." She had gone on to explain that it was his influence that had helped make the excavation of the ancient city possible.

Bump liked Luis instinctively. He was straightforward, friendly, and seemed extremely bright. He sat by him throughout the meal and was impressed with the man's apparent compassion for the people he served as their physician, which probably encompassed just about everyone in his own village and those in the surrounding areas as well. He was enthusiastic about the ancient ruins, and seemed to be held in high esteem by all those associated with the site.

Claire's affection for the man was obvious. She conversed easily with him and seemed to regard his thoughts and opinions highly. Her face was alight with energy as she explained some of the newer discoveries around the site, whether big or small.

Bump also noticed, with some relief, that she asked after the health of Luis' wife. It wasn't the first time since having met her that he found himself watching her interactions with other men closely. She was obviously enamored with Luis, and he found himself glad that the man was married.

Why? He studied Claire across the table and felt his heart give a small thump when she made a light comment about the "insurance adjuster" who was probably going to become a permanent fixture at the site. She threw a wink at him and laughed, turning her attention again to something Luis was telling her.

So what are your intentions here, St. James? Marriage and six kids? He shook his head slightly and took a long swig from his soda. Who knew what his intentions were. Before he was baptized into the LDS church, he had led a relatively simple existence. He dated women—one at a time, which was his own personal rule, and then saw each relationship through to its obvious and inevitable conclusion. They always ended, and while he'd often felt a pang or two of regret, he never quite envisioned himself as one who would eventually settle down.

Suddenly he found himself a member of a religion about which family was everything. He had viewed his first Sacrament Meeting with a fair measure of alarm. The children had been everywhere, climbing on their fathers, climbing on their mothers, climbing over the backs of the pews, crawling *under* the pews—Froot Loops and coloring books strewn across the benches. He'd never seen so many children in one place outside of an elementary school. And he hadn't been to one of those in years.

He glanced again at Claire, wondering about what kind of mother she'd be. His mouth quirked into a smile at the thought of her children, starched and pressed, their bedrooms spotless, and star charts on the fridge monitoring the progress of their good behavior. She led an organized life; he imagined she'd run an organized household as well.

And quit eating if she got stressed.

His mouth involuntarily pulled downward into a slight frown and he wondered if she well and truly knew what she was doing. She said she was feeling better, and he'd seen the evidence of that earlier. It was apparent in her demeanor and the sincerity of her smiles. And she *was* eating dinner—he'd been watching her the entire time, so he had firsthand knowledge of that fact.

But who knew, really? She was the only one who did, and he supposed he'd have to take her word for it. He wondered when his attention had shifted from responsibility for a promise made to a friend, to concern for his *own* peace of mind that she was healthy and well. She smiled at him again and said something, and he was aghast to realize he had no comprehension of the words coming out of her mouth.

He cleared his throat. "What was that?"

She leaned forward, apparently assuming he couldn't hear her over the noise of numerous other conversations occurring simultaneously in the small building. "Luis invited us to his house tomorrow for lunch after church. Would you like to go?"

He nodded, collecting his thoughts. "Church?"

Luis turned to him in explanation. "There's a new building in my town," he said. "We're big enough to be a full ward, now. Our meetings start at 12:00 noon. Would you be interested? Claire tells me you're a new convert."

"Yes, I'd like that. Oh," he said as an afterthought. "I didn't bring any appropriate church clothes. I wasn't expecting to attend . . ."

Claire smiled and waved a hand at him. "Just wear your khakis and one of those white sports shirts I saw you in," she said. "It'll be fine."

"You have church clothes?" he asked.

"Yeah, one dress. I have to hope people won't judge me too harshly, seeing me in the same thing, week after week," she laughed.

Luis smiled at her. "These people would never judge you harshly," he said.

"That's very true," Claire conceded. "Your ward has some of the sweetest people I've ever met in my life." She turned back to Bump. "So do we have a date?"

"Absolutely."

"You can bring Jon along too, if he's interested."

Bump considered the notion for a moment before answering. "I'll see if he wants to," he finally said. "I don't know, though. He may be more comfortable hanging out here, pawing through the dirt." *There was a time when I would have been, too*, he mused. He was surprised by the fact that he was actually looking forward to the services. Life certainly had a way of changing.

* * * * * *

Claire retired early to her bed after a quick shower, and sat cross-legged on the cot with her journal.

I'm feeling much, much better, she wrote, *and I'm grateful. I feel like I'm in control of things again—at least my own life, if not the things going on around me. The activity on the site is going along smoothly; and thankfully, nothing has disappeared from the lab in a long time. Bump St. James and Jon Kiersey are actually sleeping in there, bless them, and as a result I've been sleeping better at night. Things have been quiet and organized, and that's how I like it.*

I'm eating again, quite regularly, in fact, and it was much easier this time to pull myself out of this funk. Last time was so hard, and I needed so much help and moral support from everyone around me. This time, I did it with some blunt prodding from just one person.

Speaking of that one person, who shall remain nameless for the sake of my pride when I read this years from now and die of embarrassment, I think I'm totally whooped. He's funny and smart and so very, very stable. I can't believe how attractive that quality is to me. I'd never noticed it before in other men, but now that I think back on it, I wonder if some of my past relationships have failed because I felt like I was always the one carrying the load. Darren was wishy-washy, yet liked to think he was always in control. He was volatile, though, and unpredictable. His mercurial moods used to drive me insane.

THIS man, however, who shall continue to remain nameless, is stability and consistency incarnate. Of course, maybe I'm speaking too soon; I mean I barely know the man, after all, but he just seems so rock solid. He's very much in control of the situation here, which I find not only comforting but alluring.

To top it all off, he's to-die-for good looking. I'm sure if I lined up this man and his friend, and then asked Paige to pick the better-looking one, she'd pick the friend. But as for me, I don't think I've ever laid eyes on a man I've found more attractive. Now, where will all of this get me? Probably nowhere. Despite the fact that he's joined the Church, I don't think he's the marrying type. Who knows, maybe I'm reading it wrong, but I don't think he quite knows what to do with his new conversion. I pity him, in a humorous kind of way—there are nuances about the Church even I can't relate to. I can only imagine how it must seem to a man who has probably had his share of wine, women, and song . . .

Claire stretched and took a look back over her entry. She hadn't realized until she started writing just how intrigued she was by Bump St. James. She tapped her pen lid against her lips and burrowed her brow in thought.

Well, she concluded, *he'll be here for a little while, at least, and I'll enjoy whatever time I can get to look at him. I'm thinking that'll have to be enough. I barely know him, anyway, besides which I really don't have time for a man. Someday I'll head back to the States and look for a teaching position somewhere. I mean, who needs a relationship when you've got things to do?*

Chapter 14

Queliza stood outside the king's chambers, wincing at the shouting pouring out from within.

"You will not go on the next campaign," the king roared at his son. "I'll not have an entire operation placed in jeopardy because my inexperienced son is tagging along."

"But father," came the reply, "I am nearly a man. I want to follow in your footsteps."

"And you will, but when I say it shall be. Not one minute before. Now leave me."

Queliza stood to one side as the prince exited the royal chambers. He looked dejected, and her heart ached for him. "Did you really want so much to go into battle?" she asked quietly.

"No. I wanted him to see me as a man, for once." The expression on his face grew determined. "He will soon enough . . ."

* * * * * *

The ride to Luis' chapel was pleasant. The small town was situated approximately 10 miles to the south of the site, and Claire was grateful for the fact that the weather was clear and the ride uneventful. She cast a sidelong glance at the man in the passenger seat, trying to fight a blush at the memory of the things she'd written about him in her journal the night before. *It's not like he knows what you wrote, Claire,* she chastised herself. Still, she couldn't quite be sure. Those tiger-eyes of his seemed to see everything.

"So," she said, clearing her throat and breaking the silence, which was steadily getting on her nerves. She said the first thing that popped into her mind. "Are you seeing anyone?"

He raised an eyebrow and looked at her. "No, not at the moment. Are you?"

Claire made the mistake of glancing at his face. A smile had started at the corner of his mouth and he was looking at her with something that might have been suppressed amusement.

"No." What on earth had driven her to ask him a question like that? Well, the answer wasn't too far, if she dared look for it. She wanted to know if he was available. So much for her I-don't-have-time-for-a-man theory. Apparently her subconscious had other ideas. Perpetuation of the species. That must be it; it wasn't her fault, it was instinct.

"Why do you ask?" He was still looking at her, darn him, with those golden eyes and perfectly white teeth. She glanced at him again, gripping the steering wheel with one hand at twelve o'clock and striving for an appearance of nonchalance. He looked predatory, like a large cat playing with a mouse before pouncing.

"No reason, just curious." Now where was her charm when she needed it? Of all the times for it to be absent, this had to be the worst. She impatiently let out a puff of air and gritted her teeth at the fact that she was uncomfortable. "You know, people wonder . . ."

"Who's wondering?" The twitch of a smile was turning into a full-fledged grin.

"Oh, you know . . ."

"Noooo, I'm afraid I don't."

She stopped the jeep in the middle of the road and looked him full in the face, her exasperation finally freeing itself. "I am. How's that, Bump St. James? *I'm* wondering. Why? I don't really know. Maybe I was just trying to make conversation."

He appeared to be struggling to put a damper on his smile that widened with every word exploding from her mouth. "Maybe you were," he answered.

"Is that psycho, or something? To wonder about someone you're spending time with?"

"Not at all."

"Can I continue, then?"

He gestured toward the road with his hand, coughing to cover what sounded suspiciously like a laugh. "Please do."

Claire shoved the jeep into gear, wincing at the grinding sound accompanying the fact that she was too impatient to shove the clutch all the way to the floor. She glared quickly at Bump, silently daring him to make a smart comment.

He didn't say a word. He did have the audacity, however, to keep coughing.

"Well, then," she said when they were under way again, "How about your mother. Is she seeing anyone?"

"My *mother*?"

His mother? Her attempt at making it sound as though she wasn't interested in *his* social life specifically, but more the world at large, was backfiring. "I find people's lives interesting," she said, trying desperately to climb out of the hole she'd unwittingly dug for herself.

She pulled alongside a small building that was welcoming people dressed in their Sunday best. She cut the engine and finally conceded defeat, thumping her head once against the steering wheel and leaving it there. She barely suppressed a groan. His *mother*?

She closed her eyes as the sounds of his laughter burst forth. And continued. She felt her lips twitch in self-deprecating amusement and shook her head slightly, wallowing in her own idiocy. She finally lifted her head and turned at the feel of his hand on her arm, his long fingers curling softly around her biceps, and the sounds of his laughter gently fading.

"Claire," he finally said, a smile still touching his lips, "I like you too."

She scowled. "Why?"

He chuckled and slowly rubbed his hand along her bare arm, gently caressing. "I just do."

He held her eyes within his gaze, the amusement fading and darkening into something more intense. He moved toward her slowly and she felt herself leaning to meet him. She closed her eyes as he drew closer, and felt his warmth as he moved to meet her lips with his own.

She jumped, startled, and smashed her nose into his as her car door was opened from the outside. "Claire?"

She turned, stunned. "Luis?"

Luis looked past Claire at Bump, an expression of surprise crossing his features. "Oh, hello! I didn't see you—I thought Claire was alone."

Luis considered the pair in the car, seated close together, looking shocked. He cleared his throat. "Um. I'll just wait for you inside." With that he closed the door and left them alone.

Claire looked back at Bump, feeling completely bewildered. Now what?

"Nothing like a ruined moment, is there?" His hand still held her arm in its gentle grasp. He ran his fingers up and down one more time before releasing her completely. "Will you indulge me another time?" he asked, his face serious.

She released a shaky breath and nodded, swallowing her disappointment. *Why not now?* she wanted to ask, but decided her pride had been battered enough for one day. "Are you the type who has to pick his moments?" she asked on a whisper.

His eyes wandered from her eyes to her lips, and she wondered if he were going to change his mind. "Yeah," he murmured, "although now I'm wondering if I should just take them when I can get them."

A family with young children ran by the jeep, the little ones squealing with laughter as they passed. Claire blinked, and looked beyond Bump's shoulder at the people filing into the building. "I suppose we should go in," she murmured, a light frown creasing her brow.

"Yes, I suppose we should." At that, he opened his door and was out of the jeep and around to her side before her brain could suggest to her limbs that they ought to be moving.

He opened her door and offered her his hand. He grinned at her confusion. It was enough to have her shaking herself mentally and pulling herself together.

"Just because my synapses aren't firing is no reason to be smug," she told him as she took his hand and rose, shutting the car door behind her and locking it. "You should have taken your moment when you had it. Who knows when you'll get another one of those." She softened her flippancy with a wink. It took every effort she could manage to be blasé.

"Oh, I make my moments, Dr. O'Brian. There'll be others."

Hmm. Now there was something a girl couldn't very well complain about. Unfortunately, her tongue was stuck to the roof of her mouth, and any witty response she might have come up with in a less-charged setting was sadly absent.

He was looking down into her face, the smile on his lips making its way into his eyes. "Now then," he said, tucking her arm into his. "Shall we go to church?"

* * * * * *

Once inside, Bump and Claire were greeted by Luis and a woman standing close to him who Bump assumed must be Maria, his wife. A young child clung to his mother's hand. Luis extended his hand and shook Bump's, a warm smile on his face. "I'm glad you were able to make it," he said.

Bump nodded and offered his hand to Maria as Luis made the introductions. "And this young man is Marco," Luis finished, motioning to his son.

Marco solemnly extended his hand and Bump took it, trying to hide his surprise. "It's a pleasure to meet you, sir," the child said.

I'll bet this one doesn't climb over the benches, Bump mused with a smile. "It's a pleasure to meet you as well, Marco, and your English is wonderful. How old are you?"

"Six, sir."

Claire leaned close to gently run a hand over the boy's hair. "He's very grown up," she said with a smile.

"I can see that." Bump straightened and considered the child. Marco wasn't running around in circles. He wasn't screaming or crying, or demanding to be taken to the bathroom. Perhaps children had their mellow moments. It was something he'd have to consider.

"Well," Luis said, interrupting Bump's inspection of his son, "we start with Sacrament Meeting. The chapel is right over here." He started to walk, holding his wife's hand and leaving the others to follow behind. He talked over his shoulder as they went.

"We're very proud of the new building," he said. "We've waited a long time to have one this nice."

Bump looked around as they made their way to the chapel; the building was typically, tastefully new LDS. The colors were muted and coordinated in a matching scheme, and if he didn't know better he'd think he was in his chapel at home, except that this building was probably only half the size.

"It's beautiful," he said, and meant it. One thing he'd learned about the LDS way of doing things was that the Church was wise with the administration of funds, but always, *always* did it with style and taste. It mirrored his own philosophy and he regarded the new building with a sense of pride. There was a certain amount of ownership, he found, in belonging to an organization that took care of not only its own but many others, and did it well.

He made himself comfortable in the chapel on a bench next to Claire and settled in for the meeting, wondering how he'd keep his thoughts focused on the messages being delivered and not the beautiful woman by his side. When they had left the site that morning, he'd had to work to keep from staring at her.

Her hair was done up in some elegant twist thing with a clip at the back of her head and she wore a dress of forest green that was made of thin, form-fitting, wispy material. The sleeves were short and the length was long, coming to rest about an inch above her ankle when she stood. She wore trendy black shoes with clunky, wedged heels, the same kind he'd often seen Liz Saxton O'Brian wear when she had gone out on assignment for him.

Claire's arms, face, and neck were tan from long hours in the sun—he was assuming she didn't wear that hat as often as she probably should—and the rich tone of her skin offset the cool color of the jewelry she wore: a silver rope necklace, silver hoops at her ears, and a thin silver watch. On the ring finger of her right hand she wore a brilliantly red ruby in a setting that was also silver. She'd apparently scrubbed her hands, for her fingernails bore no traces of their usual dirt.

What he *really* wanted to do, he realized as he sat trying to make his way through the opening hymn, was drag her back out to the jeep and finish what he'd almost started. And then what, though? He had to maintain a working relationship with her at the site, as well as keep himself focused on his job. He didn't know her well enough to know whether or not she was into casual associations with a physical element, and much to his own surprise, he wasn't sure if that would be enough for him, even if it were for her.

And what to tell her brother, on top of it all? He couldn't very well forget the fact that the woman he was currently ogling on a daily basis was the sister of someone he respected and associated with quite regularly. He'd seen how protective Connor was of Liz, (*although*, he thought with a smile, she didn't really need most of it), and he imagined Connor wouldn't be any less so regarding his sister. *And he should be*, Bump mused. Someone you cared about deserved your loyalty and protection, whether she needed it or not. He didn't figure Connor would take it too lightly if Bump messed with his little sister and then left, never to return.

No, he decided with an inward sigh, *better keep things simple*. That way nobody got hurt and nobody got pounded on by someone's angry older brother. He would do his job so that Claire could do hers, and he would enjoy her friendship along the way. Or maybe he'd let her lead and see where she wanted to go. She certainly hadn't fought him in the jeep and he imagined that had Luis not interrupted, they might still be outside. He'd all but promised he'd try it again sometime, and she'd looked at him with those huge blue eyes, made even more intense with the accenting effects of makeup, which he'd never seen her wear, and he'd had the impression that she was more than amenable to the notion of a rain check.

Play it by ear, he finally decided, and felt better. He liked coming to some sort of resolution with any given problem, and having reached this one, he relaxed. He glanced over at her and saw her lips moving along with the words to the song but didn't hear any noise coming out.

He leaned over to her ear and whispered, "I can't hear you."

She glanced sideways and whispered back, "I can't sing."

"That makes two of us." He settled back into the seat with a smile, feeling as though he'd finally found a kindred spirit.

* * * * * *

Bump was leaving the room where the elder's quorum had met and was looking around for Claire, hoping to join her for the Gospel

Doctrine class. When he finally found her, she was walking down the hallway away from the room where Luis told him that Sunday School would be held.

"Hey," he half-hissed and jogged to catch her. "Where are you going?" Then a thought struck him; she was probably just trying to find a bathroom and here he was tagging along after her like a puppy with its tongue hanging out.

Claire turned back and smiled as he caught up to her, suddenly feeling sheepish. "I like going into the Primary room during the Junior Primary's sharing time. Those kids are so cute." She motioned to him as she continued walking. "Come with me."

He followed, trying to keep the dubious response he felt from manifesting itself outwardly on his face. The Primary room was probably the last place he'd choose to go willingly, but there was the small matter of the delectable-looking woman walking at his side. He knew in that instant that he'd not only follow her to the Primary room, but he'd stay there for as long as she wanted.

She was talking again, and he was missing it. "I substituted for Marco's class the first week I got here," she was saying. "Ever since, I've made a point of hanging out to watch them do a portion of their sharing time, and then I sneak back into Gospel Doctrine."

They reached the appointed room and walked quietly to the back. The small children, aged three to seven were seated by classes and although a bit wiggly, looked engaged in what they were hearing. As Claire and Bump sat on the back row, she leaned over to him to whisper in his ear.

"I've taught Primary on and off for years," she said, "and I've never seen such a cute group of kids."

He watched with interest as the children listened to stories and then played a game led by the Primary president, who was doing her best to keep things hopping and their interest focused when it seemed to wander. His eyes wandered over each child, scrubbed and dressed in their Sunday clothes, most of them singing when they should be singing and responding when they were asked.

He found himself understanding, truly, the word "sweet." The children were sweet and gentle and not that far removed from the presence of God. He smiled at their expressions of joy when they won the games they were playing, even when the noise bordered on raucous and the teachers were "shushing" them in an effort to calm them down.

The president again shared a story, this time holding a picture of the Savior surrounded by children. She spoke in Spanish, but he could feel the gentle spirit that enveloped the room. Following the story, the children sang a song he knew he'd heard once or twice before, perhaps in the first sacrament meeting he'd ever attended where the musical number was performed entirely by children.

I feel my Savior's love in all the world around me . . . He felt an unfamiliar sting behind his eyes as he realized the children were singing in Spanish, but he understood the words. *His Spirit warms my soul through everything I see . . .*

He glanced at Claire and saw a solitary tear trace a path down her cheek. She closed her eyes. *I feel my Savior's love; its gentleness enfolds me, and when I kneel to pray, my heart is filled with peace . . .*

He sat through the song, his jaw clenching at the rush of emotion he'd not experienced since his lessons with the missionaries and his subsequent baptism. When the song ended, he heard Claire sniff and felt her lean close to him.

"We can go now, if you'd like," she whispered.

"No," he answered. "Let's just stay in here. Do you mind?"

"Not a bit."

Chapter 15

Queliza desperately tried one more time to get the queen's attention. She was distracted with the fitting session for her new clothing, and she turned an irritated glance upon the young servant.

"Really, Queliza, I wish you would stop bothering me with such talk. It is unthinkable that the prince would attempt such a thing. I won't hear of it again."

Queliza finished her duties for the queen that afternoon and retired to her own quarters in a small corner of the palace, feeling dejected. There was always the chance that the prince would win, and then her fears would be for naught. But if he were to lose—would the king actually order the execution of his own son?

* * * * * *

How's your work coming along, Maria?" Claire asked their hostess as they sat at the Muños's dinner table.

Maria smiled a bit. "Well, it's been slow lately because of the surgery, but I'm gradually returning to most of my former activities."

"I'm happy to hear that. And I'm sure Marco is such a big help for you," Claire said with a wink at Marco.

"He is a very big helper," Maria replied and smiled at her son. "A big helper indeed."

As the meal drew to a close, Luis motioned to the table and said, "Maria, you and Claire go relax. I'll take care of this."

Not wanting to appear useless, Bump offered to help, to which Luis replied, "I'd be happy for the company."

"Come with me, Claire," Maria said as she rose. "I'll show you my latest piece of pottery." She paused to plant a kiss on her husband's cheek and gave him a grateful, "thank you," as she left the room, with Claire on her heels.

Bump made a mental note; offer to clean up after dinner—makes for a grateful wife. Well, that is, if one *wanted* a wife. He rose and began clearing the dishes from the table, noticing the details of the Muños home that had escaped him upon earlier notice. The home was nice—by far the nicest in the area, but not so large and imposing as to appear presumptuous to the other townspeople. Bump wondered how much more money Luis might be making in the States, or one of the larger cities in the country and was impressed with the fact that the man was so committed to his roots.

The home was decorated with pieces of pottery and weavings, presumably handmade by Maria herself, or perhaps relatives; and several pictures and various pieces of art adorned the walls, giving splashes of color everywhere the eye traveled. It was bright and mood lifting. He found himself noticing several pieces he'd like to add to his own sedate collection at home.

"So where did you meet your wife?" Bump asked as Luis began rinsing dishes.

Luis laughed. "Well, she grew up in a small town about an hour away from here, but we met at USC, ironically enough. We debated for a long time whether or not we'd stay there or come back home; obviously we ended up back here and haven't regretted it. At times it's been hard, but we like what we're doing."

"Well, I certainly respect your efforts. I'm sure the people here are grateful."

Luis nodded. "They need so much; I'm happy to share what I know with them." He rinsed another plate and turned the conversation toward Bump. "So where is your family from?"

"Well, I live in Seattle, Washington now, as does my mother, but she's actually British. We lived in England until my father died, then, when I was still young, we moved to the States to live with my mother's sister and her family."

"And what does your mother think of your conversion to the Church?"

Bump smiled. "She supported me, although she thought it was a bit odd and highly out of character for me to embrace anything religious . . . I keep thinking that someday I'll have to bring her to church with me. I think she'd like it."

Luis nodded. "And how has your transition been? I remember when I was baptized it took awhile for everything to sink in . . . there are so many nuances . . ."

Bump laughed. "You're definitely right about that," he said. "I've noticed it myself." He paused, not wanting to delve into his own personal thoughts, which he never shared with anyone, but sensing a familiarity with Luis that made him comfortable speaking his mind. "I don't know that I'll ever fit in to this way of life," he stated.

Luis smiled. "Which way are you talking about? The Word of Wisdom, the tithing, the chastity part . . .?"

Bump dismissed it with a flick of his hand. "No, no. That's all been relatively easy, for the most part." He thought of Claire in the other room. "But the Word of Wisdom made sense to me, and I have no problem with tithing." He paused. "It's all the little stuff. I don't see myself as much of a family man, and I definitely know that if I do get married, I can't handle six kids . . ."

Luis laughed and turned off the water, looking at Bump, his eyes full of understanding and compassion. "There's no rule anywhere that says you have to have six children. Or more. That's something between husband and wife and God. It's nobody else's business."

Bump nodded. "It's all the rest, too, though. The close association among the members in my ward; they've all been very nice and welcoming, but I don't feel like one of them. It's not their fault, I just don't feel like I'm . . . *like* them."

Luis thoughtfully turned the water back on and continued rinsing dishes. "That's because we're all different, my friend," he said. "We're not all supposed to be the same, and for all their 'togetherness,' I'll bet those people all feel 'different' as well at certain times. It's a bit odd for us as converts," he added, "because we're new to the whole thing. Many members you'll meet have grown up in the church, and Mormon culture is something they're as familiar with as breathing. It takes time, but you'll find your own rhythm before long."

Bump shrugged. "I suppose I will."

Luis smiled again. "Are you familiar with the story in Acts, where Peter has a dream of a large 'sheet' that holds many different kinds of creatures? And he's then told to preach the gospel to the gentiles? Well, I've always compared that big sheet to a large fish net that's cast over the side of a boat and brings in many different varieties of fish. The gospel is like that. It's a big net, and there's room enough for all of us, in all our varieties. We should be grateful we're all different. Makes for an interesting life that way."

Bump nodded. *It's a big net,* he repeated to himself. *And there's room enough in it for me.*

* * * * * *

Bump was quiet on the ride back to the site, and rather than embarrass herself by asking about the social lives of his other friends and family members, Claire kept silent and left him to his thoughts. They had nearly reached their destination when he finally spoke.

"How has it been for you as a lifelong Church member?" was his question.

She squinted and pursed her lips in thought. "You mean just in general or are you talking about something specific?"

"Just in general."

"Well, I've always had a testimony of it, so I've been grateful that I never had to go looking for it, but there have been times that I've found it a bit . . . challenging."

"In what way?"

She sighed. "Well, there are pros and there are cons. Even though we're all different, when you're one in ideology with someone there's common ground. That person will understand what you're about without you having to say one word. As for traits, interests, and side philosophies, if you look hard enough, you'll find people who are like you, inside the Church and outside as well."

She paused. "There's a flip side, though. Look at me," she said. "All of my high-school friends were married by age twenty-one. I'm twenty-five and still single. You know what that makes me?"

He shook his head.

"Ugly."

He laughed out loud.

She smirked. "At best, a freak. But as I've gotten older, I've made friends with people whose lives run parallel to my own, and who don't think there's something wrong with me, even though no man has seen fit to rescue me from myself."

"Is that a bit of a chip on the shoulder?"

"Well, enough people ask you if you're 'one of them man haters' and you start to put your guard up." She smiled. "How well did you know Liz, when she worked for you?"

"I knew her on a casual basis, but we never talked about anything personal."

"Well, we've compared notes on occasion. We're the same age; she married Connor at age twenty-five. For the last few years, she's endured comments and questions like the kind I often get. I don't think people mean to be spiteful or nosy, they're just curious."

Claire paused, lost in her own thoughts for a moment. "Of course I want to get married," she finally murmured. "I want that companionship. I like men; men make me laugh."

Bump cast her a wry glance. "What's so funny about men?"

"Everything." She grinned. "Men and women are different, and I happen to think that's a good thing." Her levity faded at her next thought, though she tried to keep her comments light. "I'd even like a little Marco of my own someday."

Bump nodded and lightly snorted his agreement. "*I'd* even have a Marco of my own if I could be guaranteed he'd be that well behaved."

Claire took her eyes off the road for a moment to smile at him. "You're not much used to kids, are you."

"No, not much."

"I've heard it's different when they're your own."

"I guess it must be. People keep having more."

She laughed and pulled the jeep into its parking spot near the site in a secluded patch of trees. She cut the engine and reluctantly turned to him. "Bump," she said, searching for words, "I don't know what to do with this."

"With what?" He looked at her with those golden-colored eyes and she suddenly felt very stupid.

She made a loose circle with her hand, talking as she gestured between him and herself. "This. Any of this."

He smiled. "What are you trying to say, Claire? Just spit it out."

She tipped her head to one side and felt her lips pull into a pained smile, closing her eyes for a moment before opening them and saying, "You. I don't know what to do with you. I'm no good at . . . at . . . but then maybe this is all nothing and I'm making a big deal out of it . . ."

He reached for her hand and held it loosely between his own, tracing loose circles on the back of it with his thumb. "It's not 'nothing,'" he said. "But maybe we ought to just take things a step at a time. I've never been one for beating around the bush, so I'll just tell you straight out what I'm thinking. I find you extremely attractive. I think you're smart and funny and I enjoy spending time with you."

He paused. "I don't know really what to make of things. My life has changed quite drastically in the past few months, and I'm still trying to adjust. I don't want to get . . . involved with you on a level that's too deep for either one of us to handle and end up causing you grief."

She knew her eyes were open wide and she couldn't seem to close them, even a little bit. He was by far the most straightforward man she'd ever known. Her past boyfriends had all tried to get to her in subtle ways. This man didn't seem to care to waste his time with that.

When she finally found her voice, her throat was thick with emotion. "So I wasn't imagining it, then."

"No." He smiled.

"I . . . I . . ." she paused again, fumbling to organize her thoughts.

"Just say it. Tell me exactly what you're thinking."

Fine. If he was going to push her into the blunt zone, so be it. "Okay," she said, finding strength in the honesty of her thoughts, "I'm wondering why you're even remotely attracted to me. I'm sure you've had tons of experience with tons of women and I'm wondering if you're interested in me because I'm the only woman around and you find me mildly amusing."

He stared for a moment, apparently taken aback. Then he laughed. "Claire," he said, "for starters, you're not the only woman around. There are at least three more here at the site and several villages full within a few miles' radius." He held up a hand to forestall her rebuttal. "And secondly, I don't know how you can look in the mirror every day and honestly tell me you don't know why I'm finding you attractive."

She winced, unintentionally. "I'm sure you've had better."

He shook his head. "Why are you assuming I'm some Don Juan?"

"Look at you!"

He raised his eyebrows, his eyes wide, and shrugged. "So?"

Claire closed her eyes in frustration. "I'm finding this whole conversation really bizarre," she moaned. "You've never even kissed me, for crying out loud, and I'm talking like we're . . ."

He leaned forward, tugging on her hand he still held bound between his own, and sealed his lips over hers, smothering any further comment. When he finally pulled back, several long, luscious moments later, she opened her eyes and found herself hard-pressed to draw a breath.

"There," he said, sounding none too steady himself, "now I have. Now we're involved, so keep on talking. Let's air it all right here, right now."

She sucked in a lung full of air and wondered what it was she'd been thinking about before. Bump . . . his past . . . other women . . .

"How can I possibly compete with the women you've been with before?" she whispered.

"Claire," he said softly, his face still close to hers, "listen to me and listen well. I never say anything I don't mean. If I had wanted to stay with any of the women I've had relationships with in the past, I'd still be there. I don't willingly give up anything I want. Furthermore," he added, "this is not a competition. I can guarantee you I wasn't thinking of anyone but you, just now. I know you don't know me very well, so I can understand your curiosity about my life."

Still gripping her hand, he leaned back a bit and ran his other hand through his hair. "In my life, and I'm thirty-four next month," he added as an aside, "I've had approximately three serious relationships. And contrary to what you obviously believe, I haven't been promiscuous with every woman I've ever dated. I've been selective because I take it seriously, and now the point is moot because I've made a commitment to my Heavenly Father. You don't have to worry about how you'd compare in that respect because I won't be sleeping with you, as much as I'd like to." The expression on his face was one of agitation, and it wasn't one Claire had seen on him before.

She flushed. "I didn't mean that," she said.

He looked at her, his features softening. "I know you didn't. I just don't want you thinking that if we do decide to take things to another level that I'd be comparing you to this huge, and *fabricated*, might I add, past. I am duty-bound, I take my commitments seriously, no matter what they might be, and I don't cheat. The funny thing is," he finished quietly on a wry smile, "that I'm actually excellent husband material. I just haven't ever seen myself as one."

She gave him a small nod, making herself meet his eyes despite her chagrin. "I didn't mean for you to have to divulge all of that," she murmured. "I'm really not trying to pry . . . I just don't always feel that secure when I feel *involvement* coming on. I've botched a couple of relationships, and this last one was a real doozie for me."

"Well, I'll tell you this much," he replied. "Any man who had a chance at something special with you and blew it is an idiot in the truest sense of the word."

She laughed. "That's a sweet thing to say."

"Nah, I'm not really all that sweet." He tugged on her hand again. "One more for the road," he said, and kissed her completely and thoroughly senseless. That she was able to find her way to her room on legs that felt anything but steady was a miracle.

Chapter 16

Queliza opened her door at the soft knock. The prince stood on the other side, an odd assortment of furs and cloth in his arms. She ushered him inside, where he promptly showed her his "uniform" that he was preparing for the Game. The headdress was a headband of sorts, with feathers rising from the front and a mask that obscured the upper half of his face. There were holes to make his eyes visible.

"Will you be able to see clearly with this mask covering your face?" she asked in concern.

The prince kissed her. "Yes, I will," he said. He framed her face with his hands. "I just wanted to show someone . . . I cannot wait to see the look on my father's face when he realizes who has captained the winning team . . ."

* * * * * *

Monday afternoon, Bump sat in the lab quietly observing Miguel Robaina and Sue Chastain as they went about the business of caring for the artifacts before carefully packing them for shipment to a bigger lab. He made notes in a notebook so as not to appear intrusive; they knew he was there to investigate things for an "insurance company," but had they imagined his true purpose they might have been a bit more nervous. His goal was to keep things as normal and calm as possible. People reacted more honestly that way.

As it was, Sue and Miguel conversed casually with each other, comparing notes from their respective pasts as it concerned school, family, and just general life. They had an easy manner between them and seemed to work well together. He watched Miguel, specifically, as he carefully and reverently handled the ancient items and Bump noted, as he had on other occasions, Miguel's zeal for the profession he studied. Miguel couldn't be described as a "fanatic," he supposed, but there was a light in his eyes when he was absorbed in his work that wasn't present in casual conversation.

Bump assumed it could mean one of two things. One, that Miguel really, *really* loved his job, or that two, he loved it enough to want the artifacts for himself.

He watched as the studious young man pushed his glasses further up on his nose and made notes about an ancient pottery vessel positioned on the table in front of him. One thing was for certain; Miguel was bright and dedicated. Whether or not he was an advocate of the ethical side of the archaeological field remained to be seen.

Bump turned his attention to Sue. In the course of his observations, he had realized something about her—but of course it came as no surprise. She was extremely bright. Had Bump been observing individuals who were less than brilliant, he might have allowed himself to relax and take the situation and its people at face value; as it was, he stayed on his guard. He trusted nobody. They were all smart, they all had access, and given enough time, he'd probably find that several of them had motive.

He pushed himself to his feet. "Are you going to be here for awhile, Sue?"

She nodded and smiled. "I have enough work here to keep me busy into the night," she replied, her cultured British accents reminding him of his mother.

Bump made his way out of the lab and wondered at the wisdom of leaving it, even with someone Claire trusted. There were no guarantees, and his only consolation was that for either Miguel or Sue to steal an artifact at this juncture would be completely and irrefutably stupid, given the fact that they knew that *he* knew they were the only ones in there. Comforted, superficially at least, with the fact that he knew neither Miguel nor Sue was stupid, he went in search of Claire.

When he found her, she was in conversation with Jon, who was making a sketch of the ball court in the center of the ancient plaza. She stopped mid-sentence when she spied Bump, and he fought back a smile at the gentle flush that stole across her features. He hadn't spoken to her alone since the day before, having decided she probably needed some space. *Who am I kidding,* he mused. *I needed some space, too.* The rush of feelings he had experienced concerning this woman had begun as simple physical attraction upon meeting her, and they seemed to be growing into something else, something entirely too—well, *too deep* for his comfort—with each conversation they had. There was something special about her he just really liked, he supposed. He continually told himself there was nothing strange about that.

He saw the exact moment when she fought back her blush and let her natural people-charming skills take over for her. She smiled and winked at him, nudging Jon. "Oh, look," she said. "We've been caught playing. We're supposed to be working."

Jon looked up from his sketch pad and shook his head with a smile. "You're paying me to do this," he said. "I am working."

"Well, you sure don't make it look like work." She motioned to Bump. "Come here and see this," she said.

Bump moved to stand next to Jon and looked over Jon's shoulder at the paper he held in his hand. It was a replica of the ancient temple so exact in its proportions and detail that Bump was momentarily shocked into silence.

When he finally found his voice, it was filled with incredulity, although he tried to hide it and downplay his reaction for fear Jon would never show him any of his artistic attempts again.

"That's amazing, Jon," he finally said. "You do very, *very* good work."

Jon shrugged. "It's nothing," he mumbled.

"It's definitely something," he said. He looked the younger man in the eyes and said, "You could make a serious living with this talent, do you know that? And I'm the man to help you do it, if you're interested."

"I suppose you have friends in the art world?" Jon smirked. "I don't see myself hanging out in some gallery showing off my latest pieces."

"Not all artistic talent is shown in galleries; there are jobs as commercial artists, designers, all kinds of things when you decide which direction you want to take it."

Jon's mouth formed a half-smile. "And you do know people."

Bump grinned at him. "That I do."

"Yeah," Claire interjected, "what is it about all this 'people-knowing' stuff? You mentioned that to me once before, too. You have unlimited worldwide resources?" She laughed at the last.

Jon shook his head, his smile growing. "It's not a joke," he said, despite the nudge Bump gave him with his elbow. "He does have unlimited worldwide resources. You name it, and this man knows someone who knows it, has it, or who can get it for you." He glanced at his friend with a smug grin, apparently thrilled at having turned the conversation away from himself and onto his counterpart instead.

"It's not all that big a deal," Bump muttered.

Claire stared, a smile threatening at the corners of her mouth.

Jon snorted at him. "Oh, come on. Why get all modest now? You've been happy to threaten me with your might and power on more than one occasion."

Bump shook his head with a subtle roll of the eye. "That was entirely warranted, my friend. I did it for your sake."

"Well, that may be true, but," he said, turning again to Claire, "don't let him fool you. There's not a country or an industry in the world he couldn't go to and find someone who owed him some kind of favor."

Claire eyed him speculatively. "So what's your secret?" she asked.

Enough, already, Bump decided impatiently. "I take a lot of notes," he flatly stated, hoping the discussion would be closed.

He was saved from further probing when Justin Hodges approached. When he reached Claire's side, he murmured a brief "hello" to Bump and Jon, and then turned to her, saying, "I just thought you might like to know that Etienne is on his way back."

"Joy."

Justin smiled. "I know. But we do need him here, especially for the staircase. Supposedly his family crisis has been resolved and he'll be here tomorrow."

Claire nodded. "I'd better get the red carpet ready, then," she muttered.

Bump noted the exchange and Claire's mildly hostile attitude with interest. He'd yet to meet the elusive Mr. DuBois, and was looking forward to the opportunity. Merely because Etienne hadn't been present when the most recent artifact had turned up missing didn't exonerate him in the least, as far as Bump was concerned. He could have paid someone else to do the deed in his absence, thereby making it appear as though he were innocent of all the thefts.

"This guy must like himself, huh?" Jon commented as he absently made marks on his sketch, darkening in shadows and enhancing minor details.

"Yes, you could say that," Claire replied with a small sound of disgust, as though she were trying to maintain a professional exterior but was losing the battle. "He's really good at what he does," she said on a sigh, "and he wants us all to bow down whenever he enters a room because of it. The world of Mayan epigraphy and translation has advanced by leaps and bounds in the last several decades. Roughly eighty percent of the writings are now recognizable and understood. Etienne would have us believe he alone holds the key to the remaining twenty percent."

"Between him and Devon," Justin added, "we're kept pretty well entertained."

"Speaking of," Claire interrupted, "where is she?"

Justin shrugged. "She's gone into town on a lot of errands lately with one of the other volunteers. I think she's finally feeling a little uncomfortable having been so blatantly critical and accusatory toward you," he said. "She's made herself scarce lately, and I don't think any of us are going to complain about that too much."

"No problem here," Claire said. "I keep waiting for her to get bored and go home."

Fortunately for the sake of his investigation, Bump was grateful she hadn't. Logically, his mind kept leading him back to the fact that Devon apparently hated Claire, was devoted to her uncle, and would presumably be ecstatic to see Claire fail or be blamed for the fact that priceless artifacts were missing. He made a mental note to spend some more time with the young woman when she showed her face again. And if she wouldn't talk to him, he'd recruit Jon. It had worked once before.

As Justin turned to leave the small group, Bump stopped him with a quick question. "How's Ricardo Valez doing? I'm assuming he's still in the hospital since he's not around here?"

Justin nodded. "I just saw him yesterday, in fact. He's doing moderately well, but he's pretty heavily medicated on some stuff that's knocking him flat. He has malaria from his swim in the river, and he's also got pneumonia, which I'm guessing he had from before. He's been coughing like crazy since he got here. They're keeping him at the hospital for several more days, at least. I'm amazed he took a swim in the river—he didn't grow up around here but I would think he'd have known of the malaria risk."

Claire smiled. "He's taken up swimming since going away to school and he told me when he first got here that he was going to miss it. Poor guy; I think he just threw caution to the wind and went for it."

Bump nodded. "Well, this is probably not the best of times for him, then, but I was hoping to get a chance to talk to him about what he knows. Maybe in a few days . . ."

"I'll be going into town on Thursday," Justin commented. "Ricardo may be a little more coherent by then. You're more than welcome to come with me, if I don't end up going sooner."

"That'll work. Thanks." This time when Justin turned to leave, Bump let him go. He wanted to ask Claire a question without anyone who was associated with the site overhearing. When Justin finally disappeared into his office at the far end of the ruins, Bump broached his subject with Claire.

"I need to pry into your financial life for a minute," he said without preamble.

She cocked her head to one side. "Oh, really. And what makes you think I'll tell you?" she asked with a subtle arch of her eyebrow.

Had he imagined that? Was she flirting with him? He studied her slow grin and the gentle blush that returned to her cheeks, unbidden, he was sure, and felt . . . relief. He hadn't scared her off, apparently, and for that he was grateful. However, with Jon still standing close to his right, he was reluctant to respond, although her playful comment called for it. He didn't like working for an audience.

He cleared his throat, and her broadening grin told him that she knew what he was thinking. *Well, that's fine*, he decided. *Paybacks are an option, and they're usually twice as bad.* Finding amused comfort in that thought and mentally daring her to read his mind about *that* little tidbit, he merely said, "I'm assuming archaeologists don't exactly make an enviable amount of money, is that true?"

"Well," she said on a sigh, "for the most part, yes, that's true. There are some who will become really huge and do extremely well, but the average archaeologist makes only a fair amount of money. I think it's a lot like teaching," she explained. "We do what we do because we love it. The money is a nice side bonus."

"Yes, but when it comes down to it, money is a necessity that some could become obsessed about if there wasn't enough coming in, right?"

She nodded, looking perplexed. "Yes, I suppose so. Why?"

"I'm thinking motives, here. The artifacts that have been stolen," he said. "What would they be worth?"

She shrugged slightly, her lips pursed. "Well, if you could find someone who knew their worth, and given the fact that they're recently unearthed from inside a newly discovered Mayan city, I suppose you could make quite a haul." She closed her eyes, apparently letting the notion sink in. "Someone took them for money."

"I didn't say that. Yet. I'm just trying to sort out all the options."

She rubbed her forehead with her hand. "It makes sense; I suppose I just hadn't thought of it that way. Maybe I hoped someone loved them so much he just had to have them for his own collection."

An image of Miguel's face jumped into Bump's consciousness at her suggestion, and he considered it for a moment before replying. "It's only one theory," he suggested softly. "We just have to consider every possibility."

Jon, who had until that point been quietly adding to his sketch, finally piped up. "You'd be amazed at what people will do for money," he stated. "It's a powerful motivator."

Bump turned and scrutinized his friend. He had known Jon for so long as "Doc" on the streets of Chicago, that the comments he'd heard from him lately that were lucid and made sense always stopped Bump in his tracks. His associations with the young man had been stilted, at best; he'd always been trying to reason with or get information out of a man who was perpetually drunk or high. This new sober and clean individual was perceptive, quick, and bright. Bump intended for him to stay that way.

"That's true," Bump added with a nod. "And anyway," he said to Claire, "it didn't take much reasoning to figure that the students here aren't exactly rolling in it. But I'm wondering how someone would feel with the knowledge that after school, there wasn't much monetary reward to look forward to. Wouldn't you want to secure your future a bit?"

"Not by stealing—especially something ancient and precious!"

"I know *you* wouldn't," he said. "But someone else might."

She looked off into the distance, a pained expression crossing her soft features. "I don't want it to be one of the students," she murmured. "I would be so . . . sad."

Bump eyed her with concern, wondering if he'd opened a Pandora's Box that would send her into another fasting frenzy. "It's okay," he said quickly. "I'll take care of it."

She smiled a bit at that and shook her head. "You don't have to turn yourself into a co-dependent for my sake," she said. "I really don't need to be coddled or protected." She glanced uncomfortably at Jon, who was still sketching and appeared to be trying to give her privacy without making it obvious by actually leaving. She shrugged as though unconcerned with whatever he might overhear, and said, "I'll be okay."

"So I can take you out for a hot fudge sundae after dinner tonight?"

She snorted. "Well, first of all, I haven't seen a Baskin Robbins since I left the states. And secondly," she added, "no thanks. Let's be realistic."

He nodded his approval with a slight smile of his own at her attempts to effectively deal with her problems. "That's fair," he said. "I can handle realistic."

Chapter 17

The Game was swiftly approaching. Queliza finally shared her knowledge with Palome, knowing full well he had no power to stop the event, but unable to keep her concerns to herself any longer.

Palome was shocked. "The king will be furious!"

"But if he wins, surely he will be proud?"

"The risk is great." Palome shook his head. "That reckless young fool . . ."

* * * * * *

When Bump was unable to find Claire after dinner on Monday night, he didn't have to wonder where she'd gone. As he climbed the steps of the temple, he wondered why he couldn't have become enamored of a woman who was content to stay at ground level. *Well*, he supposed, *I haven't exercised since I got here . . . I should be grateful for these little hikes.*

He reached the top and found Claire, just as he'd suspected, lying flat on her back and examining the stars. "I must be getting old," he said as he approached her. "That climb kills me."

She leaned up and rested on her elbows, smiling in greeting. "Well, then it's good for you," she said. "I'll have to come up here more often so we can be sure you stay healthy."

He sank down next to her and sat quietly for a moment before speaking. "What are you thinking about?"

She brought herself to a sitting position and hugged her knees. "I don't know; lots of things, I guess. Mostly I was thinking back on my therapy and feeling pretty proud that I'm getting things under control. I have you to thank for a large part of that," she said with a small gesture toward him, "and I'm grateful."

"I haven't done anything," he murmured.

"Just the fact that you're here helps. You're taking care of things I couldn't, and that's made a big difference." She sighed softly. "There were a lot of issues I needed to deal with the last time I got . . . sick. . . ."

"What kind of issues?"

"Nothing really awful or huge, just the fact that I'm a freak, I suppose." She softened her self-deprecatory remark with a smile. "There were some things with my mother that I had to let go of . . ." She paused for a moment. "My mother is very headstrong," she said. "Unfortunately, so am I. She wanted things to go her way, and I was determined to do them mine."

"She's not happy with what you've done?"

Claire laughed. "On the contrary, actually. She couldn't be happier. She's been my strongest advocate, and always was. We just . . . we used to butt heads a lot, and I was forever afraid that if I gave in, I was losing control of what I wanted."

Control again. Bump smiled. "So what you've learned to do is relinquish control."

"More or less. And I don't blame my mother for causing an eating disorder. It was a combination of many things, I think; her personality, meshed with mine and my penchant for perfection, my unwillingness to never accept mistakes in myself . . . it all snowballed into one big, huge mess. Combine that with the fact that I wanted to be six feet tall and walking down a runway . . ."

"Now that doesn't make much sense to me," he said. "Too many planes in the way."

Claire looked at him for a moment before tipping her head back and laughing for a good, long time. "You made a joke," she said, still laughing. "That was a good one!"

It was a stupid joke and he knew it, but it was at that moment that he decided he'd go on the stand-up comedy circuit if it would make her laugh like that again. It was a beautiful, melodic sound, and the very sights and sounds of her taking such delight in his odd attempt at humor made him want to stay up all night thinking of clever one-liners.

"It wasn't really that funny," he said, smiling at her.

She eventually quieted, but the traces of her mirth were still evident in the expression on her face. "Yes it was," she said. "And the next time I pick up a fashion magazine and feel jealous of the women on the pages, I'll envision them on the wrong kind of runway getting flattened by a plane. It'll be my new happy thought."

"That's kind of sick, you do realize that?"

"Yes I do," she replied, "but sometimes happy thoughts are few and far between, so I'll take them where I can get them."

"Your life should be full of happy thoughts," he said quietly. "Is it really so hard for you to find them?"

She sobered and evaded answering for a moment by looking heavenward. "I worry a lot," she finally said. "I worry about my parents' health. They're far away and getting older. I worry about Connor and Liz. Here I was thinking my brother was invincible and he nearly got himself killed in Peru. I worry about Paige. She's at school in California. She's young and beautiful and far from home." She paused for breath, and he didn't interrupt her thoughts.

"I worry about myself," she admitted, her voice low. "I worry that I'll never stop worrying and will get ulcers and have a heart attack by age thirty. I worry about my career, especially lately. I worry that every single artifact we dig up will be stolen. . . . Did I mention that I worry a lot?"

He smiled and shook his head, taking her hand and rubbing circles across the back of it with his thumb, much the same way he had the day before when they were alone in the jeep. "Did nobody ever tell you that eighty percent of the things we worry about never come to pass?"

She made a small sound through her nose that might have been something akin to laughter. "What about the other twenty percent, then? Twenty percent of the time, my fears will be founded in reality."

"Yes, but you know what? That's just life." His tone was kind. "And have you noticed that all of those things you just mentioned to me are things totally and completely beyond your control?"

Claire nodded. "That was part of my whole recovery process when I was in therapy," she admitted. "I had to learn to quit freaking out about things I have no control over. It's not easy, though, and sometimes I forget."

He shook his head slightly, almost to himself. "It's interesting that your worries translate themselves to an unwillingness to eat."

She shrugged lightly with a simple smile. "It's familiar," she whispered. "I can *do* something about how much I eat. You might look at me and think, 'Just eat, for crying out loud,'—I'm sure my mom did, although I never asked her outright, but it's not that simple. It's hard. When this very first happened to me in grad school, it was probably a way of crying out for attention. But the funny thing is, it's not anymore. Now it's just habit. Familiarity."

He scowled briefly. "You need someone with you, then, all the time. Why haven't you found someone you like, yet?"

She laughed. "Are you talking husband here? Oh, sure, I'll just go right out and find myself one." She shook her head, still amused, apparently. "It won't do me any good if I can't take care of this on my own. A husband can't be with me twenty-four seven, nor should he have to be. Support from loved ones and friends helps, absolutely— kind of like what your presence here has done for me, but it's gotta be something I can deal with myself or I'll never be at peace."

"And are you dealing with it?"

She looked him in the eyes and softly replied, "I am. It's hard, but I am, and I'm proud of that." He saw her eyes fill, the moonlight reflected on the gloss within. Suddenly all the poetic imagery and idiocy he'd associated with his feelings for her of late didn't seem so ridiculous. He leaned over and cupped her face in his hands, lowering his lips to hers.

It was a long, long time before he found the strength to break the contact and look carefully into her face. "That was inevitable, you know," he whispered.

She nodded, a solitary tear slipping from its home and rolling down her cheek. *Nice one, St. James*, he thought to himself with a small, uncustomary stab of panic. *Make her cry!* "Are you okay?"

She nodded, her chin lifting a notch. "I'm okay," she answered.

He realized that if nothing else, her pride would see her through. She would battle whatever emotional and personal issues she faced, and, if she relied on nothing else, pride alone would keep her strong. "I believe you," he said honestly and kissed her again, this time encircling her with his arms and pulling her close.

* * * * * *

Claire's mind was a jumble of thoughts as she finally returned to her room. Bump had escorted her there after kissing her for a long time under the stars, after which he stated that they had to leave or they'd both be sorry. She wasn't so sure she'd have been sorry, but had been grateful for his moral fortitude when hers seemed to want to be absent.

She decided it was time for a shower. A shower always cleared her thoughts. As she gathered the things she needed and made her way to the bathroom, she tried to make sense of the feelings she had for a man she barely knew. To say she was attracted to him would have been a laughable understatement. That much had been evident from the first time she'd met him and her eyes had been more than happy to go exploring of their own free will.

There was something more, though—in fact, a lot of "some-things" more. He had a mental strength that she found particularly attractive, and a no-nonsense way in which he looked at life that made things seem really very simple. She wished she had even a fraction of his apparent peace. She was sure he had "issues"; everyone had issues . . . but he seemed to keep his in check. She didn't imagine that he wallowed in them.

He was comfortable in his surroundings, as well. He was new to the ruins and the circumstances involving the staff, but he knew his work well and stepped in, taking charge without alienating anyone or obnoxiously asserting himself.

He was also extremely compassionate. She wouldn't have guessed so on their first meeting, but she'd seen his protective nature in the way he dealt with Jon Kiersey. Bump was gentle and patient without being disabling. He had also been that way with her, she realized, and she wondered if his feelings for her were merely an extension of his protective personality.

Into her mind flashed an image of him holding her, kissing her senseless not thirty minutes earlier. As she stepped into the sun-warmed water of the shower and relaxed, taking great pleasure in massaging her tired scalp, she reasoned that a man probably wouldn't have to extend such courtesies merely as an act of kindness. She'd heard

the strain in his voice when he'd insisted they part for the evening—
and she knew that, if nothing else, he was a man of his word.

She knew he didn't lie, and that he wouldn't be merely amusing
himself with her for sport, especially given the fact that he respected
and liked her brother. He may not be entirely certain what his feelings for her meant, but she didn't believe he would engage her
emotions if he didn't feel something for her in return. Especially after
all she'd shared, and the things he'd told her the day before when they
arrived home from church.

So what then, she wondered, did *she* want? Love and commitment? Marriage? She compared the feelings she was currently experiencing with those she'd had at the outset of her relationship with
Darren Stark. They had met at a dig in England that Darren was
funding and where Claire was studying for a quarter, and Darren had
showered her with attention and words of adoration. He had been
relentless in his pursuit of her, and she had often taken her school
breaks in Paris where she could spend time with him. The relationship had lasted for nearly a year when Claire had finally found the
strength to tell him it was done.

During the course of that year he had confused her and manipu-
lated her emotions to the point that she wasn't even sure what she
wanted from her life that existed outside of her profession. He was, in
truth, a weak man who preyed on those he envisioned to be weaker
than he was, yet while he had led her around in circles, he had also
misread her. Her break from the relationship had been final, and had
left him confused. He had hounded her, off and on, ever since.

In the beginning of the relationship, she had been flattered by the
attention and had been stressed enough over school that she had
allowed him to infiltrate her life in ways that she might not have,
otherwise. But with Darren, or anyone else she'd ever dated, she had
never felt the sense of security she felt in the presence of Bump St.
James. Finding someone who had her same kind of strength and
determination to do things and do them well was a novelty. It was,
she supposed, an added bonus that he wasn't neurotic about it the
way she was.

She shook her head at herself as the water ran down her head and
onto her face. *Well*, she mused, closing her eyes against the tepid

water, *I may be a freak, but I get things done. And I make people smile.* That had to count for something.

Chapter 18

The morning of the Game dawned bright and hot. Queliza stood on the fringes of the crowd as the two teams gathered, prepared to do battle. The Game was played once a year, and it was a time-honored tradition shared by many cities.

Her throat was thick and she felt faint as the teams lined up and the ball was thrown into play. The crowd displayed an excited curiosity about who the mysterious captain could be; his face was hidden, and the king had been amused enough by such antics to allow it.

She glanced at the king who was seated high on one of the two buildings that flanked the ball court, watching the proceedings with pleasure. Men would die at the finish and the winners would be heroes . . .

* * * * * *

The next morning dawned bright and early, and upon waking, Claire was greeted in the mess hall by the smug and smiling face of Etienne DuBois.

"It's so good to see you, *chére,*" he said. "And how have you fared in my absence?"

"Well," she replied, trying to pull her lips into a smile, "it's been hard, but I've managed."

She went to the counter to retrieve some cereal and milk someone else had left out, and pouring herself some, sat at one of the tables. Etienne did likewise and found a seat next to her. She decided to try to start over with the man, wondering if maybe she'd judged him harshly. Perhaps he just had many insecurities, and who didn't? Maybe his bravado was merely a way of masking those.

She glanced at him as she chomped on her Wheaties, taking in the expensive yet functional clothing and the impeccably groomed overall appearance. If Bump's theory proved correct and someone had been taking the artifacts to sell for money, then he could probably just dismiss Etienne as a possible suspect. Etienne's money came from his ancestors; he lived off family money, and lived well. He studied glyphs and made a name for himself in the archaeology field because he enjoyed it, and was good at it.

Or maybe the whole "family money" thing was just a front; could that be the case? Claire continued munching her cereal and tried not to scrutinize her companion too closely. It was he, himself, who had told the entire site and all its inhabitants that he came from old money. That may well have been a lie, she supposed. Who knew? It was getting frustrating trying to continue day by day, knowing that someone she probably worked quite closely with was responsible for making her life miserable.

Etienne and Claire both looked up as Sue and Miguel entered the building, followed closely by Justin. They all three pulled their lips back from their teeth and gritted a civil, if not entirely enthusiastic "hello" to Etienne. Etienne, in return, nodded regally to the trio and resumed eating.

When the newcomers had all chosen their cereal, they made themselves comfortable at the table where Claire and Etienne were seated; given the fact that the two other tables were empty, Claire had to assume her friends had taken pity on her.

"So, Etienne," Claire ventured when nobody seemed to want to say anything, "is everything okay at home?"

He nodded, somewhat stiffly. "There were some problems with my parents, but things are resolved, now."

"Well, we're all happy to hear that." Claire raised her eyebrows at the other three.

"Yes, we are," they echoed in unison.

Etienne seemed to shrug off his moment of discomfort and looked up with a smile. "I'm happy to be back," he said, "so I can get to work on the staircase."

Now, see, Claire? she asked herself. *He's really not so bad. He loves this work as much as the rest of us do.*

"I know that nobody here can decipher the glyphs, and I'm sure you're all anxious for me to get to work on it. It's a good thing I wasn't away for long."

Spoke too soon. Claire gritted her teeth. It wasn't so much the fact that he was right; he spoke the truth—nobody else did have the knowledge necessary to translate the ancient carvings. It was his manner and his attitude that grated on her nerves. *Nope,* she decided. She hadn't been mistaken about him at all. He was every bit as obnoxious as she had judged him to be at the first.

"Well," she said as she finished her breakfast, "you just get to work on it and enjoy. There's enough there to keep you busy for hours on end, I'm sure."

"Perhaps," he answered. "Or perhaps not. It may take me only a few minutes. I've been amazed at how quickly I've been able to decipher many of the structures here at this site."

Justin cleared his throat. "Etienne, is there a new development in the field of epigraphy that you know about and the rest of us don't?"

Etienne shrugged lightly, looking amused. "The field is growing with understanding at an amazing rate," he said with a smile. "And when you're good, you're good."

There's my cue, thought Claire. *If I stay here another minute I'll wrap my hands around his throat and squeeze.* Her resolve to leave was strengthened immeasurably when Devon Stark walked through the door looking like a beauty-pageant contestant and strutted over to the counter for some food.

"Hi everyone," she said a bit breathlessly over her shoulder. "Sorry I'm late."

Late? Claire cocked an eyebrow. It wasn't exactly as though they had assigned times for meals; they all kind of wandered in and got what they wanted, when they wanted it.

"I was talking to Bump St. James," she said as she walked over to the table, nibbling on a piece of bread. She took a seat at the table and affected what Claire assumed was supposed to be a knowledge-able expression. "He wanted my opinion on some things," she said, glancing at everyone present, her gaze finally coming to rest on Claire. "I think he trusts my perception."

Etienne gave a short bark of incredulous laughter that he didn't even try to hide, and Claire decided that had she not disliked him so much, she probably could have kissed him. He turned to Devon with a smile that clearly mocked. "My dear child," he said. "Who is this man that so trusts your perception?"

Devon tried, but didn't quite manage to mask a glare. She flushed hotly. "He's here investigating the missing artifacts on behalf of the insurance company that covers the site. He needs to find out exactly what they were, how much they were worth, and why someone would want them."

Etienne looked surprised. "Really?" He turned to Justin and Claire. "That's an odd procedure, isn't it? I've never encountered that scenario on the other sites I've been involved with."

"Have you ever been on other sites where artifacts have turned up missing, Etienne?" Claire posed the question without a flinch.

He turned his amused gaze on her face. "What are you suggesting, Dr. O'Brian?"

"Not a thing. Merely curious."

"No, as a matter of fact, I've never seen this happen before. The other sites I've worked on have been excellently managed and have appeared to be completely secure, I would suppose, given the fact that nothing ever disappeared."

Dang. He had her there. "Well," she said, "At any rate, Mr. St. James will probably want to speak with you about what you may know. Contrary to popular belief, he's been talking to *all* of us about this."

"Why bother calling him 'Mr. St. James,' Claire," Devon interrupted. "I think we all know by now that you two have moved to a first-name basis."

"Devon," Claire said evenly as she rose to clear her bowl, "don't you have some pressing business in town, or something?"

"No, Claire, as a matter of fact I don't. I think I should be here to keep an eye on things for my uncle."

Claire rinsed her bowl and placed it in the sink, where it would be washed later by Rosa, who was paid to clean up after the staff. She calmly washed her hands as well, and dried them on a dish towel before turning around. When she did, she picked up her backpack from where she had placed it next to her chair. "I'll be in the lab today," she said, directing her comment at Sue and Miguel. "Check with Justin first, and then if there's not somewhere else he wants you to be, come and find me."

The two students nodded uncomfortably and Sue shot a glare at Devon so hot that Claire would have laughed had she not been so angry herself. As it was, she merely walked serenely from the mess hall and across to the lab. When she reached the door, she put her hand on the knob and reached in her pocket for the key. The knob turned in her hand as she fumbled and she opened it in surprise.

Bump was inside, seated on a chair with his feet propped up on one of the tables.

"Devon has it out for you," he said without preamble when he saw her.

She sighed and closed the door behind her, making her way into the room and sitting next to him on another chair, dropping her pack to the floor with a *clunk*. "Tell me something I don't already know," she muttered.

"What did you do to that girl?"

A small noise of disgust escaped through Claire's teeth. "Nothing. She's hated me from the beginning."

"Did you know her when you were dating her uncle?"

Claire shook her head. "I'd never met her. The first time I ever laid eyes on her was when she joined us here at the site, much later after I'd broken things off with Darren. I can't figure out if she resents me because I once meant something to him and it makes her jealous, or if he's feeding her some line about the fact that his heart is all broken in pieces and it's my fault. Who knows what she thinks, but either way it's not pretty."

"I talked to her a little while ago," Bump commented, his eyes narrowed, "but she didn't tell me much that she hadn't already. I was hoping to get something new from her, but . . ." He stared at the door, thinking, tapping a pen against his thigh.

"Well, I have another treat in store for you," Claire said, settling back into her chair and stretching her legs. "Etienne DuBois is back in town and charming as ever. He's been told you're an insurance adjuster, and I think he questioned it. He's bright, I'll give him that, but *man*, he's obnoxious."

Bump nodded, apparently pulling his thoughts to the present. "I'll talk to him this morning, then. Where will he be working?"

"Probably on the old staircase we're just now uncovering; it's the one at the far end of the ruins to the left of the temple."

He nodded as though making a mental note of that fact. "So what's the deal with Hodges?"

"Justin?" At his nod, she shrugged lightly. "What do you mean?"

"He doesn't seem to be quite in charge, in my opinion. If I were to come in and observe how things run around here and I hadn't been told ahead of time who did what, I'd say you were the director of the site and Justin was your assistant, not the other way around."

Claire felt slightly chagrined. "Well, that's probably a personality thing," she mumbled. "I tend to take charge."

Bump laughed. "It's not that you're taking charge, it's that Hodges *isn't*. How long has he had this business? Has he done other digs on his own?"

She nodded. "He has, but none this big. I think he's a little overwhelmed with the scope of this whole project and the fact that Darren has been so strange about his requirements. We have more than enough work here for about a gazillion students and I could handle a much larger group, but Darren keeps insisting we keep it small, and won't explain why. He has a flair for the dramatic," she finished with a wry smile.

"How would you describe Hodges to someone who didn't know him?"

"Hmm. Well, I'd describe him as pretty quiet and withdrawn, but intensely devoted to his profession. That's one of the reasons I was so excited when he chose me to work with him. He's fantastic at what he does and he loves it as much as I do. He's a hard worker, very dedicated, and an extremely devoted father."

She could feel her expression hardening at her next thought. "His wife, however, is making things really hard for him. They're going through a messy divorce and she won't let him see or talk to their daughter, except on her very exacting terms. He's so quiet, even more quiet than usual, and I know he's stressing about things at home. I've heard bits of conversations he's had with his wife. They're not pretty.

"The thefts here on top of everything else have given him a lot to stew over, I think. That's probably one of the reasons I took such an aggressive stance in getting you hired to take care of all this; I didn't want Justin having one more thing to worry about." Claire frowned.

"Well, that gives me plenty to think about," he said with a hint of a smile as he brought his legs down and touched his feet to the floor. "Onward and upward." He leaned over to give Claire a soft kiss on her willing lips. "You'll be in here today, then?"

Claire nodded, dazed. He kissed her and she lost all train of thought.

He grinned. "One more," he said, and after planting another quick kiss on her mouth, he stood and walked to the door, turning back as an apparent afterthought. "Are you feeling . . . okay about things?"

She squinted. "*Us* kind of things?"

"Yeah."

She smiled. "I am."

"Good. So am I." With a wink, he turned and was gone, leaving Claire to sit staring at the spot he'd vacated and wishing he'd come back. She shook herself and finally rose from her chair, ready to begin the work she needed to complete for the day.

Chapter 19

The ball flew from one side to the other, continuously in play, never dropped. The crowd cheered and gasped when it appeared it would fall to the ground, but it didn't.

Queliza was a bundle of nerves. She jumped at the touch of a hand at her elbow. Palome. He was looking at her with a sad expression. He gave her arm a small squeeze as a gesture of support and turned his attention back to the Game.

The crowd gasped in horror as the ball was finally dropped. It fell at the feet of the mysterious captain who had hidden his face behind a mask. The moments slowed to fractions of pictures for Queliza. She leaned against Palome for support when she would have fallen to the ground.

The king descended from his throne to congratulate the winners and seal the fate of the losers. It was with some amusement that he unmasked the young captain. His face froze when he realized his son was the man behind the mask.

He stood still in shock for many long moments before he finally stated to the crowd, "Prepare for the executions . . ."

* * * * *

Bump found the man he presumed to be Etienne DuBois precisely where Claire said he'd be, examining the staircase that was currently being exhumed from the earth near the ancient temple. DuBois held a notebook in his hand and was crouched close to the carvings, making markings quickly on his paper with a pencil.

Bump approached him and stood so that he cast a shadow over the man's notebook. "Hi there," he said when DuBois looked up in irritation. Bump extended his hand but remained standing upright. "I'm Bump St. James. I'm representing the insurance company that covers these ruins and I'd like to ask you a few questions, if you don't mind."

"Bump?" Etienne DuBois stood and grasped the offered hand, a smile quirking the corners of his mouth. "This is your name?"

"That's right." He didn't bother with any explanations. He took in at a glance the man's expensive-looking khaki pants, the sandals on his feet and the neatly pressed short-sleeved shirt. Etienne's hair was wavy and combed back off a high forehead, his nose patrician and haughty—an attribute Bump was sure the Frenchman found to be a nice asset—and his eyes were an ice blue.

Bump gestured toward the ancient staircase. "You must be pretty excited about this find, here," he said, hoping to draw the man into some semblance of casual conversation.

Etienne looked at the ancient glyphs and smiled. "Yes, I am. It's an incredible thing, and Hodges was lucky to have me here already assigned to this dig when they found the staircase. If I had been working somewhere else, they might well have hired someone less qualified to decipher it."

"Indeed. I'm sure they're grateful."

Etienne eyed him carefully as though trying to decide whether or not Bump was sincere. He finally shrugged. "Well, one can never tell, but they should be."

Time to shift. "What can you tell me about the artifacts that have turned up missing in recent weeks. Anything at all?"

Etienne drew a deep breath and expelled it on a disgusted sigh. "I fear I have nothing useful to share," he said. "I have to wonder at Justin Hodges' abilities, however. I have never seen such negligence in management in my entire career."

"You think he's been negligent?"

"Certainly! How else can you account for the fact that such valuable pieces are missing? If he had tighter controls over the personnel and workers, I doubt very highly that this would have happened. As it is, he lets his second-in-command run the operation and allows a ridiculously stupid teenager to run amok amidst all of it. If he were more of a man, he'd have told Stark that there was no place for the niece and she'd have to find her experiences elsewhere."

Bump was more curious about the brief mention of Claire's role. "And you think Dr. O'Brian is overstepping her bounds?"

Etienne wrinkled his nose. "I wouldn't say that. I think this operation has needed leadership and she's stepped up and provided it. It's not her job, however. She's the on-site conservator and oversees the experiences of the masters students. She has enough to do without taking care of all the rest."

Bump eyed the man with interest. It actually sounded as though DuBois showed a sliver of respect for Claire. Maybe she had misread his obnoxious behavior and hadn't seen it as high regard.

"If she didn't have me here to take care of the interpretation of the glyphs, I feel she'd be lost. She knows she can count on me to do my job and do it well. As for the missing artifacts, well, I'll leave that up to you, Mr. Bump. I'm afraid I don't know anything at all about it."

Well, okay. So he *was* indeed obnoxious, but apparently Etienne felt he was invaluable to the good doctor, and in an odd way Bump could relate. It was nice to bask in the glow of Claire's approval, and he doubted DuBois had had the pleasure of that experience yet. He might not try so hard to convince everyone he was wonderful if she had given him the pat on the back he thought he needed from her. On the other hand, Etienne had matter-of-factly extolled his own virtues to Bump at least twice in the few minutes they'd been standing together. It likely wasn't just Claire's approval he was looking for. He'd take it wherever he could get it.

Bump began to understand the frustration experienced by the other members of the staff. It would get old after awhile. He thought of his own ego and the way he teased his friends with his arrogance. The memories nearly made him laugh out loud. Thankfully, his demeanor and personality were nothing like the Frenchman's. If they were, he might be worried. Bump was good, and he knew it, but didn't feel the need to express it to the rest of the world except in cases where he felt another person would benefit from hearing it—as had Claire when they'd first met—or in times of humor when he meant to tease. There was a distinct difference.

"Well," he said and extended his hand again, "thank you for your time. I'll let you get back to work, but I'd appreciate it if you would let me know if you think of anything that would be useful."

The Frenchman nodded once and shook Bump's hand, returning again to his work when Bump turned away. Bump walked the length of the site, glancing at the stone pillars that dotted the plaza, carved with odd pictures and faces that DuBois had probably already, if he was to be believed, deciphered and documented. He passed the ball court and its two parallel buildings that ran the length on either side, and took note of the other structures that emerged from the forest floor.

He made his way to the other end of the site where the research complex was housed, with the intention of talking briefly to Justin Hodges. He reached the small office and went to push the door, which was already partially ajar, further open. He stopped when he heard Justin's voice inside, sounding more than a little agitated. As Bump stood quietly outside, it became apparent that Justin was on the phone.

Bump felt a twinge of regret at the fact that he was eavesdropping, but didn't for a moment think of moving away from the door. It was a tool of the trade, and one he'd never turn away from. He heard only Justin's side of the conversation, but what he heard made him feel for the man.

"Trina," Justin was saying, "I just sent you the child support for this month. I've never missed, and I've never been late. I'm sending you all I have and you know that!" Pause. "I have never once shirked my responsibilities to Mandy. Never!" His voice hissed angrily and he sounded as though he were in pain. "You won't even let me talk to her, let alone see her when I'm home—how can you expect me to maintain a good relationship with her?"

Another pause. "You're not letting me, Trina. You're not letting me be a good father! I send her letters that I'm sure she never sees, I send her presents she probably never opens and I call all the time, only to be told she's outside with friends or is busy doing her homework. You can't keep doing this to me! To me and Mandy!"

Bump closed his eyes. After a few more harsh words, the phone was slammed with a loud bang, presumably onto the desk, and he heard Hodges emit a harsh sound that probably represented something between anger and grief. Bump quietly turned from the door and made his way thoughtfully to the lab, knowing full well why Claire had taken the worry and responsibility of the thefts onto her own shoulders. Hodges was dealing with an emotional maelstrom that would make any man cringe.

He shook his head as he walked, wondering if little Mandy was ever going to know her father, and feeling an odd kinship with a child he'd never met.

* * * * * *

"So tell me about your academic life," Claire said to Bump as they sat under the stars atop the steps of the ancient temple, this time including Jon as well.

"My academic life, huh? Well, let's see," Bump said. "I grew up in Seattle and went through the public school system, then went to college at the University of Washington. I majored in Criminal Justice because I thought it was interesting and had at one point entertained the notion of going to law school. After I finished my undergrad, I changed directions and did an MBA instead of law, and started my own business."

"And have you enjoyed it all?"

He nodded. "Overall, yes. I've seen some things that have made me wonder, but it's been good. I've lived a pretty good life, up to this point, and I'm content. How about yours?"

"Yeah," Jon interrupted curiously. "Aren't you a little young to be an archaeologist already?"

"Well, I was lucky," Claire said. "I knew what I wanted when I was really young so it was easy for me to stay focused and plow through it. I did early college when I was in high school and pushed straight through college and grad school after that. I haven't been out of school for very long. This is my first real 'job'." Claire turned her attention to Jon. "So tell me about you. I'm dying of curiosity."

His sad smile was evident in the darkness. "I've not done anything worth talking about," he said.

She cocked her head sympathetically to one side. "Did you go to school when you were young?"

He shrugged gently. "Off and on. I dropped out of high school when I was fifteen, so I can't even claim a high school diploma."

Her brow wrinkled. "I don't understand something," she said. "It's not that I expect someone who didn't finish high school to be all but illiterate, but you seem so much more beyond that. To look at you and hear you speak, I would never guess you hadn't graduated from college, let alone high school. You've even made references to Tom Sawyer, for crying out loud!"

Jon smiled. "I happen to like Tom Sawyer," he said. "And even though I dropped out of high school, the one thing that's probably saved me is that I like to read. I never admitted it to anyone, of course, but I did like to read, whether drunk or sober." His smile turned sheepish. "Of course, I remember the stuff I read when I was sober a little better than what I read drunk, but at least I was making an effort." He looked almost surprised. "I guess that was one good thing."

"Absolutely, it was," Claire agreed softly. "A very good thing. You can still get your GED, you know. You might take a refresher course at the local high school or community center when you get home and then consider it. I bet with a little study you'd sail right through it."

Jon shook his head a bit. "Can't you just see me sitting there, almost twenty-five years old, trying to graduate from high school?"

"A lot of people do it," Claire answered. "It's not that uncommon, you know. And I think the hardest part would probably be just getting there—making yourself do it. Once you've made the commitment and are into it, I'm sure it won't seem like such an impossible thing anymore."

Jon nodded slightly. "I'll have to look into it," he replied.

Bump nodded as well. "I think it's a good idea," he said. "I'll help you set the whole thing up when we get home. In the meantime, we probably ought to enjoy this time here as much as possible. Who knows when we'll vacation in Guatemala again."

Claire did her best not to snort, but failed miserably. "Yeah, this is quite the vacation for you both, I'm sure. This place must seem like a nuthouse."

Jon surprised her by laughing. "Actually, I was just thinking today that I've never spent so much time with relatively normal people in my life. You all squeak, compared to what I've seen."

"That may be true," Claire said with a rueful grin, "but I can't help but feel sorry for you guys. We've got quite the little soap opera going on here." She comically ticked her fingers off as she spoke. "A neurotic archaeologist recovering from an eating disorder, three poor university students, one of which is hospitalized, a site director ready to tear his heart out and then murder his estranged wife, one certain Frenchman who thinks he's God's gift to Mayan archaeological sites everywhere, and an extremely obnoxious teenager who would be better off in a mall than hanging out with a bunch of ancient ruins. Throw in a whole slew of hardworking native people who must think we're straight out of a loony bin and you've got quite a show."

Jon laughed again and Bump shook his head with a smile. "It's really not all that bad, Claire. People are interesting; I'm always amazed at differing group dynamics."

"Yeah, this would make quite the case study. We'd be written up in psych texts everywhere."

"Nah. It probably seems more pronounced to you because you're right in the middle of it. I bet you'll look back on some of these times and wish you could relive it."

At that, she reluctantly nodded. "Yes, there are parts I've really enjoyed. Most of it, in fact."

"And we'll get the rest taken care of before long. It's only a matter of time, I can feel it."

"Really?"

"Really."

Chapter 20

Queliza stood on the fringes of the activity before the ancient temple, too horrified to leave. She had caught a glimpse of the haunted look in the eyes of the prince before he was taken with his teammates to be executed.

She looked with nausea on the instruments to be used for the beheading, and the carved ceremonial knives that would be dipped in the victims' blood and buried with them.

The king had not spoken to the prince. He stood by and watched as his henchmen executed the team members one by one, and finally ended the life of his only son. His expression was wooden and hard until the workers began to clear the remains of the victims and prepare them for burial.

He stopped them as they moved to clear away his son. "The prince will be buried in the temple," he said, his voice showing its first signs of remorse, "in the inner sanctum . . ."

* * * * * *

Claire awoke the following morning to find the sky enveloped in clouds. She wasn't concerned; the country was nowhere near its customary rainy season, and she was fairly confident that the biggest problem they would face should they be surprised by a downpour was the matter of getting the computers and other equipment inside. As much as she enjoyed the bright sun, she had to admit that the gray hues in the canopy overhead enhanced the ruins and cast shadows here and there, giving the whole place an intriguing feel.

She hurriedly dressed and gathered the things she'd need for her backpack, tying her hair in its customary ponytail and making a quick pit stop at the mess hall before finding her way to the lab. She made sure Sue was securely positioned therein and didn't have immediate plans. "Tell Justin if you have to go somewhere," Claire said to her as she turned to leave. "I'll be in the temple for awhile today."

Sue grinned at her. "Couldn't stay away another day, could you?"

"Ah, you know me too well." Claire smiled in return and walked briskly toward the ancient temple, munching on an apple as she went. When she reached the massive structure, she saw Jon waiting for her. "Hi there," she called to him.

"Hi. Do you mind if I tag along?"

"Not at all! And where's Bump today? He didn't want to give it a try?"

Jon grinned. "He looked kind of green when I told him where I was going," he said on a bit of a laugh. "I think this place scares him."

Claire felt a look of disbelief cross her features. "You've gotta be kidding," she said. "That man's not afraid of anything."

"Except maybe tight spaces, would be my guess."

She looked at him quizzically. "You think?"

Jon shrugged. "Who knows. All I know is that he won't set foot in this place."

Claire smiled. "Maybe we can blackmail him with that." Her smile grew at Jon's answering laugh, and she motioned for him to follow her to the entrance of the temple. They went in, following the same tunnels as they had the first time, dodging workers with their dirt-filled wheelbarrows, until they reached the heart of the interior.

The exterior wall of the Mayan's first structure loomed above them as they made their way to the place they'd worked the first time Claire had taken Jon into the building. They passed Justin, who was on his way out, and Etienne DuBois, who had been reading and recording the glyphs on the ancient wall. He was shaking his head in amazement.

"I can't believe the fact that we still have such good paint remnants on this wall," Etienne remarked as he passed Claire. She smiled. Finally, something she found she could relate to in the Frenchman. Awe at the Mayan remains surrounding them.

"It's incredible, isn't it?" She held his gaze with her smile. "I'm wondering what we'll find inside."

At that, Etienne shrugged. "I don't know that we'll find a way to get inside," he commented. "It's looking quite solid."

"Yes, but there must be an entrance somewhere. We'll find it."

Claire deposited her pack at the same location where she and Jon had worked before and again found a lantern to position closely. They worked alongside each other in pleasant companionship, chipping away at the dirt and rock encrusted on the wall. Jon asked Claire about her reading preferences, and she shared several authors and titles that she enjoyed, feeling extremely pleased with his willingness to converse, and even more pleased that the topic of conversation was something he would benefit from. If he would keep reading and commit to working toward a GED when he returned home, she knew he'd find more faith in his own abilities.

She discovered, upon further dialogue, that his tastes and interests were wide and varied, and he seemed as surprised by that revelation as was she. She was excited for the possibilities that were his; he was like a child discovering a whole new life for himself.

He was saying something about a book he'd read in junior high school when Claire noticed a crack in the wall that seemed to run in a straight line to approximately three feet above her head when she stood. At that point, the crack turned a ninety-degree angle and ran to her left for approximately another three feet where it turned at another ninety-degree angle and ran down the wall again, until it was nearly at her eye level where it disappeared into the mound of dirt.

Narrowing her eyes, she stared at the line for a long time, running her finger along the ridge. It was wider than she'd first realized; it had to be at least a few centimeters in width; she hadn't noticed it before because it was so well disguised within the glyphs. She shifted slightly to her left where the line ran down the wall again until it disappeared. She cleared away the dirt at the level of her face, seeing more of the line exposed as she worked. She knew that it ran to the floor.

"Jon," she interrupted, her voice unintentionally hushed, "I think I've found something."

After spending considerable time in the dirt and having found nothing of interest in the time that he'd been at the site, he seemed thrilled. "What is it?" The urgency in his tone matched hers.

"Look at this," she exclaimed, her level of excitement rising. "I think it's a door!"

He stared as she ran her finger along the crack. His mouth dropped open of its own accord. "I think you're right!"

They stood motionless for a moment, staring first at the crack, then at each other. She felt her eyes opening so wide she was afraid they'd fall out. Finally spurred into action, she moved around Jon and grabbed a wheelbarrow that sat empty nearby. She also grabbed a large shovel that stood propped against the wall and ordered Jon to start digging.

"But be careful," she admonished as she went in search of more help. She ran through the maze of tunnels, dodging other workers and the jagged outcropping of rock that framed the inside of the exterior wall. By the time she reached the entrance to the temple, she was out of breath, but ran for all she was worth to Justin's office.

She found him seated at his desk, and she was so winded that she braced her hands on the other side of the desk and heaved her discovery to him in pants. "We've . . . found . . . a . . . door . . ." was all she managed.

His brow wrinkled in confusion. "A door?"

"Yes," she gulped and took a huge breath. "A door on the exterior wall of the interior temple," she managed.

Justin stood, overturning his chair. It crashed to the floor unheeded behind him. He grabbed her shoulders, his eyes wide. "Are you sure?"

She nodded. "It has to be. Come and see it!"

The pair ran quickly back to the temple and navigated their way through the tunnels on the inside. When they reached Jon, he was digging very quickly, moving as much dirt as he could without scratching or damaging the wall. The wheelbarrow was already full.

Jon stopped for a moment while Claire breathlessly showed Justin the crack along the wall. He turned and hugged her in his euphoria and she laughed, tightly squeezing back. "Can you believe it?" she asked, her voice wavering.

He shook his head. "I can't. Now we can finally see what's inside this thing!" He stood for a moment, absorbing the relevance of the find, and then turned back along the wall to recruit more help. Claire heard him calling out an order in rapid-fire Spanish, and before long, the small area contained a team of well-organized workers who filled the wheelbarrows with dirt and then moved the fill to the outside. Jon stayed with them, closest to the door, and didn't relinquish his spot for even a moment.

Claire stared at the crack in the wall that was growing longer with each disappearing shovelful of dirt. She felt tears stinging her eyes as she viewed the process. The moment was a dream come true. She asked Justin if he'd send someone for Sue and Miguel, making sure to have them lock the lab door behind them. Justin quickly dispatched a young boy to do the job.

It wasn't long before the entire doorway was revealed, and Sue and Miguel came running with Luis on their heels just as Claire and Justin were examining the door for possible signs of entry. Claire turned when she heard the others approach and beamed when she saw that Luis was with them. "I'm so glad you're here for this!" she exclaimed gladly, feeling her eyes burning again.

"So am I, Claire! You found this door just now?"

She nodded. "Now we just have to figure out how to get it open."

"This thing probably weighs a ton," Justin murmured.

And it did. It took several attempts with many strong and willing hands and the use of several crowbars before the great stone wall finally groaned, creaked, and scraped its way open. Claire figured it was probably a miracle that no fingers were smashed or lost by the time the door was lifted back and out of the way.

The noise stopped, the conversation stopped, and all was hushed. Justin turned to Claire. "You really should be the one to look first, Claire," he said. "Grab that lantern behind you."

She could barely hold the lantern as she made her way to the ancient room's entrance. When she reached it, she looked once at Justin, who nodded at her and patted her shoulder. She then raised the lantern high and forward, and peered inside.

It was unbelievably dark.

"We need another lantern," she murmured to Justin. Someone passed another lantern to him and together the two of them made their way into the dark interior, followed by Jon, Miguel, Sue, and Luis. The other volunteers who had helped move the dirt also crowded the doorway, anxious to see what lay within.

Claire glanced down at the floor, wanting to ensure that it was all there, and intact. It was made entirely of stone, and appeared solid as far as the beam of light reached. As they moved farther into the interior, they began to realize that it was actually relatively small. Claire called back over her shoulder for more light, and several more lanterns were passed into willing hands, shedding light on what lay within.

At the center of the room was an altar, and upon the altar lay a skeleton. Claire approached the altar carefully, her scientific mind making notes as she examined the bones and items that lay around it. The head had been severed from the rest of the body. Also on the altar were positioned several small pottery vessels, still vivid in the colors of their original paints despite the passage of thousands of years, and near the skull were three black metal tools that resembled carved knives.

She looked at Justin over her raised lantern. "This is just amazing," she whispered.

She heard Sue whispering somewhere behind her. "What *was* this place?"

Claire shook her head. "I don't know," she answered in hushed tones. "It could be a royal tomb," she said, closely examining the altar and items around it.

"Or it could be a sacrificial victim," Justin murmured.

Claire nodded reluctantly. "It very well could be," she agreed, "although that's certainly a lot more ghoulish, isn't it."

Justin had moved to the other side of the altar opposite Claire and was bending down to closely inspect the knife near the skull. "I can't be sure," he said, holding the lantern close, "but there may well be blood stains or other residue on these weapons."

Claire also leaned in close, and motioned for the others to move in with the light so that they all might see more clearly. The knife blades were long, approximately an inch wide at the base near the carved figures that formed the handle, and tapering to a point at the end—the whole thing from one end to the other measuring approximately twelve inches.

"I need my camera," Claire said. "It's in my backpack. Will someone get it? I also need the flash."

Jon turned and maneuvered through the crowd that had moved within the room and were gathered at the door. He returned in a moment, handing Claire her old 35mm camera and its flash. She attached the two and began snapping pictures from every possible angle.

As she moved her way around the altar, she became aware of the mass of people who had filed in behind them. She looked into the curious and expectant faces of the local volunteers and felt a surge of gratitude for their presence.

The room was eventually vacated as the staff left to return to other duties and share the news of the new find with all and sundry. Sue and Miguel also disappeared, but returned within moments equipped with notebooks and cameras. Luis stayed as well, helping them record the artifacts found, the superficial facts of the condition of the bones, and the placement of items in the ancient tomb. Jon was also gone again momentarily, but returned with Bump's hand-held video camera.

The group spent the better part of the day in the tomb, recording every last detail as meticulously as possible before carefully transfer-ring the vessels and knives into boxes to be taken to the lab where Claire could determine what kind of treatment they'd need before shipping.

The hour was much later than Claire realized by the time the small team made their way from the ancient temple, transporting the last of the finds to the lab. They were dusty, tired, and ecstatic.

Claire entered the mess hall after washing her hands and face. Maria Muñoz was at the site and had prepared a delightful-smelling meal for the staff and volunteers who still remained. After expressing her thanks, Claire stood to one side for a moment, enjoying the plea-sure written on the faces of everyone present. She didn't even feel annoyed when she looked at Etienne; she figured that was an amazing thing in and of itself. When Devon entered the room, Claire ignored her in hopes that her own spirits would remain high.

She smiled as Bump eventually materialized and made his way to her side. "Congratulations, Claire," he said, rubbing a hand down her arm. "You must be thrilled."

"I am," she said, practically feeling the glow on her face. "I'm so happy we found this today. It was the most amazing feeling ever. You should have come in and seen it for yourself!"

Bump looked slightly chagrined. "I don't do well in tight spaces," he said. "I would have, otherwise. I'll just help you celebrate out here, how's that?"

"That'll do," she said with a grin.

The impromptu celebration lasted well into the night, and many of the workers stayed much longer than they usually did to converse and share the experience with the small team of archaeologists, much to the delight of both parties. Many of the local people had their own legends about the ruins, and theory upon theory flew about in conversation as to the probable origins of the ancient tomb and its lonely inhabitant.

Claire left the party while it was in full swing, with Bump close on her heels, to retire to the lab and quickly assess the needs of the artifacts they had removed. The material of the artifacts and the climate outside the dry, airless temple dictated differing preservation techniques for each item. The general rule for conservation was to do as little as possible, and to avoid doing anything that couldn't later be undone. It was a rule she followed religiously.

Bump stayed with her in the lab, his feet propped on a far table and saying little, watching her work, uninterrupted. When she'd done what she needed to with the small and intricately painted vessels, she left them alone and turned her attention to the carved knives she was presuming were made of flint. Pulling on latex gloves, she carefully handled one knife and placed it under the all-seeing eye of a high-powered microscope. As she focused in on the tip of the blade, her suspicions were confirmed and her heart beat a little faster.

"I think we have some blood residue here," she said in a murmur, still looking through the microscope. "This is just unreal."

Bump smiled. "You're not going to sleep tonight, are you?"

She looked up with a grin. "Not much, I'm afraid."

She looked a bit longer at the blade of the knife before carefully placing it back in its secure position in some tissue paper on a shelf. "We can do DNA testing on that blood," she said, motioning to the knife, "and find the descendant of whomever that blood belonged. Isn't that just incredible?"

Bump nodded his agreement with another smile. "It is incredible," he said as he rose and made his way to her side, "and so are you." He wrapped his arms around her and pulled her close, tucking her head under his chin.

Chapter 21

The queen was ill the day following the execution. Queliza wasn't surprised. She was ill, herself. When she was summoned to the queen's side, it was all she could do to drag herself from her own room.

The queen dismissed the other servants and bade Queliza sit beside her. "I would ask a favor of you, Queliza, and if you promise me you will keep this favor, I will not have you executed."

Queliza swallowed and nodded her agreement. "I must insist that you never tell anyone you warned me that the prince intended to participate in the Game. I am sure you understand that I could face severe consequences with the king, were he to learn of such things."

Queliza knew well that the queen could end the life of a servant on a whim. "I will keep your secret, your majesty," she murmured, though in her current depression she couldn't imagine why she wished to live. The pain she felt caused her so much physical and emotional devastation she wondered if her life would be over before the day were out, simply because her heart couldn't bear the agony . . .

* * * * *

Claire awoke Thursday morning knowing something fantastic had happened but couldn't remember quite what it was. Suddenly the delicious memories of the day before came rushing back like a beautiful dream. She had found the entrance to the sacred interior Mayan temple, and had discovered a veritable treasure-trove of archaeological gems within.

She was ecstatic. She stretched languidly, enjoying the fact that she was alive and that almost all was right with the world. She didn't even allow the specter of the thefts to dampen her spirits and drag her mood downward. She quickly dressed, noting with interest the late hour on her watch. She had overslept, and by a long shot. She was a little surprised nobody had come to wake her, but figured that one day of rising later than normal wasn't bad considering the fact that she never did.

As she left her building, she turned to lock the door behind her. Taped to the outside of the door was a note, folded in half. She opened it curiously, and smiled when she read the message inside.

"Jon and I have gone into town with Justin," it read. "I'm going to interview Ricardo Valez and then spend some time with Luis. He mentioned he could use some help with one of the families in the ward that's been having a hard time lately. They're moving into a new house. We should be back late in the afternoon. Miss me, please— Bump."

Claire folded the note, still smiling, and placed it in her pocket. Bump St. James was a good man, she decided. He was thoughtful and considerate, and capable. She was impressed by the fact that he was willing to set aside whatever else he may have had planned for the day in order to help a struggling family. There was plenty going on; he could easily have declined.

She hummed softly as she walked along to the lab, and was smiling when she stepped inside. Sue and Miguel were already there working on some items that had been discovered before Wednesday's Big Find and that still needed to be documented and recorded. Devon was also inside, as were a few local volunteers who were doing small tasks that Sue had presumably assigned to them.

Claire said a friendly "hello" to all and sundry, and made her way over to the shelves where the flint knives were still resting. She looked at them with interest for a few moments before turning back to those present. "I did mention that we're not cleaning any of these, didn't I?"

Sue and Miguel both nodded. "We made sure that nobody touched them," Sue replied. "They'll just stay there until you decide when to ship them. I assume you found residue of some sort?"

Claire nodded. "I'm thinking blood, obviously. We'll have it analyzed in depth at the bigger lab." She turned to leave after making sure Sue was going to stay put. She told them she'd be inside the temple for awhile, and left instructions to have someone find her if they had questions about any of the artifacts and their various treatments.

The sky was still dark, a leftover condition from the day before, and the clouds somehow seemed a little more ominous than they had been. As she opened the door to leave the lab, she noted the condition of the weather and the wind that seemed to be picking up with each passing moment.

"Miguel," she said over her shoulder, "would you make sure the equipment outside gets put away? It's looking like rain. You can ask for some help from the volunteers if you need it."

He nodded and rose. "I'll take care of it right now," he said.

Claire walked quickly to the temple, sliding her arms into the long-sleeved flannel shirt she usually ended up tying around her waist. The temperatures were dropping uncharacteristically, besides which, she knew it would be cooler in the temple itself. She passed Etienne as she walked, calling a greeting to him and waving when he glanced at her over his shoulder.

He smiled and said "hello," and she decided to try her best to overlook his irritating behavior; in reality, he was actually a moderately nice man. He was working hard at unraveling the secrets the staircase held, and was extremely dedicated to his work, if nothing else.

Claire entered the temple and exchanged simple greetings with the staff who still plugged away at clearing the fill from the ancient building. She appreciated their efforts; they followed Justin's instructions carefully each day and kept busy, even when he was absent, as he was currently.

She wove her way carefully to the center and when she reached it, retrieved a lantern and carried it into the tomb they'd opened the day before. She entered it carefully, almost reverently, and stood there for a moment, alone, in the silence. She was in awe of the fact that she stood where the ancients once had; that whether their intentions had been good or evil, whether sanctioned by the Father or the adversary, they had once stood where she was standing and they had lives and stories of their own.

Her questions about them were endless and she doubted she'd ever receive her answers in this life, but she thanked her Father silently, nonetheless, for allowing her the opportunity to wonder about such things. Feeling a moment of profound gratitude, she thanked Him for the life she'd led, the family she had, and the very breath in her lungs.

She thanked Him for her varied opportunities, her schooling, and her work experiences. As she stood still, mentally conversing with her Maker, an image of Bump passed through her mind's eye and she thanked her Father for the associations she'd been blessed to form with good people. Her head gave a small nod as she acknowledged the fact that she'd like to know Bump St. James a whole lot better before her life was through.

Her arm eventually grew weary and she set the lantern on the ground, and as an afterthought, sat next to it on the cold, stone floor, wondering still about the temple's ancient people. "Tell me your secrets," she whispered on a plea to the silent room.

* * * * * *

Bump walked through the hospital corridors with Jon on one side and Justin Hodges on the other. As they made their way to Ricardo Valez's room, he regarded the older facilities and general feel of the place. He'd never much liked hospitals; they reminded him of his father's death.

They eventually found Valez, resting against his pillows, his complexion extremely pale. He opened his eyes when he heard the trio enter. Justin quickly and quietly explained the reason for their visit, introducing the sick man to Bump and Jon. Justin then excused himself, saying he needed to make a phone call, but that if Bump needed him for anything he'd be right outside.

Bump rested casually against the side of the bed and Jon sat in a chair that was positioned in a corner of the small room. "Hi there," Bump said and offered the man his hand.

Valez took it within his weak grasp and tried to sit up a bit. Bump helped him find the button that raised the bed into a sitting position and waited patiently until the poor man looked at least marginally comfortable. His breathing was labored and sounded heavy, and he was caught by a coughing fit that left him lying weak and looking even more pale than before. He was thin and slight of body, with dark-brown hair and eyes. He was probably a very pleasant-looking man on a healthy day.

"This won't take long," Bump apologized. "I just needed to talk to you about what you might know." He gave the insurance company spiel and asked Ricardo if he could offer any interesting details about the thefts of the artifacts.

Ricardo shook his head slightly. "I wish I could help," he said. "I couldn't believe it when they started disappearing."

Bump looked carefully at the man, attempting to judge his sincerity. It seemed genuine enough; however, Bump couldn't dismiss the fact that no more artifacts had disappeared since Valez had been laid up in the hospital. Of course, Bump and Jon had been sleeping in the lab every night, which seemed to have done the trick quite nicely.

"How well do you know the others on the staff?" Bump asked, watching his face.

Ricardo shrugged slightly. "Well enough, I suppose. I'm not much of a people person, but I've enjoyed their company, with a couple of possible exceptions." He managed a wry smile despite his fatigue. "I didn't know any of them before I arrived at the site, and I've been there for a couple of months now. I arrived at the same time as Sue Chastain and Miguel Robaina."

"And what's your general opinion of the locals? Do you know any of them well at all?"

Ricardo shook his head. "I don't know many of them well," he admitted, "but if you want my honest opinion, I'm thinking you don't need to look any farther than the regular staff."

Bump quirked an eyebrow. "What makes you say that?"

"I remember noting each time that there were never any signs of forced entry, and all of us have access to all of the building keys. Anyone with a key could have easily slipped into the lab and taken things. And another thing I noticed," he added, "is that the artifacts taken were interesting pieces themselves."

Bump remembered Claire saying much the same thing when he had first arrived.

"What makes them interesting?"

"Well, the first few that disappeared were interesting pieces of pottery, mostly intact with very few chips or breaks, and I think a tool was also taken at one point. But one of the pottery vessels had especially caught my eye and I was sorry to see it stolen." At that, Ricardo collapsed into a coughing fit, and Bump was forced to wait patiently for the man to continue.

"Anyway," he said after taking a drink of water from a cup near his bed, "the bulk of the pieces stolen before were simple in design and décor as far as the glyphs painted onto the sides. They were all symbols that Etienne had been able to translate and decipher. The one that *I* found the most interesting, personally, was one that had so many odd and undecipherable symbols that even the mighty DuBois couldn't decode it." He coughed again.

"Now," he continued, "it could be just coincidence that this particular pot disappeared, but at the time, there were also several other pieces on the shelves similar to those already taken. And this one that was so unique in its glyphs appeared at first glance to be pretty much like the others. Whoever took the difficult one knew something about it."

"So you think it was selected very specifically, not just randomly?"

Valez nodded. "I think whoever took that one knew exactly what he or she was looking for. Which is not to say that the other thefts weren't specific, and it could have been that this particular one was snatched at random, but somehow I doubt it." He scrunched his nose. "If I remember correctly, Claire had it positioned toward the back of the shelves; it wasn't out in the open where someone who was looking for just anything would have reached out and grabbed it."

Bump absorbed the information slowly, piecing things together as he sat quietly by the side of the sick man. "Well," he finally said, "that definitely gives me some things to think about, Ricardo. Thank you for your help."

He rose from the bed and motioned to Jon. "We'll be leaving, now. Is there anything I can get for you before we go?"

Ricardo pushed the button that lowered his bed back into its former position. "No thanks," he said. "Maybe you could just tell everyone 'hello' for me, and I hope to be back soon."

"I will. Thanks again."

They left the hospital in silence. Justin dropped Bump and Jon off at Luis' residence and then explained he had some things to do in town. Bump mentioned that Luis had offered to take them back to the site when they were finished for the day, at which Justin said his good-byes and left. Bump watched the slump of the man's shoulders as he drove away, feeling a fresh wave of pity for the burden Justin must be carrying, wondering if he'd ever have a normal relationship with his daughter.

* * * * * *

Claire left the temple feeling content. She smiled as she stepped out into the rain, which didn't dampen her spirits in the least. The ancient tomb hadn't yielded any fantastic secrets, not that she'd expected it to, but that was okay. Sometimes the formulation of theories was half the fun. She could imagine what had gone on all those years ago and wonder what life had been like for the people who inhabited the land she currently trod upon.

It didn't take long before she was soaked to the skin, the rain seeming to come down harder and faster with each step. By the time she reached the lab, she was dripping wet. She opened the lab door and closed it quickly behind her, shuddering and murmuring an "Oh!" aloud.

She turned and set her backpack on the floor, and looked up, expecting to see Sue and Miguel hard at work. They weren't in the lab. None of the volunteers were in there either.

But Devon was.

She was seated at one of the tables. In one of her hands was an ancient flint knife. In the other hand was a rag. Next to her elbow on the table was an open container of cleaning solution.

The other two flint knives retrieved from the temple the day before lay on the table, glistening with moisture. Claire's breath caught in her throat, and for a moment she couldn't formulate a coherent thought, let alone words.

Devon eyed her with disdain. "Hello, Claire," she finally said as she resumed her scrubbing of the ancient knife. "You'd think a grown woman would know better than to let herself get soaked in a rain-storm."

"What . . . what . . ." Claire stumbled slowly toward the girl, feeling as though she were dreaming and unable to run. She could barely make her feet move. "What . . . what . . . are . . . you . . . *doing?*"

Devon eyed her strangely. "What do you mean, what am I doing? I'm doing your students' job, that's what. They left with all this work still to do. They're in the mess hall having lunch. I decided to get things moving so my uncle will have something to show for this pathetic dig. These artifacts need to be shipped out soon, am I right about that, *doctor* Claire? Seems to me you're too busy getting cozy with the insurance adjuster to remember your job."

Claire had finally reached the opposite side of the table at which Devon was seated. She blindly reached her arm forward and grabbed the knife from the girl's hand with all her strength. She also scooped the other two knives from the table and collapsed to her knees, clutching the ancient metal to her chest.

Her words were thick in her throat and she could barely get them past her tongue, which seemed to have lost all use. Devon was blinking in surprise, which quickly turned to unmistakable anger.

"What do you think you're doing?" the girl shrieked, her eyes blazing.

"Devon," Claire managed to finally spit through her clenched teeth, "tell me you didn't just clean all these knives!"

"Of course I did! They're filthy and they need to be shipped out. I've seen you do enough cleaning in here to do it myself! You ought to be grateful I'm helping out around here!"

Claire felt a burning in her chest and wondered if she were truly going to experience heart failure. "Did you realize," she bit off harshly, "that there was blood residue on these knives? That we were going to have them carefully studied at another lab?!"

Devon sniffed, but began to lose some of her heated color. "Blood, that's gross," she said. "Who wants a bloody knife?"

"*The entire archaeological world, you miserable little witch!* You have just scrubbed away blood belonging to people who lived here in these ruins *ages* ago! *Do you realize what you've done?*!" Claire choked on the last, finally shedding the tears that had started in her soul and worked their way to the surface.

Devon paled visibly. "I didn't . . . know . . ."

"That's a vicious lie!" Claire shouted. "You were in this lab this morning when I specifically reminded Sue and Miguel to make sure nobody cleaned this stuff!" Her breath was coming in short, harsh sobs and the tears by now coursed a steady stream down her face.

Devon jumped up, knocking her chair over as she moved, and ran from the lab, slamming the door behind her.

Claire bent forward, still kneeling, the ancient knives still clutched to her chest. She huddled over, grief wracking her small frame at the loss, which was not only scientific, but more importantly to her, personal. She coughed and choked, her sobs bursting forth with a violence she hadn't imagined possible. She felt the pressure building up behind her eyes and it hurt.

The nausea was unexpected, however. Still hugging the knives, she crawled to a garbage can at the end of the table and threw up what little she'd eaten, feeling like her head would surely explode. When she was finally finished, she pulled herself up into a standing position by using one of the shelves as leverage, and clutched numbly for a clean rag. She wiped her face, still tormented by sobs that would surely never cease.

She stumbled from the lab and out into the driving rain, which was coming down in sheets so thick she could barely see to make her way into Justin's office. Once there, she slammed the door behind her and locked it, diving immediately for the phone and dialing the phone number she knew from memory but didn't think she'd be calling again any time soon.

Darren's sleepy voice answered on the other end. "Hello?"

"Darren," Claire bit off, trying to control her voice enough to be understood.

"Claire? Is that you?"

She cut off a sob and took a deep breath. "Yes, it's me. Your niece . . ." she began, but couldn't continue.

"What's wrong with Devon?" The alarm in Darren's voice was apparent, and Claire despised him for it. In her anger and grief, she didn't want *anyone* caring about the welfare of the younger woman.

"Nothing's *wrong* with her," Claire sobbed out on a shout, "except that she just *destroyed* the most amazing find I've ever seen!" She briefly told Darren what had transpired, her words punctuated with cries of rage and sorrow.

"I'll tell you what, Claire," Darren said quietly. "You come to Paris, right now, and we'll talk about this. If you come here, I'll agree to send her home."

Claire paused, alarm bells sounding through the fog that had enveloped her head since she saw Devon with a rag in one hand and a priceless piece of history in the other. "Why?" she finally asked. "Why, Darren? Why do I have to go to Paris—why can't you just send her home now?"

She hated that she was pleading, hated that he somehow, once again, seemed to have the upper hand. When he spoke again, his voice was calm and quiet. "Because I want to see you again, Claire— you ended this and you never gave me a chance to say good-bye. If it has to be this way, so be it, I'll use it. You either come and see me, or Devon stays. And I'll back whatever defense she uses to explain why she did what she did. And wouldn't it be sad if the site had to be shut down at this point because the funding was pulled?"

Claire's meager control snapped. "Fine!" she shouted, still crying, squeezing the knives she still held in one hand so hard that it was beginning to hurt. "You want me in Paris, I'll be there on the next plane I can get myself on! I'd like to know one thing, though—are these threats of yours supposed to endear you to me? Am I supposed to just profess my love for a man who's trying to sabotage my entire career?"

"You just get here, Claire, and I'll give you twenty-four hours to do it. If you're not here, all hell breaks loose."

Claire slammed the phone back into place and sat back in Justin's chair, dazed. What had just happened? She absently looked down at her right hand which was fisted so tightly around the knives that her fingers were white. She slowly opened her hand to reveal several small red lines where she'd cut herself.

At least there's blood now. Just a few thousand years too new. Her tears fell afresh and she stood, again squeezing her hand around the artifacts and grateful for the pain it caused; it kept her moving. If she stopped, she might not do what she had stupidly committed herself to, and then the entire site would be shut down for who knew how long.

Of course, she tried to reason as she stepped back out into the rain and started toward her small room, now that the site was fully operational and going forward, new funding might not be so hard to come by. But there was no guarantee she'd be allowed to continue working on it, and that thought hurt beyond comprehension.

She finally reached her building and fumbled in her pocket for her key. Finding it, she entered and began throwing clothes and other items necessary for travel into a large duffel bag. She grabbed her purse and extracted her wallet and passport. Stuffing them on top, she zipped the whole thing shut.

She was just turning to leave when Sue and Miguel appeared in her doorway, their eyes huge. "What's going on?" Sue demanded, utterly bewildered.

"I'm going to Paris," Claire muttered flatly. "Devon ruined the knives, so her uncle said if I go talk with him about some things, he'll make her go home." *And he won't put us all out of work.*

"Oh, Claire." Sue looked sick. Miguel looked furious.

"*What* did she do?" he asked.

Claire slowly opened her hand, which still held the carved knives. She had packed her entire bag with her free left hand. "She scrubbed off all the ancient residue," she answered numbly. "The new blood is mine." She reluctantly handed the knives over to him. "Will you put these back where they go in the lab?"

"Oh, NO!" Sue's exclamation mirrored Claire's own horror. "Why?"

Claire shrugged. "She thought she was being useful. Who knows."

Sue closed her eyes. "I locked the lab when we went to lunch," she moaned. "Devon passed us on the way into the mess hall—she was just leaving—and she said she was going to her room for awhile. She must have gotten a key from Justin's office!"

"Well, however she did it," Claire answered, "the damage is done." She moved past the stunned pair and out again into the rain. As an afterthought, she walked back inside and grabbed a notebook that lay atop her locker, and hastily scribbled a note. She folded it in four and handed it to Sue.

"Will you give this to Bump St. James for me?" she asked. At Sue's somber nod, she turned and left. "I'm taking one of the jeeps," she yelled over her shoulder through the storm. "Tell Justin he can pick it up at the airport."

* * * * * *

Several hours later, Claire settled back into her seat on a 747, trying to get comfortable for a long transatlantic flight. After leaving the site, she had driven the hour it had taken to reach the small airport near the site, which, thanks to a wallet full of credit cards, had then arranged to have her flown to a larger airport in Guatemala City, and then on to Miami, from which she had recently departed.

She was exhausted, filthy, and still damp. She hadn't bothered to check her duffel bag and had instead stashed it in the overhead compartment. Once the plane reached sufficient altitude and the seat-belt signs turned off, she reluctantly rose and pawed through her bag for her small makeup bag she remembered having packed in her fury.

Carrying it with her, she walked down the narrow aisle and into the cramped bathroom. She took one look at her face and groaned. *When have I ever looked this bad?* Opening the bag, she extracted a small brush and began repairing the damage as best she could. She removed the elastic that held her ponytail in place, and brushed through the snarls until it was smooth. She then took a stiff paper towel and dampened it, thoroughly scrubbing her face from forehead to neck, and around the back of her ears.

She pulled a bottle of moisturizer from her bag and smoothed on a thin layer, sighing as she did so and beginning to feel a bit more human. She then thoroughly and completely scrubbed her hands, ridding her fingernails of their customary dirt, and applied a generous layer of hand lotion, taking comfort in the repetitive motion her hands made as she twisted and intertwined her fingers.

When she felt a painful stinging, she looked at the palm of her right hand, the angry criss-crossing of red marks painful evidence of her prior anger and frustration. It had numbed a bit, and didn't feel quite as raw. It still hurt, though. She felt horribly . . . sad.

Claire made her way back to her seat and replaced her makeup bag, sliding into her row and taking the seat next to the window. The flight was amazingly, blissfully, sparse. There were very few passengers, and none at all on the row where Claire sat. She looked out the plane window and into the darkening night. Before long it would be black, and Claire would close the window shade because that void, all that nothingness outside the plane would make her nervous.

For the last few moments, however, until twilight turned into night, she stared outside and leaned her head against the plastic. *Why, Father,* began her sad prayer. *Why did this have to happen? It was a priceless piece of the past! Could you not have warned me to prevent it? I would have listened!*

A lone tear slipped and ran down her cheek. Just when she thought she'd cried an entire river and was all dried up, the source somehow replenished itself. She bit her lip and caught her breath, not wanting to weep anymore. Her eyelids were already swollen and her face bore bright pinpricks of red—evidence of the tiny capillaries she'd burst when she threw up. Her mind had registered all that when she washed her face in the bathroom, but she hadn't wanted to consider all the pathetic details.

Now she faced a new concern; her defenses were down and she had to deal with Darren Stark. She wasn't worried she'd fall back under his spell; she was beyond immune to his pseudo-charm and his manipulative manner. She didn't want to grovel, though, and she didn't want him to see her with her pride in tatters.

She closed her eyes and sighed, her breath catching on itself and making her sound, even to her own ears, like a child who has cried herself to sleep.

I want Bump. I wish I had waited to see him before I left.

But she had to acknowledge the very real possibility that he might have tried, and succeeded, in talking her out of going. She knew she had to confront Darren once and for all, face-to-face, and getting rid of Devon in the process would be a beautiful bonus. It was funny; she was already missing Bump with a pang that surprised her. How could she possibly love a man after knowing him for a period of, what, only a couple of weeks?

But she did. *I guess the last laugh is on me,* she mused, feeling pathetic all over again. Several of her high-school friends had known their husbands for a period of only a few months before they had married. She'd always considered it ridiculous; how on earth could a woman know her true feelings for a man in such an alarmingly short time?

Life must come full circle, she thought, another tear slipping past her closed eyelids. Maybe it was just lust, she reasoned. That was a very powerful thing. Or maybe she was getting desperate for a relationship and had jumped at the first attractive man who paid her any attention.

Don't be stupid, her heart argued, and she knew it was right. She might not know Bump inside and out, but she knew enough to love what she saw. And she wanted more.

She felt miserable and alone. And exhausted. Just when she feared she'd never find any rest, she felt the presence of her late grandfather; she felt him sitting next to her and holding her hand, which lay limp and sore in her lap.

She didn't open her eyes; she didn't want to look at the seat next to her and find it empty. She knew he was there, and it was enough.

What's it all about, Claire? she heard him whisper.

Ah, Grandpa. Another tear fell. *It's about life kicking my butt again.*

The sounds of his gentle laughter echoed in her head. *Only if you let it, Claire my girl, only if you let it.*

Chapter 22

A week following the Game, Palome found Queliza seated by herself under a blanket of stars on the steps of one of the buildings near the ball court. She sat looking at the court, unblinking, and her thoughts were her own.

She managed a weak smile when he sat beside her and took her hand in his own, offering comfort the only way he knew how . . . with his own gentle presence . . .

* * * * * *

"She's *where?*"

Sue Chastain looked miserable. Miguel Robaina, standing uncomfortably next to her didn't look much better. "She's on her way to Paris."

"Why?" The question came out flat and hard. Bump did his best to keep from roaring at the sad-looking pair and waited as patiently as he could until Sue formulated her words.

She took a deep breath and told him a story that had him clenching his jaw and seeing red. He took a deep breath and tried to come up with some kind of game plan, but his mind was blank, and underneath his inability to think was an odd fear he couldn't quite define.

"She's meeting Stark, you said?"

Sue nodded, her face pained. She looked quickly over her shoulder. "He told her he'd send Devon home if she went to Paris to discuss some things. Oh," she said, reaching into her pocket and extracting a folded piece of paper, "and she said to give you this."

Bump quickly unfolded the paper and scanned the note that had been hastily scrawled hours before, the resulting penmanship so bad he could barely read it.

"I have to talk to Darren so he won't shut down the site," it said. "Things are so bad right now I can't even think. I'll call you as soon as I can. Miss me please. Claire."

Bump turned with a curse and made his way across the damp earth to Justin Hodges' office. The light was on inside and he didn't even bother with a knock. He stormed in and sat heavily on one of the chairs facing Justin's desk.

Justin sat behind the desk, pinching the bridge of his nose. He didn't seem surprised at Bump's noisy entry; he raised his eyes to him and said, "I take it you found out about Claire."

"Yeah, I did. You want to tell me what is going on here?"

Justin tipped his head back and rotated it around on his neck, looking as sick as Bump felt. "I wish I knew." He shook his head. "Things are so far out of control around here . . ."

Bump fought the urge to deliver the man a setback he'd probably never recover from and left his admission alone. That Justin had left so many burdens on Claire's shoulders for so long was a matter that could be addressed in the future. For the time being, Bump's sole concern was Claire, herself.

"Had she already gone when you got back here today?" Bump's eyebrows were fiercely drawn as he wondered how quickly he could get a flight to Paris.

"Yes, she was. I got all the information we have from Sue and Miguel, and Devon's locked herself in her room. She refuses to come out."

"Probably the first smart thing she's ever done. She ought to stay in there until she rots." Bump rose from his chair and added, "Let me know if Claire calls; I want to talk to her."

Justin nodded and placed his elbows on the desk, resting his head in his hands. Bump left him and walked to his room, his hands shoved deep in his pockets, experiencing a feeling of such helplessness he didn't know what to do with it. It was a foreign thing; he was always the man with the answers, he always knew what to do.

He opened the door to his room and found Jon sitting on his cot, looking more than a little worried, himself. "What are you going to do?" was the first question out of the man's mouth.

Bump sank down onto his own cot, resting his elbows on his knees. "I don't know."

The silence that followed was deafening. "You don't know?" finally came the incredulous reply. "What, are you kidding me?"

Bump's answer was much sharper than he intended. "No, I'm not kidding! Until I hear from Claire I won't know exactly what's happening, and I can't afford to leave the site now if she's got things under control and will be back within a day or two."

"You really think she's got things under control? She's going to see an old lover, who not only wasn't happy about being jilted, apparently, but has been messing with her head ever since. First, by funding this site, and secondly by sticking his spawn-of-Satan niece right under her nose!"

Bump was struck by two things simultaneously. The first was amazement at the level of Jon's perception. The second was an inward flinching as he realized everything Jon had said was right, and that Claire probably was walking into a viper's nest with her defenses down. When Sue had caught his attention the moment Luis dropped him off at the site, she mentioned that Claire had been an emotional mess when she left.

That didn't bode well for her. It wouldn't have for anyone.

Jon was still staring at him. "So are you going after her or what?"

Bump closed his eyes. Finally, he shook his head. "Not yet. I'll wait until she calls."

Jon swore and stood, pacing the small length of the room. "I think you're nuts, man. She's gonna need help."

"Maybe. Or maybe not. She may prefer to do this alone."

Jon stopped pacing and shook his head. "I'm going for a run," he stated and changed his shoes, heading out the door without another word.

Bump put his head in his hands and sighed. He was concerned that a young man under his emotional care was headed out into the Guatemalan night with nothing but a pair of running shoes on his feet. It was dark out there, and largely unfamiliar; Bump hoped he'd find his way back. And his other, bigger concern was that a woman who had come to mean the world to him was flying farther and farther away from him with each passing moment and headed into what could be very real danger.

And he wasn't chasing after her, which went against every instinct he'd ever possessed.

He hoped with all he was worth that his overriding, if somewhat contradictory, intuition that she be allowed the freedom to handle it alone was correct. If one hair on her head were harmed . . . the very thought made his stomach churn. *Well, one thing's for sure*, he mused. *If Stark causes her any harm, I'll hunt him down myself and ruin him. I'll make him wish he'd never even heard the name Claire O'Brian.*

He thought of the myriad ways he could devastate Stark, from financial to physical, and took ghoulish pleasure at the thought of seeing him cry if he caused Claire any more pain. Bump St. James was a force to be reckoned with, and he knew it. Jon had been right, much to Bump's chagrin, the day he had bragged on his friend's behalf to Claire; there weren't too many places in the world where Bump didn't know someone who would help him with whatever he asked.

On that thought, an idea sparked and spurred him into the action that had evaded him from the moment Sue Chastain had tearfully told him that Claire was gone. He grabbed his mobile phone and his Palm Pilot™. Quickly retrieving the number of a police detective in Paris he'd met several years before but with whom he still kept in occasional contact, he called the man and let it ring several times before it was finally answered.

"Jean-Pierre," he began, "it's Bump."

* * * * * *

Claire awoke to the droning sound of the plane engines. She glanced at her watch and noted she'd slept for several hours, but had to stifle a groan at the realization she still had another five or six hours in the plane. She stretched her tired body and yawned, feeling hungry for the first time in hours. She decided to flag down the next flight attendant she saw and ask about getting some peanuts, if nothing else.

She stood and opened the overhead bin, again unzipping her duffel bag and retrieving her wallet. Sitting back in her seat, she pulled out a credit card and went through the necessary motions to make a couple of phone calls she knew she could no longer put off.

The first call was to Darren Stark. When he answered the phone, she said numbly, "I'm on my way. Where are you staying?"

She could hear the smile in his voice. "The apartment on the Seine," he said. "I believe you know where it is. Should I pick you up at the airport?"

"No. I'll book a room at a hotel and come to you. Now why don't you call Devon and tell her you're sending her home."

He laughed. "You don't really expect me to do that until we've talked, do you? Don't be silly. I'll see you when you arrive. Don't make me wait too long."

She disconnected the call with a small *hiss* and narrowed her eyes, feeling her whole face contort into a tight mask of rage. She closed her eyes and forced herself to relax, taking a deep breath. As much as she looked forward to the next call, she was also dreading it.

She didn't know Bump well enough to know how he'd handle the situation. Had she been in a different frame of mind, she'd have laughed. Her feelings for the man were more involved than any she'd ever had for anyone she'd dated, even those relationships that had lasted for quite awhile. Yet she didn't even know how he reacted to stress, to the unexpected.

She punched in the numbers to the office at the dig and waited for the call to be answered. When it was, she heard Justin's weary voice on the other end.

"Claire!" He all but shouted her name when he realized who she was.

"I'm okay," she answered when he began shooting rapid-fire questions at her about her welfare. She briefly explained what was happening, and then bit her lip. "Um, Justin . . . is Bump St. James around?"

"Yes, he is. As a matter of fact, he wanted me to let him know when you called. He came in a few minutes ago and gave me his mobile number. Do you want to call that number or should I go get him for you; he can just talk to you on this phone . . ."

"No, why don't you give me his number. That'll be easier." She wrote down the phone number he read off to her and she thanked him, reassuring him again that she'd be okay.

"Claire," Justin said just before hanging up, "be careful. I wouldn't trust Stark for one minute. I never have. He's . . . he's . . . well, just be careful."

Claire emitted a harsh, humorless laugh. "I know that firsthand, Justin. I will be careful."

She ended the call and punched the numbers of Bump's phone, holding her breath and waiting for an explosion.

* * * * * *

When Bump's phone rang, he was sitting atop the steps of the ancient temple, looking at the cloudless sky. He nearly jumped out of his skin at the intruding noise—something he couldn't ever remember having happened in his life; his heart began to pound when he realized that it was probably Claire.

"Hello?"

"Bump. It's Claire."

He closed his eyes, amazed at his physical reaction; his surge of adrenaline had left him feeling weak. "Well, well," he answered, trying to keep his voice steady. "Things weren't exciting enough around here for you, huh? Had to hop a plane to Paris?"

She laughed, sounding relieved, oddly enough, and he was happy to note that the sound seemed genuine. She was tough; her pride was probably holding her together pretty well.

"Well, you know me. I just can't hack too much routine."

He snorted at that, knowing her well enough to realize that her type thrived on routine. He sobered, mentally cursing the fact that he was so far away from her. "So, how are you? Sue told me everything."

She sighed. "I'm okay. I'm sick about it all, but I'm okay. I keep telling myself that there are worse things in life than ruined artifacts. They're not even really ruined, just a portion of the find is. We still have the artifacts themselves." She sighed again. "I remember reading somewhere that in life there are three kinds of lumps: a lump in the oatmeal, a lump in the throat, and a lump in the breast. I figure this is probably a lump-in-the-throat kind of a thing."

He smiled. "That's a good analogy. I'll bet at the time, though, you probably wanted to stab Devon through the heart with one of those old knives."

She made a sound of obvious disgust. "What do you mean 'one'? I'd have used all three."

He laughed out loud, missing her and wishing she were sitting with him under the stars as they'd done before. "Well, she's been holed up in her room since this morning; I bet she'll probably leave of her own accord, even if Stark doesn't give her the boot."

"Let's hope so. I don't want this whole stupid trip to be in vain."

Jon's words came back in full force, and Bump hesitated, wanting to ask, but not wanting to invade her space. "Are you going to be okay with all of this?" he finally ventured. "I mean really okay? Can you handle Stark?"

She sighed again. "Yeah. It has to be done or he's not going to leave me alone." Her voice lowered a pitch and he had to strain to hear her. "He's not going to give up until I tell him straight to his face that it's done. I think that's what this *whole* thing, all this time, has been leading up to."

He was equally as quiet when he answered. "And what if he doesn't take that as a good enough answer? What will you do?"

She replied without missing a beat. "Then I come home, file a restraining order on him and get myself a Permit to Carry Concealed."

Bump laughed out loud again. "I can just see you with a gun strapped around your ankle."

He could hear the smile in her voice when she answered. "Don't you find that alluring? Some men think that chicks with guns are really cool."

He sobered. "I find you alluring in any way, shape, or form, in any given scenario. I'd take you any way I could get you."

He heard the hitch in her breath, and wondered if she were crying. "I know that what you're doing right now, Claire, is trying to put some closure on an old relationship, and I won't try to make things more complicated for you. But I can't pretend that you don't mean something to me."

He paused, wanting to say what he needed to without burdening her with more than she was capable of handling at the moment. "You get this finished, and we'll take it from there. I'll be here when you get back, even if things are wrapped up on the investigative end."

"I appreciate that," she answered back softly. "I . . . I wish you were with me."

"Say the word and I'll get on the next plane out of here."

He could imagine her shaking her head with her eyes closed, a small smile playing ruefully at the corner of her mouth. "I need to do this alone," she replied.

"Okay. But," he added, "don't be surprised if you see a blonde guy, about six feet tall, short hair, lanky build, most likely wearing John Lennon glasses, trailing you around."

"What?"

"He's a friend of mine on the Paris police force, and he owes me a favor. His name is Jean-Pierre; I asked him to keep tabs on you, gave him your name and description, all of that. He'll just keep an eye on things."

She laughed, long and hard. "Jon was right. People everywhere owe you favors! Well," she said, finally sobering, "I'll just pretend he's not there. Will that work?"

"That'll work."

"Okay, then . . ." She trailed off, prolonging the inevitable end to the conversation.

"Yeah . . ."

She sighed. "I'll call you when I get things settled."

"You do that. I'll keep my phone with me at all times."

"Okay. I . . . take care."

"I will, Claire. You too."

He involuntarily winced as the call was disconnected, and felt a heavy weight in his heart. He wasn't used to leaving things up to other people. But, he had to remind himself, it wasn't his life. It was hers. And he had to respect her wishes to handle it alone. Had it been up to him, he knew exactly how he'd handle Stark; he'd walk into the man's house, threaten him in a very subtle way with bodily harm if he didn't get his niece off the dig and remove himself from Claire's life. If that didn't work, he'd threaten financial ruin, which usually had a way of getting people's attention.

It wasn't up to him, however, and it really wasn't any of his business. Her life would shortly be his business though, he vowed, and this would be the last time she'd take off without him to do something that threatened her safety. He couldn't explain it; it was insane to his own sense of logic, but he loved her. He loved her and wanted to be with her forever.

If one of his friends or acquaintances were to say to him, *Hey, I just met this woman a couple of weeks ago and I love her and want to be with her for the rest of my life,* he'd have snorted in derision. The very concept was laughable, especially given the fact that he'd never envisioned himself married at all, but there it was.

He knew she'd had issues and problems in the past. He knew that her struggles to be happy and content and *eat,* for crying out loud, were a daily thing, and that she was a perfectionist to a fault. He knew that getting past all the surface layers and initial infatuation would reveal a person that often doubted herself, despite her enormous intellect and capabilities, and one who would need reassurance from someone she held in high esteem that life really is okay. That it's not always perfect, but that it's not meant to be, either.

He didn't care. He didn't care if she turned out to be the type who harped because he left a pair of socks laying on the bedroom floor. If that were the case, he'd pick them up, put them in the laundry basket and then tickle her until she laughed herself silly and admitted she loved him.

He clenched his teeth together and stared upward at a filmy cloud that had formed and moved like a white silk scarf against the stars. Maybe her feelings didn't match the depth of his and she would never tell him she loved him. He wasn't sure what he'd do, in that case. It wasn't like he could call in a favor from one of his myriad worldwide contacts to take care of that particular problem. He had no way of making her love him.

The thought that she might not *ever* love him was unthinkable. She might not love him now, but he wasn't about to go down without a fight.

Chapter 23

The days followed one another, as days do, and Queliza eventually returned to her former activities with some semblance of normalcy, if not a light heart. She kept the queen's secret, and the look of understanding that occasionally passed between them reminded her of her position, and the necessity for secrecy. She shared an odd kinship with the queen; their lives both hung in the balance—hinged on the same awful thoughts . . .

* * * * * *

I'm here," Claire said to Darren, who had picked up the phone on the first ring. "I just checked in to the hotel and I'd like to get cleaned up a bit." She paused. "I'm also exhausted. I'd like to sleep for a couple of hours if you think you can handle that." She lightly smacked her forehead and reminded herself that she ought to at least *try* to stay in his good graces if she hoped to accomplish anything for the sake of the site.

"Well, Claire," came the dry reply, "I think I can handle that. It's 3:00 right now, how about I have a driver there to pick you up at 6:00? We can have dinner and talk." He sounded so cordial, so polite and charming. He was again the man she thought she'd fallen in love with, and it made her skin crawl.

"I'll be ready at 6:00. I'm at the Ritz."

"My, my. Somebody must be paying you well."

"Oh, I'm not paying. I've stayed here before, remember? The concierge recognized me and showed me to my usual suite. You'll be receiving the bill soon, I'm sure."

She hung up the phone on the sound of his laughter and rubbed her burning eyes. She made her way into the beautifully appointed bathroom, took a steaming hot shower and then wrapped herself in a fluffy white bathrobe. She wandered into the bedroom and fell across the large bed, falling asleep almost instantaneously.

When she awoke, she glanced at the clock with bleary eyes that barely opened. It was 5:30. Moaning, she rolled over onto her back and looked at the ceiling, wondering how she'd find the wherewithal to pull the evening off. She dragged herself into a sitting position and groaned, touching her feet to the floor and shuffling her way back into the bathroom, where she critically examined her reflection in the mirror.

Her eyelids were so swollen she looked like she'd been hit in the face. That would simply *never* do. She picked up the phone extension next to the vanity and requested a spoon.

"Yes ma'am, right away," the voice answered without missing a beat. Moments later, a knock at her door produced the requested spoon. She took it, murmuring her thanks and wishing she didn't look so pathetic.

She wandered back into the bathroom and ran the back of the spoon under a steady stream of cold water and dried it off with a tissue. Holding the shockingly cold metal to her eyelid, she looked at herself in the mirror with the one eye she had open and slightly shook her head. Years of schooling and proving herself to the world, and this was what she was reduced to—standing in a bathroom in Paris, alone and tense, trying to diminish the swelling in her eyelids by holding a cold spoon to her face.

She repeated the motion again and again, and was rewarded with her efforts as she scrutinized her eyelids and realized the process was working. It made them slightly red, but at least they weren't three times their normal puffiness. It was a beauty tip from a magazine she'd read years earlier, and it was one she'd had to use on a few occasions, unfortunately. She washed her face with a cold washcloth and was relieved to see that very few of the small red dots that had resulted from her vomiting were still visible.

She quickly applied her makeup, noting with disinterest that it was a process most women probably could have accomplished in their sleep. When she was working in the field, she only wore makeup on Sundays, and then only when there was a church in the vicinity for her to attend. Yet in spite of the infrequency with which she applied the stuff, it was like riding a bike; she never forgot how, and the motions always seemed familiar.

To hide the distress her eyelids had undergone from the shock of cold metal, she dusted a neutral color of shadow overtop, and fringed her already thick, black lashes with mascara. She then brushed her teeth and applied a layer of dark lipstick to her lips.

She stood back, critically examining herself in the mirror. The corner of her mouth quirked into a smug smile. Other than the fact that she appeared a bit tired, she looked good. Mentally thanking her lucky stars that she had such good hair, she lifted the complimentary blow dryer from its cradle on the wall and worked on the portion of her hair that hadn't dried while she slept. She lightly fluffed her bangs with her fingers and allowed the rest to flow thick and straight down her back.

Wandering back into the living area of the suite where she'd dumped her duffel bag on arrival, she pawed through her belongings and realized the only clothing she had were the things she wore every day at the ruins. Hardly the thing needed to convince an old boyfriend that even though the relationship was finished, she still needed his money. She laughed out loud at the absurdity of the situation and reached for the nearest phone, calling the gift shop and asking that they send up a tasteful, simple black evening dress and shoes to go with it.

She gave the woman her size, doing the best she could with her limited French, and hung up the phone after leaving instructions that the bill be sent to Darren Stark. She wouldn't keep the things; she'd leave them in the hotel room when she left, if nothing else, but she wasn't about to spend her own money on things she would not have ordinarily had to buy if Darren hadn't forced her into an impossible position.

The woman at the gift shop worked magic; in just a few minutes, a black dress, matching shoes, and black hose appeared at her door. She generously tipped the man waiting expectantly in the hallway, giving him double what she would have because she realized he was the same person who had delivered her spoon, and she'd forgotten to pay him at the time, much to her present chagrin.

With steady hands, Claire dressed herself and then stood before a full-length mirror. The dress was a soft velvet, the sleeves short and the length resting just above her knee. The black hose were nearly sheer, and the shoes were black pumps with a small heel. The entire ensemble was simple and tasteful, just as she'd requested, and she felt armed to do battle in it. Had she worn her everyday white T-shirt and khakis she'd have felt dowdy next to Darren's usual attire of the most expensive things available on the men's market, and that wouldn't have served her purpose well at all.

Just before she had time to pace, a ring of the phone notified her of the arrival of Darren's car. She gave herself one last glance in the mirror, sighed and straightened her shoulders, and headed out the door.

* * * * * *

Seeing Darren again was like an unpleasant fist in the stomach. He was maybe an inch shy of six feet, with a handsome face—so handsome he was almost pretty—short dark-blonde hair and brown eyes. All the old memories came flooding back; his obsessive need to control everything she did—where she went and with whom—his desire to mold her thoughts so that they would match his, his whining and whipped puppy-dog look when she didn't act the way he thought she should.

She had enjoyed his company at first, but realized after the fact that it was because she had been mesmerized by his wealth and apparent power, and he treated her like a queen. Until she started expressing opinions that conflicted with his. Then he acted like a spoiled child. It was too much to bear, and nauseating on top of it. She'd stretched it out for as long as she could stand it, and then, with a phone call, had ended the entire relationship.

Her family had despised both him and the fact that he tried so hard to turn her into someone she wasn't. They had been relieved when she brought a conclusion to the whole farce. Now she stood in the living room of his lavishly furnished apartment on the Left Bank of the Seine, wondering for all she was worth what she'd gotten herself into.

"You look . . . wonderful," he breathed, standing several feet away from her with his hands in his pockets. His mouth turned upward into a smile that she had once found attractive. "Your hair has grown since I saw you last."

She nodded, but said nothing.

"You look like a dark-haired *La Femme Nikita*," he stated.

Yeah, minus the six-foot height and the gun. Okay, enough chit chat. "What is it you want from me, Darren?" she asked, pleased that her voice was steady and she was holding the anger at bay.

His expression changed from a leer to one of extreme disappointment. "Can we at least have dinner together?"

What was she, some kind of beast? He'd never really harmed her, and the break-up hadn't caused her pain; it had brought her relief. Since he didn't seem to be handling it as well, the least she could do was be cordial. She tried to relax her stance and expression. "Sure," she said. "Dinner would be fine."

"Good. I thought we'd eat in, and I had my cook prepare your favorite dinner. Do you still favor pasta?"

She nodded and tried to smile. "That sounds wonderful."

"I remember you liking spaghetti with red sauce; I thought we'd try a variation this time and had cook prepare a delicious creamy white sauce instead. I know you like to watch your waistline, but it doesn't hurt to indulge every now and then, does it?" He approached her and took her hand, placing it in the crook of his arm. He walked her down the hallway and into the dining room.

"Great," she murmured, her smile, which was weak to begin with, laboring under the strain of trying to exist. *Just what I need—white sauce loaded in fat.* In all the time she'd spent with Darren she'd never once told him about her eating disorder; she'd let him assume she was extremely image conscious and kept her secrets to herself.

It was funny, she mused as she let herself be led into the dining room, she hadn't known Bump more than a week before she was blurting all of her emotional garbage to him. What had made the difference? She'd been angry, that much had been true, but she had shared details about it afterward that she could have kept private, had she chosen.

She sat in the chair placed to the right of the head of the long, mahogany dining-room table and let her thoughts reside with Bump for awhile before pulling herself back to the present. Darren sat in his place at the head and signaled to one of his servants for dinner to be served.

Claire shook her head slightly. The man had more money than he knew what to do with, an apartment in Paris, one in New York, one in L.A., a large villa in an area on the outskirts of Paris, and a veritable castle on the Italian Riviera. He was a wealthy American, the money was family money from generations past, and she couldn't think of a thing he *ever* did for work. He indulged his passion for archaeological finds by giving money generously and ingratiating himself in the lives of those in the archaeological field who had the most clout.

The works of art adorning his apartments were exquisite; she knew firsthand as she'd been in each of them, and he had an army of servants year round at each residence, keeping the homes in top condition and ready for his presence at a moment's notice. He'd never had to work for anything in his life, and perhaps that was one of the reasons he didn't mesh with her. She worked hard at everything she tried.

The first course was served—a delicious green salad that was almost too beautiful to eat. As Darren loaded his fork, he looked up at Claire and asked, "So, what have you been doing these days?"

She stared. *What have I been doing? Trying to keep an archaeological site from getting run into the ground by theft and disorganization!* And disorganized it definitely had become. When the artifacts started missing, little by little Justin had pulled back from full command of the site. It was as though he couldn't handle work-related problems on top of those he was experiencing in his personal life. Claire had done the best she could, but now was left to wonder if her best hadn't been nearly good enough.

"Oh, you know, the usual," she replied and stuffed some salad into her mouth before something horribly sarcastic popped out. "You?"

He shrugged. "I keep myself busy," he said. His next remark was stated casually, but loaded with meaning. "And I understand you've gotten to know the Private Investigator quite well."

She quirked an eyebrow, momentarily stunned into silence. She finally cleared her throat. "And how would you know this?"

"I have eyes and ears everywhere, Claire. You know that."

"So tell me, Darren, do you always send your nieces to do your dirty work?"

He shot her a look she couldn't quite read. "I'm sure I don't know what you mean."

"I'm sure you do. Now what is it you wanted me to do or say before you agree to send Devon home and keep funding the site?" So much for her attempts to enjoy a civilized dinner. Might as well get right to the point.

He sighed and laid down his fork. "I don't know, Claire. I guess I had hoped that if we spent some time together that you might . . . that we might . . ."

She watched him expectantly, not offering to rescue him from what he was trying so hard not to say. *Spit it out*, she wanted to tell him, and thought fondly of the source of the phrase. Bump wouldn't have a hard time telling her what he was thinking. He'd have said it outright.

"What, get back together?" she finally stated. She took a drink of water and braced herself for whatever was bound to follow. Regardless of what happened with the site, she couldn't sacrifice herself on the altar of Meaningless Relationships merely to get something in return. She would never consider selling her body to someone; she figured it wasn't any better to sell her soul.

"Darren," she said quietly, setting her water glass gently on the table, "it's done. We're done. I can't stay with you or start things again with you because . . ." she paused, not wanting to be so blunt that she was hurtful. "It's just not there, Darren. We're too different. This relationship wasn't working for me, and I wasn't happy in it."

He regarded her quietly for a moment before speaking. "I can buy you the world," he said. "Anything at all, I will get for you."

"There's a name for women who can be bought," she said, "and I like to think it doesn't apply to me."

He seemed almost amused. "You honestly think I consider you in that light? We dated each other for almost a year, and in that time you never slept with me, no matter how hard I tried."

She shook her head. "It's not only about sex. I won't be emotionally bought." She stopped speaking as their pasta was brought to the table. She looked down at the beautiful meal, swallowing hard.

Darren looked distracted and didn't notice her perusal of the plate of food. "I'm not trying to buy you, Claire. I just thought we had something that was *worth* something."

She shook her head softly. "It just didn't work for me," she repeated. "There are so many women who would probably look at me right now and think I must be out of my mind, but I can't resume any kind of relationship with you other than professional. You don't know how hard this is for me to do, knowing there's a chance you'll shut down the entire site in Guatemala, but I just can't go back to the way things were before."

"I could change," he said, looking his sad, pathetic best. And who knew—maybe he was sincere.

Again, she shook her head. "But I can't," she said. "And it would never work."

He looked at her thoughtfully for a moment, his expression painting a more confused than pained look, as though he truly couldn't understand why she was saying such absurd things. "So this is really it?"

"Yes, this is really it." She looked at him sympathetically. He was used to having whatever he wanted. It was no wonder he figured if he set his price high enough, she'd eventually cave. "I'm sorry."

He brushed it aside, apparently shaking himself out of his "confused mode" and transferring back into "charming mode." He picked up his fork and twirled the pasta around it. "Well, we can at least enjoy this dinner together, then."

She smiled. "We can." She paused. "But Darren, I have to know, what are your intentions concerning the site?"

He pouted. "Do we have to discuss this now?"

"I'd like to."

"Well," he sighed, "I suppose the decent thing to do would be to send Devon home and let you get back to work."

She couldn't believe her good fortune. She had to remind herself to breathe when she realized she was holding her breath. "Do you mean that?"

"Yes, I mean that. I'll call her in the morning and you can go back whenever you'd like."

It was too easy. Much too easy. All he'd wanted was a to-his-face end to the relationship? She couldn't put her finger on it, but there was something she didn't trust. Something in his face, she supposed. She'd always found it to be a bit weak and lacking in character.

"I appreciate that," she said cautiously, waiting for the other shoe to drop. It didn't, so she picked up her fork as well and twirled the creamy pasta around it. She put the bite in her mouth and savored the wonderfully delectable flavor for a moment before chewing and allowing it to slide down her throat.

She glanced back down at the plate, and against her will, mentally calculated the fat grams and calories. She realized there was no way she'd be able to eat another bite, in spite of all her good intentions. Some habits died hard, she supposed, and the current situation in which she found herself was stressful beyond belief. In the height of her disorder, she'd not have been able to choke down that first bite. The fact that she'd even attempted *one*, she figured, was a sign of improvement.

She reached for a dinner roll and tore off a piece, eating it one small bite at a time and exchanging as much small talk as she could with her "date," making the roll last until he finished his own plate of food.

Chapter 24

The days melted into weeks, and Queliza felt herself healing. She missed what might have been, but often found herself angry with the young man who had so rashly gambled with his own life.

She spent much time with Palome, enjoying the comfortable feel of their friendship, and laughing again; she had not felt she would ever again find anything humorous. He was good and kind and he cared for her greatly. She was grateful for the friendship; it helped her feel like living again . . .

* * * * * *

This piece of art is a recent acquisition," Darren said to Claire as they wandered through the room he referred to as his "Art Museum." It was a large room that held several pieces of art; some Claire liked, others she found a bit ridiculous. The room was one of Darren's things of pride and joy, and she indulged his desire to show her all of his newest pieces.

"It's very interesting," she replied, looking at a framed painting that resembled something she'd painted in first grade. "And you paid how much for that one?"

"A quarter of a million," he answered smugly. "Quite a steal, actually."

"Hmm."

They were interrupted by one of his staff, who approached him with an "urgent" phone call that was apparently sensitive in nature.

"You'll excuse me for a minute?" Darren asked solicitously, as though they were casual acquaintances who shared an extremely polite association.

"Of course."

He left the room and she wandered down the wall, viewing pieces she'd never seen before, and several she remembered from the last time she'd visited him in that apartment. She stopped at the long end of the room, looking at a simple country scene, simplistic and oddly out of place in the room.

Acting purely on instinct, she removed the painting and revealed the safe that was built into the wall behind it. He'd shown it to her before on a few occasions, taking great pride in allowing her to take a peek at whatever treasure he currently kept inside before moving it to a more secure location.

She spun the dial, wondering if he'd changed the combination. He'd asked her for her measurements one day, and she'd laughingly supplied them, wondering why he cared. He could look at her to see the proportions of her body; it hadn't made sense until he revealed that her measurements would "always and forever" be the combination to this particular safe.

She landed on each of the numbers, thinking that he'd surely have changed them after she told him she wanted nothing further to do with him. To her surprise, it swung open easily and noiselessly. A small noise escaped her lips and she looked over her shoulder in shock, hoping he wouldn't choose that particular moment to reappear and catch her breaking into his treasure trove.

She swung her head back around quickly, intent on closing the safe back up when her eye caught sight of two lone objects positioned inside.

They were ancient clay pots, cracked and broken in places, bearing ancient Mayan glyphs still vivid in their paint. Pots Claire herself had retrieved from a burial chamber at Corazon de la Ceiba.

Her breath caught and stuck in her lungs. She felt like they were on fire. She stared at the pots, one trembling hand reaching forward of its own accord to brush the side of the one closest to the entrance of the safe. She saw her hand touching the ancient vessel and wondered what it was that kept her from clutching the object and running into the street as far away from the house as possible.

Reason prevailed, and she blinked slowly, withdrawing her hand and leaving the pots in their resting place. What Darren had planned for them, she had no idea. She closed the safe, spun the dial to be sure it was locked, and replaced the painting. She sank onto a nearby bench Darren had placed strategically in the room for relaxed viewing pleasure.

Darren was behind the thefts.

She buried her head in her hands and tried to absorb the cold, hard reality. But he hadn't worked alone. Someone at the site must have been taking the artifacts into town and shipping them to him. Someone she knew and trusted.

Or didn't trust. She could think of two people specifically that she'd had her doubts about from the beginning. One was a spoiled girl who wanted Claire's demise. The other was a man who had recently spent time in Paris, under the guise of "family trouble." Or could it be that he was visiting his employer, delivering artifacts?

She raised her head, wondering how she should proceed. If she confronted Darren with it, surely he wouldn't just say, "You're right, I was wrong, and I'm sorry. Here, why don't you take these artifacts back with you and I won't take any more." No, more likely than not, he'd club her over the head with something large and hard to keep her from squealing the truth. He was spoiled and willful, not unlike his niece, and he wasn't going to get in trouble and then go quietly.

Her best bet, she decided, was to play dumb, get out, and call Bump. He'd tell her how to proceed from that point, whether it meant going back to Guatemala and taking care of it from there, or talking to Bump's friend, Jean-Pierre, before leaving Paris.

She waited. And waited. Darren never materialized. She rose from the hard bench and left the room, wandering the lower level of the apartment, and not finding him anywhere. She smiled at the "butler," who smiled slightly in return but said nothing to her, and on trembling legs climbed the stairs leading to the second story of the home. Once at the top, she walked slowly and noiselessly down the thickly carpeted hallway, pausing at Darren's bedroom door, and hearing nothing, continuing down the hall to his study.

She stood outside the study door, her hand poised to knock. She was prepared to enter, tell him her head hurt dreadfully and jet lag was taking its toll, and then flee like a madwoman to her hotel room. His voice sounded from inside the room, and her hand halted its progress.

He sounded agitated. "I don't care who's sleeping in there," he said. "I'm shipping the two pieces I have now to my villa in Italy and I want at least two new pieces to replace them." There was a pause; he must have been on the phone, she reasoned when she didn't hear a voice in response.

"There's enough chaos in that place now with everything that's happened for you to slip in sometime and get me something new. In fact," he continued, his voice growing in an odd excitement, "I want the knives."

Another pause ensued as Claire slowly began to piece together the bits of conversation she was hearing. "Well you'd better figure something out! I've been waiting and waiting, and you're scared of some private investigator who's decided to sleep in the lab." His voice no longer held the note of excitement; it had changed swiftly to anger.

"In two days," he barked, "I'll have someone at the small airport to meet you and pick up the knives. Be there at 10:00 in the morning. Am I clear? Good. Now don't call me again. I'll contact you."

Claire whirled away from the door and tore down the hallway, moving her way down the stairs so quickly she was afraid she'd break her neck if she fell. Once at the bottom, she ran as quietly as possible back into the Art room, thankful she hadn't encountered any servants along the way who could attest to the fact that she'd been eavesdropping.

She tried to slow her erratic breathing and kept her back to the door. Darren entered moments later; if he suspected she'd overheard him, he showed no signs. His face was composed and she turned as he approached her.

"Are you well, Claire? You look a bit flushed."

She grasped at the comment, thankful for an excuse to leave. "Actually, I'm not feeling all that great, Darren. I think the jet lag is catching up with me, or something. I'd like to go back to my hotel, if you don't mind."

He smiled regretfully. "But I do mind. I cannot, in good conscience, let you go back to your hotel alone if you're sick." He grasped her arm, his fingers firm and unyielding.

"Darren. What are you doing?" She tried to keep her voice even as she attempted to withdraw her arm.

"Did you forget about the security camera, Claire?" He pointed to a camera mounted in a corner of the room, pointing directly at the safe she'd unlocked minutes before. "No, no," he continued as he forcefully walked her out of the room despite the fact that she was now dragging her heels. "You'll have to stay here for awhile, I'm afraid. Until I decide how to handle this."

"Stop it! Darren, let me go!" She began screaming for help; surely one of his army would help her. She tried desperately to get away, sliding down onto the floor in her attempt, twisting and thrashing out as wildly as she could.

He barked out a name in French, and the butler materialized. He spoke rapidly to the man who grabbed Claire's thrashing feet and hoisted her off the ground as Darren grabbed her under the arms. They carried her up the stairs, twisting and screaming the entire way.

Once at the top, they carried her to a guest room that was positioned between the master suite and Darren's study. Throwing her upon the bed, they quickly exited the room, slamming the door and turning a key in the lock before she could scramble after them.

I'll break it down! I'll break it down with my bare hands! Her mind scrambled about in panic, knowing that Darren was far too cowardly to let her live if he thought she'd endanger his own freedom by telling others she knew who was behind the thefts at Corazon. She pounded on the door with her fists, running at it again and again, smashing into it so hard with her shoulder that she jarred her head and made herself dizzy.

Claire, stop! Some rational part of her mind screamed at her to slow down and think. *Think, think, think* . . . She paced the length of the room, trying to gather her scattered thoughts. Her breath came in uneven gasps and she wanted to crumble to the floor. She might have, had she not realized if she did, she'd never get out of the house.

The windows! She ran to the windows that faced the street and looked out. And down. It was a long way to the ground, but Darren, true to his sense of beauty, had planted a rose bush that climbed the side of the house, right next to the window, on a trellis.

She turned the lock on the window, hoping that Darren hadn't set the house alarm in an effort to hear her trying to escape. It was still early evening—*please, please don't let him think of setting the alarm!* The window pushed outward from the house, barely giving her room for her to squeeze her body through, once she mustered up the courage to do so.

She glanced across the street and spied a car parked a short distance from the house. Inside the car was a man with sandy hair and John Lennon glasses. Jean-Pierre? Dare she hope Bump's friend had actually followed her to the apartment? She waved, hoping to catch his attention.

The man in the car opened the door and stood. Yup. Roughly six feet and lanky. He approached the house and she waved at him to be cautious. He entered the yard and quickly moved against the side of the house, creeping past the lower windows in an effort to remain invisible to any inhabitants keeping vigil downstairs.

When he finally reached the base of the rose trellis below, he softly called up to her. "Claire?" he said in barely more than a whisper.

She nodded, close to tears with relief.

"I'm Jean-Pierre. Bump St. James called me last night."

"I know," she whispered back, her voice wavering dangerously. "Do you think you can help me out of here? They've got me locked in."

Jean-Pierre nodded and verbally guided her out of the window and down the trellis, which bowed precariously under her weight but didn't break. When she finally reached the ground, her arms and hands were bleeding and scratched from the mass of thorns she'd crawled through.

She flattened herself against the house next to Jean-Pierre and he grasped her hand, instructing her in heavily accented English to follow him to the car. They bent down as they passed the windows on the lower level, finally making it out of the small yard and across the street to Jean-Pierre's car.

He ushered her inside and climbed into the driver's seat, grabbing his radio communicator and calling for, what Claire assumed, was probably reinforcements. Once finished, he turned to her.

"It's nice to meet a friend of Bump St. James," he said with a smile. "I'm sorry we couldn't have met under less stressful circumstances."

She smiled back and felt the tears well in her eyes. "I'm glad you were here," she said, embarrassed to be crying in front of a total stranger.

He seemed to sense her need to metaphorically shift gears. He began asking her questions in a business-like tone. "Now, am I to understand that this man locked you in his house?"

She nodded, and briefly explained her association with Darren, up to and including the fact that he was the one responsible for the thefts at the site.

"And you can identify these artifacts?"

"Absolutely."

"Well, with your abduction alone, we have enough to arrest him. We'll deal with the artifacts as well . . . will you give your testimony at the police headquarters?"

She nodded again. "One thing, though," she said, her mind cranking a million miles an hour. "Someone at the site is also working with him. I heard him give instructions to someone in Guatemala for the day after tomorrow. Is there any way we can keep the news of this arrest a secret from those at the site until we find out who it is that's planning on following these instructions?"

"You have no idea who it could be?"

She paused. "Well, I have a few, but nothing certain. I need to get back there as quickly as possible."

He nodded his agreement. "I don't see that there should be any problems," he said and turned to look over his shoulder as two marked police cars approached them and parked. He opened his door and stood; she did likewise and followed him to speak with the other officers.

Jean-Pierre spoke rapidly in French to the other four officers now standing in front of the house. He gestured to Claire repeatedly and apparently gave suggestions as to how to proceed; the men nodded their agreement and answered him back. Jean-Pierre turned to Claire and placed a gentle hand on her shoulder. "We're going to arrest him for kidnapping," he said. "I saw you leaving through the window, so I was a witness, and you'll give your statement at headquarters, then you'll be free to go."

She nodded, glancing at the upstairs window, which still gaped open, and the beautiful roses she'd crushed and broken on her descent to the ground. Her last view of the apartment as she left with Jean-Pierre in his car was a belligerent-looking Darren Stark, gesturing angrily in denial at the police officers who were attempting to place him under arrest.

Chapter 25

Queliza accepted Palome's hand as they walked along a remote path one day after her duties for the queen were finished. She relished his nearness and realized that she wanted him in her life always. When had that happened? She'd loved him as a dear friend for years; she'd only just realized since the prince's death exactly how much Palome meant to her.

She thought of the fact that she might have someday been queen, and oddly enough, she didn't find regret in what might have been. Instead, she envisioned her life void of Palome, and felt . . . empty. She was not happy the prince was gone—she still thought of him and marveled at the waste of his life, but she considered her feelings for her dear, lifelong friend, and realized they were deeper and more real than any she had thought she had for the prince . . .

* * * * * *

So what does it look like?" Jon asked Bump, looking over Bump's shoulder at the computer screen.

"Well," Bump answered, tapping a few keys, "it looks like Etienne's family is facing certain financial ruin." He had placed a few phone calls to some people in influential positions in the banking business who "owed him some favors." The fruits of those searches, conducted on a hunch, resulted in an email sent to him from an associate, outlining the recent demise of the DuBois family portfolio.

"So if Etienne is the one behind the thefts and is doing it for large sums of money," Bump mused, "it makes sense. He's a man of intense pride and arrogance; there's no way he's going to want people knowing his family is broke."

"So how will you handle it from here?"

"I'm thinking about that." Bump's phone rang and he grabbed it quickly before it could ring twice.

"Claire." He felt a physical relief at the sound of her voice. "Where are you?"

"I'm on another plane," she answered, sounding tired, but well.

"Already? You're not at least staying the night in Paris? What time is it there?"

She laughed a little. "It's two in the morning in Paris. I considered staying the night, but I really need to be in Guatemala. You're not going to believe the story I have for you."

Bump listened with growing rage as Claire told her story, sparing no details. He shook his head in shock when she finished and was hard-pressed to find a reply.

"Bump?"

"Yeah." He rubbed his eyes, trying to still the angry pulse that was pounding in his forehead. "Claire," he said in measured tones, "are you okay?"

"I am," she answered. "I've got some scratches from the thorns on the rose bush," she tried to laugh, "but other than that I'm fine, if not a little tired." She paused. "Are you mad?"

"Claire, I'm so mad I could pound my way through a wall."

"You're mad at me?"

"No, I'm not mad at you! You know, when I found out you'd left, I swore to myself that if Stark laid a hand on you, I'd either ruin him or kill him."

He was shocked to hear her laugh. "Well, that'll have to wait," she said. "He's not going anywhere for the time being; I gave a statement to the police and they've got him locked up good and tight. But you'll have to wait on the ruining and killing part. We've got someone a little closer to home to catch."

She again recounted the details of the phone conversation she'd overheard. When she finished, he shared what he'd learned about Etienne DuBois. "It may be nothing but coincidence," he said, "but I doubt it."

"I still think it's Devon," she insisted stubbornly.

"It could be," he agreed, "but I don't quite think so." He told her of the conversation he'd had in the hospital with Ricardo Valez. "It seems to confirm your suspicion early on that whoever took the stuff knew what he was looking for. Unless her uncle was giving her specific instructions, I doubt it was Devon. She doesn't have the smarts to pull it off."

"Well, maybe not, but do you remember all that time before and during last Sunday when she was gone from the site? She could have been at the airport delivering the artifacts she'd been stealing and squirreling away somewhere."

His brows drew together in a frown. "I don't know. Besides, someone would have had to drive her there."

Claire scoffed. "Are you kidding? Darren saw to it that she had an international driver's license. Illegally, of course. She's only seventeen. Aside from that, though, she knows physically how to drive a car— even if she didn't have a license I don't see that stopping her from delivering goodies to her precious uncle." She paused. "They're two of a kind, that pair."

He listened to her ensuing silence, which spoke volumes. "I'm glad you're coming back," he said quietly. At that, Jon, who had been eagerly listening to the details of the conversation, although one-sided, gave Bump some privacy by leaving the room. Bump barely noticed. "I've missed you."

"I've missed you, too. I can't tell you how much." She yawned.

"You're tired," he said. "Get some sleep. We'll talk when you get here."

"Okay." She sounded reluctant. "I don't want to hang up," she admitted sleepily.

He smiled. "I don't either. But I'm going to, so you can rest. I'll see you soon. Call me with your flight plans into the small airport and I'll meet you there."

* * * * * *

It was late afternoon of the following day when Bump met Claire at the little airport. She stepped off the plane looking exhausted, but more beautiful than any woman he could remember. He moved forward to take her duffel bag and encircled her with his other arm, lifting her high and squeezing. She returned the embrace by throwing both arms around his neck.

When he lowered her to the ground, he kissed her senseless in front of the pilot and a few other passengers who looked on with grins. He finally pulled back, looking into her face. "Are you all right?"

She smiled. "I am now."

He walked her to the jeep and drove the hour to the site, holding her hand and glancing at her while she fitfully dozed in and out of sleep. She tried, to her credit, to hold up her end of the conversation, but failed miserably.

When they reached the site, the staff, minus Devon, were all seated in the mess hall, having dinner. A cheer from Miguel, Sue, and Etienne erupted when she entered, and they clamored around her, openly thrilled to have her back amongst them.

She sat at the table and told them a nice, big lie about how things had transpired in France. She said that Darren had agreed to send Devon home, but wanted to wait a few days. She told them that he wanted Devon to meet him in Italy so he could baby her for awhile to lessen the sting of being removed from the site.

In reality, Claire and Bump had agreed that to blow the whistle on her at this point would be counterproductive given the fact that someone from the dig would leave the site by, presumably, nine o'clock the next morning to deliver the knives to the airport by ten. That someone could well be Devon.

Or it could be Etienne. Claire watched him surreptitiously as the group conversed and wondered if he were desperately trying to revive his family's finances by stealing the artifacts for Darren and accepting a nice chunk of change in return. She wondered if Bump had thought to check DuBois' bank account to see if he'd made any large deposits in the recent past.

When she asked him that very thing later this evening, he responded with a nod.

"I don't have that information yet, though. I'm expecting it by tomorrow. Of course, we may know by then . . ."

She rolled her eyes in fatigue and frustration. "Man, I hope so. This wondering is driving me nuts."

They were seated atop the steps of the ancient temple again, looking up at the stars. Claire yawned. "I'm so sorry," she said. "I'm pathetic company."

He smiled at her and lay back on the stone, bending one arm under his head and stretching out his other one and patting the ground near his shoulder. "Come here," he said.

She snuggled close and rested her head against his shoulder, savoring his nearness and his warmth. "This probably isn't very comfortable for you," she said.

"I'll manage." His voice rumbled in his chest and she sighed.

"I'm so glad to be back," she mumbled.

He kissed her hair. "Me too," he whispered.

Although uncomfortable on the hard stone, he lay for a long time, thinking things through. He let her sleep for some time before finally waking her and walking her back to her room. He saw her safely tucked in before retiring to the lab.

Jon was out running, who knew where, and the lab was quiet. Bump flipped the switch and looked over to the shelves where the artifacts were housed. The knives were gone. He nodded in satisfaction. All was going to plan, then. He'd purposefully left the lab for a significant period of time, making sure nobody else was going to be in there either. Someone had taken the knives, according to Darren's instructions, and would leave the site in the morning to deliver them.

It was unsettling, he had to admit, thinking that somebody he'd associated closely with in the past weeks was stealing the priceless objects. What it meant was that somebody on the staff was casting ethics aside and committing a huge archaeological no-no. One of the things he so respected about Claire was her intense love for her profession and her deep and abiding respect for the morality associated with it. She would rather die than steal an artifact; on that fact he would wager his life.

He sat in the quiet, thinking, reflecting on conversations he'd had with all those involved at the site. He discarded any emotion he might feel, whether positive or negative, and looked carefully at all the facts. As the moments ticked by, his thoughts became more narrow and focused, and he considered each of the key players he'd interviewed: Justin Hodges, Etienne DuBois, Ricardo Valez, Miguel Robaina, Sue Chastain, Devon Stark, and even Luis Muños.

He'd promised Claire he'd have the mystery solved in no time, and as he mentally reviewed his list of suspects, he eventually pinpointed who he believed to be the culprit. The fact that they'd know for sure who that person was by morning was irrelevant; his instincts were rarely wrong, and he knew with absolute certainty who they'd find delivering the knives to the airport.

He considered waking Claire to share his suspicions, but he decided against it. Claire was too emotionally involved. He knew if he told her who it was, she'd immediately confront the thief and demand answers.

Jon eventually returned from his run and showered, settling down for the night in the cot near Bump's. They purposefully slept near the door; it was the only entrance or exit. Before long, Bump heard Jon's even breathing and knew he was asleep. He envied the other man his peace. He lay awake for a long time into the night, wondering if he'd be correct about who amongst the staff would prove him or herself a betrayer come morning. He'd be surprised if he were proven wrong.

* * * * * *

When morning dawned, Claire awoke with a start, her heart pounding, knowing that something was about to happen. It took her several long moments, blinking in the dim morning light, to remember what that was supposed to be.

The airport. She checked her watch, dismayed to realize it was only six A.M. She had at least a good three hours before *somebody* would leave the site, knives in tow, and head for the small airport.

She sat for a moment staring straight ahead at nothing in partic-ular. It was then she realized she felt good; she was rested and ready to tackle the day. She wasn't exactly hungry, but that was okay. The small knot in her stomach was to be expected. She rose from her bed, already feeling the warmth that would undoubtedly soon envelop the site, and dressed in a pair of jeans shorts and a white T-shirt. She didn't bother with the pants she usually wore when she knew she'd be spending time on her knees on the ground; she didn't figure she'd be doing much digging until the next day, at least.

Who knew how things would play out? *Let's see. The man whose money was funding this site is behind bars in Paris. The man who's RUNNING the site is on the verge of a nervous breakdown, and in a few hours, somebody is going to be arrested.*

Bump had told her the night before that he'd contacted the local authorities and brought them up to speed on the recent happenings. They were to be waiting at the airport at ten o'clock to take the necessary action once they realized who they were after.

Claire left her small room, locking her door behind her and venturing out into the ancient plaza. She walked along the ball court, looking at the buildings flanking it on either side as she moved, wondering for the millionth time about the people who had played the ancient game that exacted such stiff penalties for the losers.

She continued walking slowly around the site, looking carefully at the ancient, sometimes crumbling buildings that flanked the edges of the valley floor. It all seemed so very odd—the juxtaposition of modern equipment and stakes with string attached jammed into the ground was such an interesting blending of past and present. She wondered if the ancients would have cared that people thousands of years later would be so curious about their lives.

As she made her way back around toward the modern research buildings, Claire noticed that someone else was up and moving around as well. She smiled as she approached him.

"Hi there," she said.

Bump smiled in greeting. "You look rested," he noted.

She nodded. "I feel pretty good, considering . . ."

"So what are you going to do for two and a half more hours?"

"I don't know." She shrugged. "I can't concentrate on work, really. I'll probably just end up wandering around aimlessly . . ."

He laughed and took her hand. "Let's go hang out in the ball court," he said and led her to the center of the Plaza. They sat against the wall of the court that still offered some shade, and leaned back.

For the first time since she'd met him, Claire felt extremely awkward. What to say? *I haven't known you long at all, but I think you're wonderful. In fact, I love you. Are you sure you never want to get married?*

He seemed to notice her distress. With his mouth quirked, looking slightly amused, he said, "Is there something you'd like to say?"

She shrugged. "Oh, I don't know. There's a lot going on these days . . . I'm not exactly sure where my thoughts are . . ."

"Why don't you just tell me what you're thinking."

"Ha. I don't think so."

He laughed. "That sounds promising; now you *have* to tell me."

She ruefully smiled and shook her head. "I'd hate to embarrass myself."

"It's getting even better."

"How about you tell me what *you're* thinking."

"Hmm." He paused and picked up her hand, interlacing their fingers and tracing patterns on the back of her hand with his other forefinger. "If I told you what I'm thinking you'd go running for your room as fast as you could."

"Really?" She grinned.

"Really." He put her hand, still entwined with his own, to his lips and softly kissed the back where he'd been tracing it. "I think I've gone slightly insane," he said.

She glanced at his mouth, which was still lightly touching her skin. She swallowed. "Insane?"

"Mmm hmm. I've finally met the woman to end all women. I never thought that would happen for me."

"I see." She swallowed again, trying to feel a little less self-conscious. *Liz would know what to do in a situation like this*, she mused. Connor's wife was a natural-born man magnet, and she was witty, polished, and sure of herself.

Claire, on the other hand, felt dumb. The O'Brian charm had fled.

"Wouldn't you like to know a little more about her?" Bump slowly kissed each knuckle.

"Do I know her?"

"Oh, I think you do. She's extremely smart, she's very funny, and she's beautiful, on top of it all. She has a passion for her job and for people that amazes me every day. She sucked me in with her enormous blue eyes from the first moment I met her, and she hasn't let go, since."

Claire mentally cursed as she felt her eyes burn; she'd cried enough in the last two days to fill a lake, and she was sick of doing it. But she couldn't quell the emotion that rose to the surface at his gentle words and the down-to-earth way in which he'd said them—as if it were fact; there was no debate, it was all truth.

She'd dated a lot of frogs in her life, hoping to find a prince that would match her and mesh well with her personality. It seemed he had finally arrived. But he had mentioned before that he didn't see himself ever married, and it was ultimately what she wanted. It was time; she was through going to bed alone, through having nobody close enough to confide in on a regular basis. But she wouldn't settle for less than complete commitment. She wanted someone who was ready to seal his soul to hers for eternity, and she didn't know if Bump was, or ever would be, ready for that.

A tear fell from her eye and rolled in a solitary path down her cheek.

He noticed, and leaned his cheek against her hand, regarding her closely with those eyes that glowed like a tiger's. "What are you thinking?" he whispered.

"I'm wondering what you want out of life," she whispered back.

"I want you."

Her breath caught and she blinked, sending several more tears down her cheeks to follow the first one. "For how long?"

"Forever."

Chapter 26

Palome seemed to sense Queliza's mood. As they walked back toward the plaza, now deserted under the late night sky, they stopped near the ball court.

"Does it cause you pain to be here?" he asked.

"No," she answered. "Not as it did before. I am free of what were most likely girlish imaginings." Her face turned upward toward him, and at her silent invitation, he leaned forward to kiss her gently on her lips.

"I have waited all my life to ask you this question, Queliza—will you be my wife?"

She smiled. "Yes, Palome. I would be honored . . ."

* * * * *

She shook her head, still looking at his eyes, which hadn't moved a fraction from her own. "Why?"

At that, he laughed. "I'm amazed you have to ask." He slowly sobered. "Because I love you."

She bent her knees to her chest, her free elbow resting atop one knee. She buried her forehead in her free hand and slowly shook her head. "You don't know me that well," she muttered. "And the sad truth is that I love you too. I'm afraid, though, that eventually you'll decide I'm a freak and you'll leave, and it'll break my heart."

"Oh, no problems there," he replied. "I already know you're a freak."

She stared.

"I'm kidding." He smiled. "And you're not really a freak, you know. We've all got stuff to deal with; it just so happens that I know about yours beforehand, and that should make it easier in the long run." He paused. "Do you remember the night I told you about my dad passing away?"

She nodded, wiping at her cheek.

"I never tell anyone anything personal. Ever. I can't remember the last time I shared something like that with someone." He paused, waiting for some kind of response. When she just sat there, he continued. "My point is, that I've trusted you from the beginning. You were easy to talk to, and I've admired your grit and your strength from the very start."

She snorted lightly. "Yeah. My strength."

"You don't see it?"

"When I get stressed, I quit eating. What kind of strength is that?"

He finally looked exasperated. "Claire, what I find incredible is that you kept this site afloat, kept people happy, kept them organized and on task, and still managed to do all the details of your own job on an empty stomach. That's what amazes me. You never, ever quit. You never give up, and when I first got here, I saw you putting on a brave face and using your charm to keep people happy and calm, when inside it was killing you." He kissed the back of her hand again. "That, my friend, is strength."

Claire sat still for a moment, thinking over the things he'd said and feeling a warmth inside that she wasn't sure she'd ever experienced. Even when her parents had told her she was wonderful, she hadn't paid much attention because she figured they had to say that. They were her parents, for crying out loud. But from Bump, it felt different. She realized she was indeed the woman he had described, and it felt good.

"Thank you for that," she said. "I do appreciate it. You don't strike me, though, as the type who jumps right into relationships— especially the kind with words like 'forever' attached. We hardly know each other."

He sighed and leaned his head back against the stone wall. "I know," he said. "And I'm not going to say that this hasn't caught me by surprise. But," he paused for a moment, "last night when we were up by the temple and you were asleep on my arm, I . . ."

She glanced at him, surprised beyond words to see his eyes filmed over.

"I felt like my dad was there." He stopped again, his jaw working silently. "He's been with me a lot, lately; first with the missionaries, then at my baptism, and again last night. When I feel him with me, I know things are right." He laughed a little, and continued. "It's not like I don't make a move unless I feel like he sanctions it, but it's nice to have his blessing. It's like I know I'm doing the right thing if he approves."

He turned to look at her. "You know?"

She nodded. "I do. I think the veil between this life and the next is very thin."

"What's even more amazing," he stated, "is that I'd like to be a father." He shook his head as though he were surprised, himself. "The other day when we helped Luis move that family from their old house into the new one—in the pouring rain, might I add—I watched little Marco. He was trying so hard to be helpful like his dad; he's just a great kid. I'd like one."

She quirked her mouth into a smile. "One, huh?"

"Do you want a lot?" He looked fairly alarmed.

She laughed and squeezed his hand with her own. "No, maybe just a few. I don't know. I think it's one of those things that just kind of works itself out. I know people who have wanted lots of kids and had only a couple, and some who planned on one and had five."

He took a deep breath. "I think I could do two."

She laughed again, long and hard. "Two is good."

When her laughter subsided, he looked at her for a moment before saying, "Well, we're alone and we're surrounded by things you love; this is probably a really good time. Last night I was thinking about where I'd like to propose to you . . ." He paused at her look of surprise, then continued.

"I was thinking that before you agreed to marry a man you might like to know his real name."

She caught her breath and felt her eyes widen. Finally! She nodded dumbly.

He looked embarrassed.

"It's Nigel," he finally muttered.

She stared at him, not uttering a sound.

He snorted. "See what I mean?"

"Nigel?" she finally asked. "You have a beautiful name like Nigel and you choose to have people address you as '*Bump*'?"

"Yeah. You just proved my point. It's 'beautiful.' My mother always said the same thing."

"I think I'd like to meet your mother. She sounds like a woman I'd like."

"I'm sure you'd get along just great, but it doesn't change the fact that I don't like my name. And besides," he added, his voice lowering a bit, "my nickname was the one thing I still had from my dad."

Bless his heart, she thought. "Then by all means, you were right in keeping it." She turned his face toward hers and kissed him, for the first time initiating the contact herself. "I don't blame you a bit."

"So now that you know my secret," he said when she pulled back, looking more than a little pleased she'd kissed him first, "do you think you'd like to marry me?"

"Absolutely. And maybe I can call you 'Nigel' every now and then?"

He grinned. "You can call me whatever you want."

They heard voices beyond the ball court, signaling that others in the camp were awake and making their way toward breakfast. He motioned with his head that they join the others and stood, pulling her up with him.

"So what other interesting things am I going to learn about you, now?" she asked as they wandered toward the mess hall.

"Well, I used to have long hair I wore in a ponytail."

"Are you serious?" She looked up at him in surprise. "I can't even picture that!"

He looked thoughtful for a moment. "I had it cut when I went to Peru to get your brother and Liz. I've kept it short ever since, but maybe I'll let it go again . . ."

She laughed. "Then we can share scrunchies."

He looked at her out of the corner of his eye. "I don't think we'll go *that* far . . ."

* * * * * *

Claire's mood dampened significantly over the course of the morning. She and Bump ate in the mess hall with the rest of the staff, barring Devon, who was still in her room, apparently. Claire kept looking into the faces of the others present and wondered if one of them was guilty. She felt a little chagrined in hoping Devon was the responsible party, but couldn't discount Bump's other theories concerning motive and opportunity. They'd *all* had opportunity; there was no question about that.

After they all finished eating, they dispersed to see to separate duties. Sue noted Claire's attire and asked, "You're not digging today then, Claire?"

"Maybe a little bit later," she said. "I think I'll spend some time in the lab today."

She and Bump watched the staff depart, and Bump said quietly, "In about fifteen minutes, someone's going to leave."

As it turned out, a few "someones" left. When nine o'clock finally rolled around, Devon had disappeared, without telling anyone where she was going, Etienne was gone, Justin was gone, and Miguel was gone. Two of the site's jeeps were also missing. The only person accounted for was Sue, who was working in the lab and said she didn't know where anyone was.

"This is nuts," Claire muttered to Bump and Jon as the three of them climbed into the remaining jeep. "Where is everyone?"

"I don't know. But I bet we'll soon find out." Bump positioned himself behind the wheel and maneuvered the vehicle away from the site and down the road toward the small airport.

Bump and Claire shared the news of their engagement with Jon, accepting his surprised congratulations; then they all fell silent.

They reached the airport quickly; the ride took only an hour but seemed like an eternity to Claire. Bump, anxious himself, had been heavy on the accelerator. There was only one road to the place and they didn't pass anyone from the site. Whoever was set to meet Darren's middleman had been way ahead of them. This fact was evidenced by the presence of one of the missing jeeps that was parked near the airport hangar, but nobody was in the vehicle.

Bump parked a bit away from it and the trio carefully made their way to the hangar, Claire holding her breath and wondering who she'd find inside. When they finally rounded the corner of the building and peered within, the person currently talking with the police, looking weary and sick, was not who Claire had expected to see.

Justin.

At the sight of him, she felt her legs collapse and she sank to the ground on her knees, her breath knocked from her lungs. Bump quickly grasped her beneath her arms, and he and Jon dragged her back around the side of the building, away from the view of those inside.

Claire struggled to breathe. Bump shoved her head between her knees, and she heard him say to Jon, "Maybe it's a mistake. Go find out." Funny. Bump didn't seem surprised.

Bump briskly rubbed Claire's back, ordering her as he did so, "Breathe, Claire. Breathe!"

She sucked in as much air as she could and it came out on a ragged moan.

"Don't jump to conclusions," he said. "Maybe he's here for another reason."

She looked up at the sound of footsteps. Jon rounded the corner, his expression grim. He shook his head and crouched down next to her. "It's him," he said quietly. "The police have confiscated the knives; he had them wrapped in a package, ready to hand them over to someone coming in on the next plane. Should be here in a few minutes." He looked pained. "I'm sorry, Claire."

She collapsed against Bump's side, the tears finally falling. "How could he do this? *How could he do this?*"

Bump continued rubbing her back. "He's been under a lot of stress, Claire. You know that. People do strange things when they feel like they have no other options. He's probably needing money to give his wife. Who knows."

She struggled to rise, against Bump's wishes, and shook him gently off. "I want to talk to him for a minute," she said through her tears, looking down at him.

He stood and examined her critically. "Are you sure?"

She nodded and stiffened her spine, walking around the corner and into the hangar. When Justin saw her, his face turned ashen.

The police began to cut her off as she approached him, but relented when they saw her face and she asked if she could speak to him for just a moment. Justin said something to the men in Spanish; they stepped back and let her talk.

She stood in front of Justin, feeling her pain etched on her face. "Oh, Justin," she finally said. "Why?"

She saw tears form in his eyes and perceived his pain as a mirror of her own. "I needed money," he said, choked, "and Stark offered a lot of it if I'd send him some pieces for his own private collection." He shook his head. "It was the reason he wanted to keep the operation small. He figured the fewer staff we had, the fewer people he'd have to 'take care of' if word ever leaked. He had to have *some* students on hand to avoid suspicion . . ."

He shook his head again, his tears flowing freely. "I'm so sorry, Claire, for the pain this has caused you. I would have spared you that, if I could."

"But why did you agree to have Bump come and investigate? You knew what was going on all along!"

He offered a sad smile. "I couldn't very well refuse, could I? You'd have wondered why. Stark told me to stay calm about it—that Bump would probably discover nothing and then leave."

Claire narrowed her eyes in disgust as she thought of Darren Stark—spoiled, naïve and arrogant to the last. She looked again at Justin's pale face and felt her compassion stir, despite her shock and pain.

"Was the money for your wife?" she asked.

He nodded miserably. "She wanted more than I had, and said if I couldn't come up with more, she'd never let me see Mandy. Looks like that'll happen anyway."

Claire shook her head. "We'll figure something out, Justin. I'll testify for you."

He shook his head, his chin bumping up a notch. "I would never ask that of you, Claire. I've committed a horrendous breach of ethics and made you miserable in the process."

"Well, nonetheless, I hold Darren responsible for the bulk of this. We'll get things figured out." After casting him a pained, if sympathetic look, she turned and left the hangar. She found Bump and Jon waiting just outside. They all three climbed wordlessly into the jeep. The only time Claire broke the silence was to say to Bump, "You knew."

He nodded.

"Since when?"

"Last night."

"How did you know?"

He shrugged apologetically. "I thought about it for awhile. I knew he needed money to keep his wife happy, and that he probably thought that was the only way he could hope to see his daughter again." He paused, then said gently, "I'm sorry. With all the stress he was under, his priorities got mixed up."

She closed her eyes. "Well," she finally stated, "thanks for not telling me."

He looked at her, searching for sarcasm and ready to explain himself.

She shook her head. "I mean it. I'm glad I didn't know."

He nodded, and they drove the rest of the way back to the site in silence.

Chapter 27

The wedding ceremony for the astronomer's son and the queen's hand-maiden was a simple affair, conducted in the beauty of the countryside, far from the city plaza, and attended by workers who had known Queliza's parents. She imagined them there with her as she contentedly pledged her love to her lifelong friend . . .

* * * * * *

C laire allowed herself the luxury of crying herself to sleep that night. The next morning when she awoke, she worked her magic on her swollen eyelids with an ice cold spoon, gave herself a stern lecture in the mirror, and went out to face the day.

Upon their return the day before, she had gathered the staff together, relieved to find them all returned from their errands, and told them the news, beginning with her trip to Paris and its results, and ended with the happenings of the morning. They were shocked, stunned, and received the news in disbelief.

Devon had cried and raged that her uncle would never do such a thing as lock someone in a room, at which point Claire had thrust her arms in the girl's face, stating, "These are the scratches from the thorns I had to crawl through to get out of your uncle's house. He's in jail, Devon, and you're going home. I'm calling your mother as soon as we're finished talking."

Her heart had softened a bit at the girl's obvious grief, and she added, "I'm sorry, Devon. I'm sorry things had to turn out this way. You need to be home with your parents, now." Devon had nodded numbly, and hadn't protested any further when Claire had contacted her parents and made arrangements for her to fly home.

Sue and Miguel had been understandably devastated; there were classes dedicated completely to ethics that both students had taken, and they were shocked and dismayed that Justin would succumb to the pressure of betraying those ethics.

Claire had gently tried to explain why it had happened and what Justin's motivation had been, but the discussion was a painful one for her as well, and at the end she'd simply concluded by telling them all, "We'll get over this. Time heals all wounds." It sounded trite, even to her own ears, but it was the best she could come up with.

Etienne had been shocked as well. It was one of the few times she'd seen him speechless. He'd mumbled a few words of disbelief, and when the small meeting had disbanded he made his way to his room, expressing a desire to be alone. His one question before he had left was, "There was a pot, Claire, that was stolen. It was the one I had been looking forward to deciphering."

Claire had nodded her understanding. "The one with the confusing glyphs?"

"Yes. Do you suppose there's a chance we'll ever see it again?"

"Well, to my knowledge, Darren kept everything. So we should see it again at some point; I'm sure everything will be returned eventually."

Bump had gone to the hospital with Jon to explain the situation to Ricardo Valez. Bump later told Claire that Valez had been as shocked as everyone else to realize it was Justin who had taken the things from the lab. Ricardo informed Bump that his doctor had given him a nearly clean bill of health, and that he'd be released from the hospital soon, after which he'd return to school.

Claire had then spent the afternoon with Luis, whom Bump had called upon their return, and a local government official Luis knew. It was decided that the site would close temporarily until another organization or university agreed to open it back up and restore it as a fully operational site. The situation had been explained to the local workers and staff; Claire had felt the humiliation burning in her face as she'd sat with them while Luis did the talking. She felt responsible for the fact that foreigners had not only invaded their precious space, but had botched it, as well. One of the "foremen" of sorts who was involved directly under Justin with the excavation on the ancient temple was kind enough to note her discomfort and express his gratitude to her for respecting their land and their history.

She had nodded gratefully and thanked him. He then expressed his hopes that she would return to help finish the job she'd started.

As she reflected on the events of the previous day, her mind still reeling, she packed her belongings and prepared to leave. Once she finished her task, she stepped out into the bright morning sunlight and again made a slow walk around the ruins, as she'd done so many times before. She didn't want to think about the fact that she was leaving; she wondered if she'd ever see the place again. She and Bump hadn't gotten far enough into their plans for the future to know what she'd end up doing.

She'd loved her position as a teacher, and had always planned on applying at a university somewhere in the States to stay in the field. But the land itself was incredible, and as she wandered to the ancient temple, she found herself wishing she could stay there forever. She didn't doubt that the ancient society that inhabited it was probably barbaric beyond her wildest imaginings, but the things they'd left behind were so very amazing they took her breath away. Blood, sweat, and literally *lives* had been spent to build this place into what it was. She would miss it horribly.

But there was Bump. Nigel. She smiled as she thought of him. She knew she'd be able to find archaeological sites of interest and people anxious to learn about them regardless of where they lived. It was with some surprise that she envisioned herself in Guatemala without him, and that *that* picture wasn't at all acceptable to her. She wanted to share her life with him, and she figured that meant compromise.

He did a lot of travel, she reasoned as she approached the ancient temple and stood at the entrance. She was sure he wouldn't mind a trip here on occasion. She'd seen the easy way in which he'd adapted to his surroundings; she imagined he may have even come to enjoy the place as well.

The temple was empty; it seemed strange without its usual team of workers, talking and laughing together, carting wheelbarrows full of dirt out of the enormous structure. She thought of the empty tomb deep within the bowels of the building, of the skeleton that had been carefully removed and sent to a larger lab for examination, and the knives and pottery discovered with it. She thought of the knives themselves with a pang of regret. The find that they had presented at first was partially ruined, but the fact that the world still had them to look at and learn from was a good thing.

She approached Bump's and Jon's "dorm" room, not wanting to wake them, but feeling edgy and needing to talk to someone. She instead changed directions and headed into Justin's office, ignoring the flash of pain she felt as she looked at his belongings, and sitting in his chair. She reached for the phone and impulsively dialed her sister's phone number.

Paige answered the phone sounding alert, as she always did.

"Paige," Claire said, "Don't you ever sleep?"

"Claire! Hi! What are you doing?"

"I'm headed home, soon," Claire answered, and filled her sister in on the recent happenings in her life. Paige listened with sympathy and more than a little shock when Claire announced her engagement.

"Wow," she said. "You just met him, huh?"

Claire thumped her head forward on the desk with a groan. "I know," she muttered.

Paige laughed long and hard until Claire finally snapped, "Oh, enough!"

She could still hear the mirth in her sister's voice as Paige said, "You're going to have to eat a lot of crow, you know. You're going to hear about it from all your high-school friends."

"Maybe they won't have to know."

Paige paused for a moment, apparently thinking. "Claire," she finally said, "are you sure about this guy?" Claire guessed she was probably thinking about her last serious relationship.

"I'm absolutely sure," she answered quietly. "This feels very, very right. It never quite did with Darren."

"Well then, I'm happy for you. I'll be home soon for a quick vacation; we can catch up then."

"Okay. I love you, Paige."

"I love you too. Take care of yourself."

"Oh! I almost forgot; one of Bump's good friends—the guy I mentioned, the artist?"

"Yeah?"

"You'd die to see him. He's *so* your type."

"Really?"

"Really."

Paige sounded openly curious. "Are you going to introduce me to him?"

"I'm sure you'll meet him at some point. He's got some issues, though . . ."

Paige laughed. "Well, don't we all."

Not like these, we don't. But, Claire reasoned, Jon could probably use a friend like Paige. She'd be good for him. "We'll see," she finally said, and then admonished her sister to get some sleep.

"It's only midnight," Paige answered. "I still have a lot to do."

Claire shook her head. Paige had the energy of two people and needed half the sleep of one normal person. She hung up the phone after bidding her sister farewell and sat back in the chair with a smile on her face.

Paige always made her happy.

As the staff eventually rose and packed their belongings, Claire gathered everyone together in the mess hall for one final meal. "If I can help it," she said to them as they finished, "we'll all see each other again, and maybe even here."

Sue hugged her with tears in her eyes, and Miguel embraced her as well, if not a bit awkwardly. Etienne gave her a big squeeze and told her that she'd done well. She was grateful for the support and sorry to see them go, even the high and mighty Frenchman.

Devon approached her somewhat anxiously after everyone else had cleared away to bid one more farewell to the site. "Claire," she said, "I'm really sorry." At that, her eyes welled with tears and she looked away, fidgeting with her fingers. "I didn't mean to cause trouble for you . . . I didn't know . . ." She took a deep breath, still not looking at Claire's face. "My uncle told me you had broken his heart, and he wanted me to watch you to see if I could get you to talk about him. He was hoping you'd eventually go back to him . . . I couldn't do what he wanted, though. I got so mad every time I looked at you and thought about you hurting him that I didn't want you anywhere near him."

She brushed absently at a tear and shrugged, finally looking back at Claire. "Anyway, I just wanted to say I'm sorry. Especially about the knives. I really didn't mean to ruin them."

Claire softened her expression. "It's okay, Devon. This has been a hard time for all of us, and I'm guessing you'll probably be happy to go home."

At the girl's miserable nod, Claire smiled. "An archaeological dig isn't really all that glamorous, is it?"

"No. It's a lot dirtier than I thought it would be."

Claire laughed. "Well," she said, "your house is going to seem especially nice to go home to, now."

She watched the girl retreat to her room and thoughtfully asked for forgiveness if she'd judged Devon harshly. True, she'd been obnoxious and horrid, but she was also very young and had just learned a very harsh lesson about someone she had adored.

Claire finally gathered everyone together for one last picture in front of the temple. They took turns snapping photographs; Claire asked specifically that Sue take a picture of her standing between Bump and Jon, her arms around both of them. As painful as parts of the whole ordeal had been, she wanted to remember the strength she'd derived from not only Bump and Jon, but the whole odd assortment of people that comprised the staff.

They eventually wandered back to their rooms to make a final sweep for belongings. Claire collected her things, her brow furrowed deep in thought, and took them to the jeep. The plan was for everyone to fly out together from the small airport and make the necessary and connecting flights out of Guatemala City.

As the staff climbed into the vehicles, she made sure everyone was accounted for with all their gear. Finally feeling as though her work was done, she glanced back at the site one last time, feeling a tug on her heart.

Chapter 28

The years were kind to Palome and Queliza . . . they survived the tyranny that accompanied the seizure of their city, and the death of the king and queen. The ancient temple guarding the remains of the young prince was covered over by new construction at the behest of the new ruling monarch, but the original temple was left intact beneath because of its extraordinary beauty.

Palome became the court astronomer after the death of his father, and he and his beloved wife enjoyed many years together in relative peace, despite the hostile and brutal conditions of the society surrounding them . . .

* * * * * *

Claire, that is a rock and a half." Paige dumped her suitcase to the ground and held Claire's left hand in her own, scrutinizing the diamond that adorned her sister's finger. Paige was dressed casually in a crisp T-shirt, shorts, and pristine white sneakers. She wore no socks, but around her ankle was a braided hemp anklet that complemented the darker shades of her tanned legs. Her other adornments were simple; she sported small gold hoops at her ears and a thin, gold-rope chain around her neck. Her black hair was styled in a way that complemented her active lifestyle to perfection. She wore it extremely short—had she been a child, she might have been mistaken for a little boy. The cap of glossy straight hair was buzzed just above her ears and up the back of her neck.

Claire smiled fondly at her, feeling the same lift to her spirits she always did when Paige was around. In Claire's estimation, Paige always looked beautiful, even dressed as simply as she currently was, because she was a person who was comfortable in her own skin.

Paige continued scrutinizing Claire's engagement ring with her head cocked to one side and her eyes wide. "I'll say this much for the man; he's got excellent taste."

Claire smiled. "He does, doesn't he?" She was currently visiting her parents' home in Logan, Utah, and Paige, true to her word, had flown in for a quick vacation from school so they could spend some time together.

Earlier that day, Claire's mother had called her to the door; a delivery had come for Claire. It turned out to be two dozen red roses and a two-carat diamond set in a combination of platinum and yellow gold. It was breathtaking, and exactly what Claire would have picked for herself, had she gone ring shopping.

The card that accompanied the delivery merely said, "I'll see you soon. Miss me, please. Nigel." She had smiled at that, feeling a warmth that began in her heart and spread throughout her entire body.

Upon leaving Guatemala, Claire had decided to return home to regroup and spend some time with her family. Bump had business obligations to take care of in Seattle; they planned to meet within a few weeks' time, and thus far the separation had all but killed Claire. She missed Bump with an intensity that surprised her.

They had spoken briefly about their engagement and possible wedding dates. "I have to be a member for a year to take you to the temple," Bump had said softly to her as they flew home, "and you deserve nothing less. The problem is, I don't think I can wait that long and still be worthy."

Claire had laughed. He hadn't.

"And," he continued, "if the only way to be sure we keep our hands off each other is for me to stay in Seattle and you to be *wherever*, well, I don't like that option either."

"So let's get married now," she had said simply.

He looked concerned, for her sake, and she was touched. "Are you sure? I mean, you've planned on a temple marriage your whole life."

"And I'll get one," she'd answered. "A year after we're married civilly. I don't want to wait either, and it's stupid to play with fire."

He'd brought her fingers to his lips. "I will get you there," he'd said, his eyes seriously regarding her face. "It's important to me, too."

She knew it was. He had told her once that he was duty-bound and loyal, and she didn't doubt it a bit. She was also impressed with the intensity of his testimony of the gospel. He was like a solid rock, and she loved him for his consistency and his strength. She trusted him with her life.

Paige's voice brought her out of her musings and back to the present. "So tell me again when this is going to happen?"

"In two weeks. Do you think you can swing some more vacation time?"

"Yeah, I'm sure I can. Why?" Paige shoved her suitcase out of the way and moved into the living room where they'd played as children, sitting on the couch and patting the spot next to her.

Claire sank down and settled back into the cushions, feeling as comfortable with Paige as she always had. "We're getting married in Guatemala. Luis Muños has secured permission for us to do the ceremony at Corazon de la Ceiba." She shook her head. "I didn't even know about it, but Bump made all the arrangements. He called Luis and then got hold of Mom and Dad, asking what they thought and to see if they'd mind traveling that far for the wedding."

Paige's eyes widened. "I can't wait to meet this guy," she said. "He sounds really cool."

"He is. This whole thing has just progressed along so naturally . . . I can't even describe it. It's like I've known him forever. It feels right."

Paige's deep blue eyes, a mirror of Claire's own, filmed over. "Oh, Claire," she said. "I'm thrilled for you. Jealous, for me, but thrilled for you."

Claire laughed and leaned over, catching her sister in a warm embrace. "I'm thrilled, too."

They were interrupted by the ring of the phone. Her mother walked into the living room, talking as she came around the corner and stopping short when she spied the two girls on the couch. "Paige! When did you get here?"

Paige rose with a grin and hugged her mother. "Just barely. I've been checking out the boulder on Claire's finger."

"I know, isn't it something?" As if remembering she came into the room for a specific purpose, Hannah O'Brian glanced at the phone and then handed it to Claire. "It's for you," she said, and dragged Paige into the kitchen, berating her for not having come to see her mother the very minute she walked in the door.

Claire smiled and put the phone to her ear. "Hello?"

"Dr. O'Brian? This is Kevin Sabien from the Alta State University Anthropology department. How are you doing today?"

Claire swallowed, her heart giving a thump. "I'm fine, thanks."

"I won't keep you long; the reason I'm calling is to let you know that our university has recently been given the go-ahead to resume excavation of Corazon de la Ceiba. We heard about the trouble before, and I wanted to let you know how sorry I am that you were caught up in such an ugly mess. Your reputation precedes you; you've made quite a name for yourself."

Her mouth felt completely dry. "Thank you very much," was all she managed to say.

"Anyway, the true purpose for my call is to ask if you're interested in going back as the on-site conservator. We'd really like to have you there, and as it's going to be much broader in spectrum this time, involving many students and a much larger staff, we figured we'd try to get you aboard to help the rest of us who don't know the site at all."

She sat silent for a moment before finally finding the words to reply. "You know, I'm really not sure where I'll be in the next little while," she said. "I'm getting married in two weeks, and we haven't really discussed the details of our living situation . . ." *Boy, do I sound lame. I'm getting married and don't even know where I'll be living?*

She thought of the job being offered her, this time under much better and more secure circumstances, and felt her heart constrict. But she then thought of Bump and weighed the options.

In the end, it wasn't much of a contest at all. She felt a bit of a pang at her answer, but it wasn't pain filled and she didn't regret it. "As much as I'd love to tell you yes right away, it's really something I need to discuss with my fiancé first. I don't even know what his plans for the immediate future are, but I'll let you know as soon as I can so you can start looking for someone else if you need to."

"Well," came the answer, "I'm really hoping it'll work out for you that you can do this. We'd really love to have you there." There was a slight pause and Claire heard the rustling of paper on the other end. "I have some recommendations here for various epigraphers; I wonder if you'd care to tell me who you'd hire if it were up to you?"

Claire smiled. "Etienne DuBois, without a doubt. He's fantastic, and he knows his stuff. He was also there with me so he's familiar with the site. He was hard at work deciphering the staircase before we left; I'm sure he'd love the chance to resume his work."

"I'll definitely keep that in mind. Thanks. Let me give you my number so you can call me when you know what you'll be doing."

Claire walked into the kitchen with the phone and grabbed a notebook and pen, jotting the man's phone number down. She thanked him for his offer and promised to get back with him soon.

* * * * * *

Bump sat in his apartment looking out into the dark Seattle night. The rain spattered against his windows—big surprise there, and it was cool outside. Jon was out running, also a big surprise, and Bump sat alone in one of his large, overstuffed chairs, his legs propped on the equally overstuffed ottoman.

He'd just spoken with Claire. His fiancée. He smiled and leaned his head back, closing his eyes and envisioning her face. He had missed her so much since they'd been back in the States that he'd begun to wonder where his manhood had fled. He felt horribly lonely without her, and missed her easy smile and witty sense of humor. He missed the way she could make a whole roomful of people smile, just by being who she was.

So the good doctor had been offered a position at Corazon. He wasn't the least bit surprised. He knew she was good, and he knew other people knew it as well. Her success and intelligence in her field filled him with such pride he felt he could burst with it.

When she called him earlier, she had begun the conversation casually, discussing a little bit of everything and nothing, and when he'd asked if anything else were new, she'd said, "Well, I did get a phone call today from Alta State . . ."

She'd been so sure to make him understand that he was more important to her than the site, and that it hadn't even been an issue for her, but he heard the warmth in her voice when she'd spoken of the ruins, and he knew what the place meant to her. He'd seen her in action at Corazon, and he knew how much she loved it.

He smiled when he thought of her trying so hard to think of his feelings; she was sweet, and he loved her for it. But facts were facts, and the facts here clearly stated that Claire O'Brian was an excellent archaeologist, and she was needed in the field.

He turned his head when Jon entered the apartment, sweaty and tired. He sank down into a chair opposite Bump and sighed. Bump smiled at him. "Good run?"

"Good run."

"How would you feel about another trip?"

He cocked one eyebrow. "Another one?" He shrugged. "Sure."

"Don't you even want to know where?"

"You kept me plenty well entertained on the last one; I figure I can trust your judgement."

Bump laid out the details of a plan he was just beginning to formulate in his mind. When Jon rose and went to shower, Bump also left the comfort of his chair and reached for his phone. He glanced at his watch and hoped he wouldn't have too much trouble tracking down one Kevin Sabien, professor of Anthropology.

Chapter 29

The court astronomer was revered and respected, as was his wife who always carried herself with dignity and grace. Their children were bright, and grew to positions of nobility within the court. Upon their deaths, in later years, the astronomer and his wife were given burials of honor in tombs dug at the base of the temple, as a reward for their loyalty to their rulers and their commitment to life in the midst of a society that rarely valued it.

* * * * * *

The Guatemalan weather was cooperating beautifully; the sky was a deep blue, the clouds puffy and white, and the sun had decided to be merciful and spare the wedding party below it the scorching heat that would surely follow later in the day.

Claire stood next to her groom at the base of the ancient temple, before the bishop from Luis' ward. Behind them, seated in chairs, were Claire's family: her parents, Paige, and Connor and Liz. Beside Claire's mother sat Bump's mother, Ruth. She was a gentle woman with a beautifully soft, British voice. Claire looked forward to knowing her better in the days to follow.

Jon Kiersey was also amongst those seated. He looked happy for the moment, if not entirely content. His eyes still held the haunted look Claire had noticed when she first met him. When she had asked if he was still drawing, he'd clearly been uncomfortable in answering, but stated that he had been, and that he planned to continue. She'd noticed Paige's curious perusal of him when they'd met the day before the ceremony. She introduced the pair, and had left Paige to work her magic with the O'Brian charm, which, Claire had always felt, Paige possessed in larger amounts than the rest of the family members combined. The last snippet of conversation she had heard between Paige and Jon as she turned to help her mother with some flower arrangements were tentative plans to go for a run together later in the week.

Luis, Maria, and Marco were also present, as were several of the other ward members Claire had come to know in her time spent in Guatemala. Bump had specifically asked that the family he and Luis had helped move be invited to attend; he seemed to have formed a special attachment to them.

The ceremony was simple and elegant. Claire wasn't scared, although her nerves hadn't been content to leave her completely alone. She felt a small knot in her stomach that she figured would probably keep her from eating for at least a few hours.

However, when she looked at Bump at the conclusion of the short exchange she felt so excited she thought her heart would probably burst. When he finally kissed her and the crowd cheered, the knot in her stomach slowly released itself a bit and she figured she might even be able to manage a small piece of wedding cake.

The small wedding party celebrated for the better part of the day. Receptions were to follow in Logan and again in Seattle, but for the time being, the environment was small and intimate, and Claire felt it was absolutely perfect. She was so happy to be at Corazon; happy to be there for a time of very real celebration, and happy that the specters of the past weren't hanging over the place like a cloud.

It was dusk by the time everyone decided to head back to their various homes and hotel rooms. They all kissed Claire good-bye and her eyes grew misty at the love and support she felt from each. Connor took his turn after Liz had enveloped her in a big hug. He kissed her cheek and whispered his love for her in her ear. "I'm proud of you," he said. "Of everything you've done."

He then turned to Bump and shook his hand. "Nigel, huh?"

Bump cringed. He had allowed the bishop to use his formal name during the ceremony. "Yeah," he sighed. "My secret's out now."

"Well," Connor said, "it's really not that bad. The way you've always talked about your name, I was expecting it to be something like 'Percy'."

Bump laughed. "No, it's not that bad."

Claire put her arm around her husband's waist and gave him a squeeze. "It's not bad at all," she said. "I rather like it, in fact."

Liz shook her head. "All that time, and nobody ever knew his name. You know, it's funny," she said, turning specifically to Claire, "Connor said if anybody could get Bump's name out of him, it would be you."

Bump grinned. "He was right."

Bump and Claire followed their guests away from the site in their rental car. As he maneuvered the car down the street and toward Luis's town, Claire couldn't contain her curiosity any longer.

"Okay. Enough secrecy. You've been here for the past two weeks, and I know you weren't doing wedding preparations because my mom, Paige, Maria, and I did all that when we got here. What have you been up to?"

He glanced at her with a smile. "It's still a secret," he said. "It's a secret until we get there."

She sighed impatiently.

"So," he said, attempting to turn her attention elsewhere, "do you think your family approves of me?"

She snorted. "They approve so much I think they like you better than they like me, now. Especially Paige. She thinks you walk on water. And Connor and Liz were already a given, of course."

"Well, good. And for what it's worth, my mother thinks you're wonderful. She told me so this morning before the wedding."

"Oh, I'm glad. I've heard mother-in-law horror stories." She paused. "And what about your dad? Do you think he'd have approved?"

Bump smiled. "I know he does."

Claire slid closer to him on the seat and snuggled next to him as he put his arm across the back of the seat. She was quiet until they approached Luis and Maria's neighborhood.

She looked at him in some surprise. "We're staying with Luis and Maria?"

He laughed. "I like them, but there's no way I'm sharing our wedding night with anyone." He instead passed by the Muños's street and continued on to the next one where several new houses were under construction. He pulled the car to a stop in front of a brand-new home at the end of the street.

Her brow creased in a frown. "Whose house is this?"

He unbuckled his seatbelt and hers, and opening his door, pulled her along behind him. He placed a finger over her lips when she'd have asked more questions and instead led her up the walk, unlocking the door and ushering her inside before him.

The interior of the home was much like Luis and Maria's. In fact, Claire recognized several pieces of art Maria had created and shown her awhile back. The home itself smelled new; it was pristine in its white paint, and tastefully decorated with furniture and décor rich in earth tones and reds.

Bump gently nudged her forward and they walked through the living room and into the kitchen, which contained decorations in keeping with those she'd already seen, the appliances new and shiny and the floor a beautiful red Spanish tile. They walked through the kitchen, Bump still not saying a word, and down a small hallway that revealed three bedrooms and a bathroom. He led her back into the living room before he finally allowed her to speak.

Claire turned around and faced her husband. "Okay," she stated. "Whose house is this?"

He smiled. "It's ours."

She stared, uncomprehending. "Ours?"

"Yes, it's ours. And you should be grateful I got it all taken care of for you in terms of decorating and furnishing, because you only have a week and a half before you start work."

She shook her head. "You're speaking in riddles. Spit it out."

He laughed and took her by the shoulders, his hands running down the length of her arms, past the short sleeves of her wedding dress and coming to a stop at her hands where he intertwined her fingers with his. He leaned over and kissed her, releasing her hands and pulling her close against the length of his body.

He pulled back slightly and smiled into her dazed face. "I hope you don't think I'm trying to rule you with a heavy hand, now, but I took the liberty of getting you a job."

He urged her to sit with him on the couch before explaining fully. "The night you called me in Seattle about the position Alta State offered you, I tracked down Kevin Sabien and told him we were planning on living for awhile in Guatemala. I also told him I was sure you'd love to take the position he'd offered you, but asked if he'd keep it a secret so I could give it to you as part of my wedding present. The other part," he said with a gesture, "is this."

Her jaw dropped open and she was at a total and complete loss for words. When she finally did speak, her throat was clogged with tears. "You've done all this for me? But what about your business? What about your life? I kind of assumed we'd live in Seattle . . ." she smacked his chest, "and every time in the last two weeks I've tried to discuss it with you, you've blown me off!"

He grabbed her hand with a gentle smile. "I had to," he said. "It would have spoiled the surprise. I hope you're happy with it, because I'll tell ya, I've never been so excited to give someone something in my entire life!"

She laughed, the tears escaping her eyes and falling. "I am happy with it." She threw her arms up around his neck and pulled him close. "I'm so happy with it I could die. But," she said, pulling back, "how did you arrange all this on such short notice? Let me guess; somebody here owed you some favors?"

"No, but it helps to tip big. And as for my stuff back home, it's really no big deal. I have a business associate who will take care of the PI business while we're gone. I'll go back every now and then for a day or two just to check on things, but other than that, there's plenty I can do from here. I do a lot of investigative work that involves my computer, and that I can do from anywhere."

His mouth quirked into a smile. "Besides, this place kind of grew on me. My motives are probably a bit selfish; I wanted to spend some more time here as well. And I think it'll be good for Jon. He's going to stay in Guatemala for a little while, but we'll find arrangements for him. I don't want you thinking we're a package deal; Jon and I do actually lead separate lives."

She frowned. "But he needs a lot of support right now—we've got plenty of room here. I don't mind if he stays with us."

"Are you sure?"

She nodded. "Absolutely. I like him. And besides, I'm trying to decide whether or not to push Paige on him. She's good for people."

His nod was a bit reluctant. "Yeah, she probably is, but Jon's not just anybody. He's lived through some stuff he may never be able to forget."

"You don't think he's good enough for her?"

"I wouldn't say that; I just don't know how much past muck she would want to deal with in a relationship."

"Well, she's pretty even tempered. And the thing that's always made me jealous is that the even-tempered part equates to 'perpetually happy.' That girl rarely has any serious down moods. She might be good for someone like Jon."

"Yeah, or he could drag her down with him."

She shrugged. "Maybe. But she's pretty strong. Who knows." She paused for a moment, remembering there was something she wanted to tell him. "Oh!" She snapped her fingers. "That was it. Just before we left home I got a call from Justin. He's still here in Guatemala and is in jail; I think they're trying to decide what to do with him. Hopefully the jail time he's already served will lessen any kind of sentence he incurs." She shook her head. "I feel really badly for him now that the whole thing is over. He didn't say anything to me, but I'm sure his wife is having fits now that the father of her child is sitting in a Guatemalan jail. He'll be lucky if he ever sees that kid again. I'm going to follow things and see if I can't help out somehow, even if it's only as a character witness."

She was thoughtful for a moment. She'd also heard that Darren Stark was going to be in jail for a long, long time, for kidnapping and also for the archaeological thefts. The jurisdiction of both his and Justin's cases was still being ironed out. She was glad, however, that Darren's days with archaeology were finished.

"I'll tell you what," Bump said as he rose and pulled Claire off the couch. He started down the hallway, pulling her behind him as he went. "How about we stop talking and go check out our new bedroom. I had all of the bedroom furniture shipped in from Seattle. I don't know if you noticed it when we walked through, but I picked it out with you in mind. It's all light wood, very classic and simple, yet elegant."

"You think I'll like it, then?" She grinned mischievously as he pulled her into the bedroom and began slowly removing the pins that held her hair in a twist on her head.

"Oh yeah," he murmured with a smile. "I think you'll like it a lot."

PHOTO BY ROBERT CASEY

AUTHOR'S NOTES

Writing this book has been such an enjoyable experience for me because I am so intrigued by the field of archaeology. I greatly admire the men and women who share a fascination for things long buried and gone, and their passion for preserving and holding sacred these things.

I must beg indulgence if there are archaeological facts or scenes in this book that are not in keeping with reality, and ask that the reader chalk any inconsistencies up to "creative license" taken by the author. I have tried to be as authentic as possible, yet still create situations that would work with my plot.

The sub-plot that runs parallel to the main story is meant to reflect Mayan discoveries dating well after Moroni buried the plates. I was reluctant to create a story based on Book of Mormon events and people in those time periods for fear of taking liberties with their thoughts and lives.

The ancient city of Corazon de la Ceiba is also a product of the author's imagination, as is the town in which Luis and Maria Muños reside.

AN EXCERPT FROM THE LONG-AWAITED SEQUEL TO
SECRETS OF THE HEART, A NOVEL BY JOANN JOLLEY

PROMISES
of the HEART

PROLOGUE

"You're thinking about him, aren't you?"

Paula Donroe winced as her son's deep voice pulled her back to the present. "Hmm? I suppose," she murmured, setting the bulky Sunbeam® iron on its heel. It teetered for a second at one end of the long, fabric-covered ironing board, then settled into a statue-like stillness.

"Figures," Scott muttered as he slouched against the door frame of his mother's bedroom.

Paula took a deep breath before turning to face her tall, sullen, sixteen-year-old son. *Easy does it,* she silently cautioned herself. *We've all been through an emotional wringer lately, and he's probably hurting just as much as the rest of us. Maybe more . . . he was there when the shot was fired, after all.* An achingly familiar surge of grief rippled through her chest at the thought, and a moment later she felt an empathetic smile rise to her lips. "What do you mean, sweetie?"

"Nuthin'. It's all you ever think about." He stretched out one leg, dug the heel of his sneaker into the carpet, and dragged his foot slowly backward to make a long, wide furrow in the deep pile.

"Well, Scotty," she said, moving close enough to see the sparse patches of adolescent stubble on his chin, "it's only been a few weeks. We all need a little time, don't you think?" She reached out to touch his shoulder and felt the lean, hard muscles tense beneath his oversized yellow T-shirt.

"Yeah." He set his jaw in a rigid line and stared at the floor.

"You know, honey," she ventured, "if you'd like to talk about it, we could always—"

"Nuthin' to talk about." He shrugged away her hand and smoothed the carpet with a circular motion of his foot. "I gotta go."

Paula sighed. *Maybe next week . . . next month . . . next year.* "Okay. Mind if I ask where you're off to so early on a Saturday morning?" She steeled herself for the all-too-familiar response.

"The clubhouse."

"I see." Her voice was deliberately pleasant, even though she wanted to lash out at him, tell him he should find better things to do with his life than spend every waking moment with that useless gang of his. *But you can't risk driving him even further away,* she reminded herself. *Just love him and be patient—remember the eternal perspective. Let him know you care, and eventually he might return the favor.* "And how are the Crawlers doing these days?"

"Cool."

"That's nice, dear." *Patience—that's the key. Perhaps one day he'll actually speak to you in sentences of more than three words.* "Try to be home at a reasonable hour, will you?"

"Right," he growled, disappearing quickly into the hall. A few seconds later, she heard the front door slam.

Shaking her head, Paula turned back to the ironing board. She carefully smoothed the crinkled front panel of a pale-blue oxford shirt, dampened it with a spray bottle, and lowered the iron to the fabric. A slow hissing sound accompanied a few light bursts of steam as the rumpled cotton cloth yielded to the hot metal and tightened, then relaxed into a polished, wrinkle-free surface.

For some unexplained reason, this simple act of ironing had, over the last month or so, become a comfortable and comforting routine for Paula. She had moved the ironing board upstairs to her bedroom, where she now stood facing the open window overlooking the front yard of her suburban home in Woodland Hills, California. In this peaceful setting, she would sometimes spend hours banishing the wrinkles from a large assortment of shirts, blouses, and slacks. Her favorite was 100% cotton. None of the permanent-press garments would rumple enough to give her the satisfaction of restoring their original crispness. But cotton—there was a fabric she could really work with. Its wrinkles were so deep and defined that by the time she had sprayed and ironed and smoothed and creased, she was in absolute control. Maybe that was it—the sense of control. It was what she needed most in her life at the moment. If she couldn't quite get the wrinkles in her mind and heart straightened out, at least she could take care of the wrinkles in her laundry.

On this Saturday morning in mid-January, Paula now returned to the thoughts that had absorbed her before Scott's interruption. Yes, she'd been thinking about him—about *both* of them. Her mind roamed over the details of her life since that bleak day in early November when her world had changed forever. TJ, her bright, funny, basketball-crazy twelve-year-old son, had been shot in a random act of violence as he and Scott and some friends had cruised the streets of downtown Los Angeles. He had lived less than a day; and in many ways Paula had felt that his senseless death was her fault. They had argued that morning because he wanted to join the Mormon Church. Paula had flatly refused to give her permission, and TJ, in his frustration, had taken off with Scott. Hours later, the final moments of his life had played themselves out in a cold, indifferent hospital room.

But it hasn't been all bad, Paula reminded herself as she nudged the tip of the iron into a v-shaped pleat on the back of the shirt. *There have been miracles, too.* She smiled, relaxing a little as the warmer memories took hold. After TJ's death, the Mormon missionaries, Elders Richland and Stucki, had taught her the gospel, and she had finally come to understand why her young son had been so determined to join the Church: it was *true*. On a golden morning just before Thanksgiving, she and Millie, her housekeeper and friend, had been baptized. TJ had been there, too, dressed in white, a joyful grin illuminating his freckled face. Paula had seen him.

Then had come the greatest miracle of all. "I still can't believe it," Paula whispered softly as she pressed the hot iron against the shirt's

collar. For the thousandth time, she relived the   heart-stopping
moment when she had realized that Elder Mark Richland, the tall,
clear-eyed, earnest young missionary who had agonized over TJ's
death and moved Paula to tears with his testimony, was her son. Her
son! Her heart had told her it was true the moment she'd seen a
distinctive bumble-bee-shaped birthmark on the inside of his elbow
when he removed his suit jacket during Thanksgiving dinner.
Twenty-two years earlier, in the wake of the tragic death of her young
husband and estrangement from her parents, she had pressed trembling lips to that birthmark just moments before giving up her day-
old baby for adoption. Unknown to her, a Mormon family in Idaho
had raised him to be an extraordinary young man; and then some
divine force beyond any human comprehension had brought him to
California and back into Paula's life. "Thank you, Father," she
breathed.

As quickly as it had come, her expression of gratitude was
submerged in a wave of doubt, even despair. *But where is he now?* she
questioned silently. She knew where he was, of course—home on a
farm just outside Roberts, Idaho, where he'd been since the first of
December, the final day of his mission. They had stood together in
the Los Angeles airport saying their good-byes, she knowing the
marvelous secret of his parentage, wondering when and how she
would ever be able to tell him. Then, placing his lips close to her ear,
he had whispered that *he knew.* He had seen the look in her eyes that
Thanksgiving Day, had discerned the meaning in her subtle questions
about his family, and now confirmed the joyful truth at their moment
of parting. When she'd caught her breath, they had embraced, wept,
promised to stay in touch. Knowing he was on his way to a long-
awaited family reunion, she would stand back and let him make the
first contact. "Call . . . write . . . whatever," she had whispered.
"Whenever you're ready. I'll be waiting."

"I will," he had promised.

Paula's brow furrowed, and the iron stopped its rhythmic back-
and-forth motion. *That was six weeks ago,* she mused. *Christmas, New
Year's . . . times I would have expected a call, or at least a card. What's
going on?* She plunged deeper into thought, considering all the trou-
bling possibilities. *Is he ill? Has he decided he doesn't want me in his life*

after all? Has he told his parents, and have they forbidden him to contact me? Do I mean anything at all to him, or am I just another notch on his missionary name tag? Will I ever see or hear—

"Ow-w-w!" Paula smelled the seared flesh on one side of her finger almost at the same instant she felt the white-hot pain. "Nice move, Donroe," she sputtered as a fiery red welt erupted and spread itself alongside her knuckle. "What were you thinking? That's your problem, you know—you were thinking *too much.*" Her reflexes took over, and she raised the finger to her lips and sucked hard. With her other hand, she yanked on the iron's garish blue cord until the socket gave up and let go. Lifting the iron, she saw an angry brown scorch mark on the shirt's pale-blue sleeve. "So much for being in control," she muttered.

With her throbbing finger still pressed to her lips, she set the iron on its heel and moved a few steps to her bed. Sinking onto the polished-cotton comforter, she began to rock back and forth, her eyes closed tightly in an effort to shut out the pain. *Get a grip, girl,* she chided. *It's only a little burn.* But somehow this minor insult to her flesh was the last straw, and a suffocating wave of grief and helplessness washed over her. Hot tears coursed down her cheeks as she thought of her three sons—TJ, who now lay beneath a mound of cold earth in the Rolling Hills Cemetery; Scott, who seemed to be moving further away from her by the minute; and Mark Richland, the precious child she had found but now seemed to have lost again. "What's it all for, Heavenly Father?" she sobbed. "What's it all for?"

Falling back against the pillows, Paula yielded to the emotion of the moment. She wept until exhaustion stilled her slender body and she fell into a heavy, dreamless sleep.